If he moved quickly enough he might be able to assume a new disguise

As he stepped through the doorway, he heard a shout from his right. He'd been spotted. He lunged for the door, but this time the effort proved too much. His left leg suddenly gave out and he tumbled to the side with a cry of pain. A shot rang out and something struck him hard on the shoulder, spinning him out of control.

Alex managed to get his 9 mm out of the holster. He heard cursing and shouts, but for some reason the words wouldn't register. He crashed into the wall and pain shot through his shoulder, already soaked in blood. He gritted his teeth and tried to stand, but his legs would not support him. He raised his gun, watching for movement.

Two men appeared, crouching low and moving down opposite sides of the passageway. He took aim at the man on the left and fired, saw the round strike him mid-chest and blow him off his feet. Alex tried to roll to his right, but somewhere between his brain and his legs, the signal went haywire. What was supposed to be a smooth roll turned into a flop and he landed heavily as another searing pain brushed his temple.

Everything went black.

Other title[s] in this series:

ROOM 59

out OF time

cliff RYDER

A GOLD EAGLE BOOK FROM
WORLDWIDE®

TORONTO • NEW YORK • LONDON
AMSTERDAM • PARIS • SYDNEY • HAMBURG
STOCKHOLM • ATHENS • TOKYO • MILAN
MADRID • WARSAW • BUDAPEST • AUCKLAND

First edition April 2008

ISBN-13: 978-0-373-63266-4
ISBN-10:   0-373-63266-5

OUT OF TIME

Special thanks and acknowledgment to
Garrett Dylan for his contribution to this work.

Printed in U.S.A.

out OF time

1

Alex Tempest leaned on a dirt-crusted stone wall, head lowered, trying to control his breathing and ignore the pain. His legs felt like gelatin and sent sharp, stabbing jolts of agony into his hips; his head spun with a sudden wave of nausea. Every muscle was bowstring tight and his heartbeat ragged—every sound brought a flinch and a shift of disoriented senses.

The sun had begun to set over the Mexico City skyline, but the heat continued to roll off the streets in waves. On the floor of a villa just outside of town, Vincenzo Carrera lay dead in a pool of blood. His men hadn't stopped to clear away the body, the blood or any of the evidence. They hadn't even disposed of the kilo-sized bag of cocaine, blown to bits and strewed across the inlaid mosaic of Carrera's garden. The powder floated about like fine drifts of snow. Carrera would never spend the money he'd expected to make on that sale. He would not make his reservations at La Villa Cordoba, nor his date with his wife and young daughter the following day at the beach.

All that remained of Carrera was his well-oiled organization, designed to sell drugs and kill or destroy anything that got in its way. It wasn't supposed to have mattered. In, remove the target and out. That was the plan. That was always the plan. Alex wasn't known as "the Chameleon" without good reason. He had worked his way into incredibly tight spots, killed and disappeared countless times. This wasn't even one of his more difficult assignments.

But something had gone wrong. Something had been going wrong for some time, in fact, and though he'd tried to ignore it, it only grew worse as each day passed. This time it had nearly cost him both the success of his mission and his life.

As he waited for the shadows to deepen and his legs to stop shaking, he went over the mission again, trying to see if there was anything he could have done differently, trying to see where he'd gone wrong. Somewhere there was an error, a stupid error and he hated stupidity almost as much as he hated the trembling in his normally steady hand.

The earlier stages had gone exactly as he'd foreseen. It wasn't his first trip to Mexico City and his old contacts were in place. He'd managed to infiltrate the lower levels of Carrera's organization without incident, had marked his time and his place. It had taken two weeks of careful watching and listening to be certain he had it right.

Carrera had been too arrogant to distance himself from his business and his organization was too dangerous to be left without close control. It had only been a matter of time until a deal went down and Alex was close enough to the center of the operation to pin it down. They weren't secretive in their activities once inside the walls of Carrera's villa. Whom did they have to fear? Enough of the local *policia* were on the take to ensure secure operations and no business ever took place on the streets or in an unsecured location. Again, what would be the purpose?

Alex had slipped into the deep center of the garden shortly before the deal was set to go down, his tan skin darkened with a touch of makeup and his clothing already a perfect match to what the guards of the villa were wearing. There were five posts along the villa's wall and he'd placed himself very near one of these. The guard hadn't seen or heard him—he was searching for threats from outside the villa, not from within.

Just before 5:00 p.m., he'd slipped up behind the

guard, slit his throat and took his place, watching the streets beyond the walls carefully. He moved and acted exactly as the guard would have—a professional doing his job. There was no reason anyone would look at him twice and no one had. The damned plan was perfect.

At five o'clock sharp, Carrera appeared in the garden. He sat where he sat every afternoon, and a young girl brought refreshments. He ate fruit, and he laughed with the two bodyguards who were never far from his side. They were short, squat men with dark hair, dark glasses and no smiles. They made a quick sweep of the garden. They glanced up at each guard post. They didn't take any special notice of Alex. He paid no attention to them, willing them to see only what he wanted them to see—a guard on duty.

At half past five, a long white sedan wound its way up the long driveway to the villa. It stopped just shy of the iron gates. Men poured out of twin guard shacks on either side of the gate, scanning the passengers, opening the trunk and searching quickly, checking the engine and sweeping beneath the undercarriage with mirrors. Slick, quick and efficient. Alex appreciated that—under other circumstances he might have admired it.

The gates opened and the car slid in, moving at a leisurely pace. Alex watched, lost sight of the vehicle and turned his attention back to the streets.

For the moment, his duty was to protect. He kept his rifle, a modified Russian SVN-98, with the barrel tipped toward the street, but low enough that anyone watching from beyond the fence couldn't see it. They knew, of course. The police knew, the locals knew, everyone knew better than to approach the fence, but that was no reason to let down the guard. He knew what was expected, and that was what he became. It was how he operated, how he survived.

The Chameleon absorbed his environment, took on its colors.

The deal went down moments later. There were no formalities. Carrera's men escorted a small party from the villa to the garden. There were three men. One carried a banded metal case. The other two were mirror images of Carrera's men—short, squat, expressionless. They didn't glance around, but Alex knew they were aware of every detail. Their lives and the life of their leader depended on it. It was all like clockwork, and that was what was supposed to make it simple.

The money was counted. The drugs were presented for inspection. Carrera lounged in a chair, indifferent to the proceedings. The man who had carried the case moments before scooped a small sample onto his finger, tasted it quickly, then pulled a smaller case from his pocket. He took out a glass bottle, dropped a bit of the powder into it, added liquid and shook. That was the moment.

Alex knew that no one would be able to resist watching that bottle. Either the drugs were good, and the white sedan would glide back out the gates the way it glided in, leaving Carrera to count the cash, or it was a setup, an ambush meant to send some message to a lesser dealer or a competitor. It mattered little to Alex. Every set of eyes was locked on the bottle, and in that moment, he struck.

He shifted the rifle in the blink of an eye and sighted in on Carrera through the integrated scope. There was no time to hesitate, but Alex was a crack shot. It was thirty feet down the opposite side of the wall, but he'd already rigged a line. The entire operation should have taken, by his calculation, about forty seconds.

The crosshairs rested on Carrera's heart, and Alex curled his finger around the trigger, preparing to gently squeeze off the single round that would end Carrera's life. Except, at that moment, his hand began to shake. Not a small tremor, but an uncontrollable spasm that wrenched his fingers into a locked claw. He fought to control it, and pulled the trigger instinctively. The slug slammed into the bag of cocaine and sent a cloud of powder into the air. In that momentary confusion, cursing to himself, he resighted, pulled the trigger again, and blood spouted from Carrera's temple—the only part of him that was visible above the tabletop.

Carrera was dead, but the damage to the mission was done. Men were already on the move.

Alex dropped the gun and grabbed at his line. He slid down quickly, rappelling down the sheer stone face. The muscles of his hand clenched again, so tight that he nearly cried out. He dropped too quickly and fought for control. He heard voices calling out in the distance. He heard gunfire, probably the buyer's men crossing with Carrera's in the confusion. He heard the roar of an engine, and he knew they'd seen him. He hadn't gotten over the wall quickly enough.

He hit the ground moving far too quickly. He braced, released the line and rolled, but pain shot through his legs—more pain than there should have been—and it was all he could do to keep his feet. There was a hundred yards before he'd be near any sort of cover. The first side street consisted of lines of small houses, all the same, most of them uninhabited. The few that weren't empty held Carrera's men and their families. It was a small demilitarized zone, more for camouflage than habitation.

Behind the second house on the left side of the street, he'd parked a Ducati dirt bike, small, powerful and maneuverable. He heard sounds of pursuit, too close. As he ran, he tossed aside his jacket and shirt. Dangling from the handlebars he'd left a dirty serape that many of the natives here wore. He whipped it over his shoulders, slid his arms in and dropped heavily onto the bike. His legs tingled as though they'd fallen asleep, and ice picks stabbed at his hips. His vision darkened for a moment from the sudden pain, and he nearly blacked out. He gritted his teeth, punched himself in the thigh repeatedly and kicked the engine to life.

He spun out and around the corner as the first wave of Carrera's men swept out the gates and into the streets, searching for likely targets. It was five miles to the center of the city, where the streets would be busy with people and tourists *and* where the police would have to make at least an attempt to pay attention. Alex blinked and gripped the handlebars tighter, his hands like talons. His eyesight blurred and it was all that he could do to keep the Ducati upright.

For a time he operated on pure instinct, and the bursts of gunfire and the roar of engines at his heels became the sounds of dreams on awakening—distant and unreal. He was the Chameleon, and he needed only to disappear.

He dumped the bike at the edge of a small market, running between carts overladen with fruits and vegetables, and ducking in and out of alleys. At six feet one inch, he wasn't small enough to remain unseen in a doorway or tucked behind some clutter in the alley. He kept moving, ignoring the protests of his body, knowing that it didn't matter where he ended up, only that they not find him. The crowded streets were his best chance of blending in and eventually disappearing.

A car roared by the mouth of the alley where he stood. There was no way to know for sure if it was one of Carrera's. He had to assume that it was. Alex took a deep breath, steadied himself and pushed off the wall. He stumbled at first, then found his stride and, hanging close to the wall, stepped confidently into the street. Just ahead was a small cantina with tables looking out onto the street. He lowered his head and stepped inside.

The urge to turn and scan the street was strong, but he ignored it, walking into the shadows near the rear of the bar and taking a seat. Anything he did that might bring attention to himself would be a mistake. He needed to become what he appeared to be—a tired worker in from the fields, looking for a place to wait out the last heat of the day and enjoy a drink. His clothing, the makeup he wore and even the contact lenses that turned his normally pale blue eyes a dark brown color would all serve to make him look more like a native. He ordered beer in fluent, unaccented Spanish and slouched over it. Occasionally, he turned toward the door and glanced at the street, but he was careful to make such motions inconspicuous and innocuous. There was nothing to be gained by moving now. His best bet for survival was staying put, and the way he was feeling, the rest was a blessing. There was no way to deny it—something was wrong. He had to get out of Mexico and back home. He had to see a doctor. There was no longer any way to deny the sudden, excruciating pains or the uncontrollable trembling in his hands. His physical conditioning had not slacked off, and yet he seemed to spend most of his energy trying to concentrate, or fighting the pain in his legs.

Something had gone horribly wrong and his life too often depended on the skills of his body. A mistake in his line of work could easily prove fatal. And, if he was honest with himself, the missions were often too important to the safety of the world for him to fail.

The bartender polished the copper-and-brass beer taps. He paid no more attention to Alex than he did to the tables or the chairs. Alex looked into the mirror on the other side of the bar, his eyes mocking him in the reflection. There was nothing in the image to indicate that something was wrong with him, but he stared at the image as if it were a puzzle, as if maybe, if he stared long enough he could make the pieces fit back together. Alex sipped his beer and thought quietly. A young boy wandered in, looking for an easy mark or a free meal.

The boy looked sidelong at him, but didn't approach immediately. Alex met the boy's gaze and nodded him over. With a quick glance at the bartender, who seemed not to notice, the boy complied.

In a disinterested voice, Alex asked if he was hungry. The boy didn't answer, but instead glanced at the floor. Alex spoke quickly, explaining what he needed. He slid a few pesos across the table.

The boy eyed them for a moment, considering. It had to be one of the strangest requests he'd heard, but he wanted the money. He reached out, and as he did, Alex caught his wrist in a snake-fast grab.

He held the boy's gaze, and studied him. There was fear, and a bit of pride, but they weren't the dead, street eyes of one of Carrera's boys. Maybe he was just out for an evening's adventure, or maybe his parents worked late and left him to fend for himself. Whatever the story, he would do as he was told for the money, and that was enough. Alex released him and nodded again. The boy disappeared.

Alex rose, slouched over the bar and ordered a second beer. He took the chance to glance out at the street, but he saw nothing out of place. They weren't going door to door searching for him. Not yet anyway. But it was time for another change, and then it was time for him to disappear.

Despite the problems, the mission *could* be considered a success. The head of the snake had been removed, and Carrera's business would be taken over by someone else. Fights and power struggles would cause a shift at the top. And whoever ended up running it would have to rebuild. It would be a long time before they managed to work up to the threat Carrerra had become to the government, if they ever did. More than likely, wars would erupt among the underlings; lieutenants and street gangs would vie for control of their little parts of the business until it fractured. Most of the drug gangs were held together by violence, the threat of violence and fear of one leader. When that leader was gone, the disintegration was almost always just a matter of time.

He finished his beer, marking the time the boy had been gone. Just as he began to think he'd slipped up again, the boy ducked back into the cantina. He carried a package wrapped in brown paper and moved a little uncertainly. He dropped the parcel on the table in front of Alex, who tore open the corner, looked inside, smiled thinly and nodded. Alex reached into his pocket and pulled out a few more coins. He slid them across to the boy, who took them quickly. For the first time since the two had met, Alex saw a toothy grin emerge from the lonely shadows of the young face. Then the boy turned and exited so quickly and silently he might never have been there at all.

Nonchalantly, Alex took the package and walked through the beaded curtains at the rear of the building and entered the men's room. Less than five minutes later he emerged wearing a bright red T-shirt with the Union Jack flag emblazoned across the front. His dark hair was tousled. The contacts were gone, returning his eyes to their natural blue color, and the makeup had been washed off his face, lightening his skin tone by several shades. He wore cheap mirrored sunglasses and in all respects now looked like a tourist rather than a native.

Without even glancing at the curtain, he entered the kitchen, crossed to the rear exit and slipped out into another alley. He was feeling better, and his thoughts had returned to the mechanical, clockwork efficiency of his art. There were streets at both ends of the alley. One was busier, and he chose it. He stopped just inside the mouth of the alley and waited.

Moments later, a brightly colored taxi rolled slowly by. There were religious icons on the dashboard, bright, reflective stickers on the bumpers and enough chains dangling from the rear-view mirror to obscure half the windshield. Alex sauntered out of the alley, picked up his pace and raised his hand. The taxi was moving slowly, and the driver caught sight of him, pulling to the curb. Alex slipped open the rear door.

He heard quick footsteps behind him and heavy breath. He didn't turn. He slipped into the backseat.

"Airport," he said softly. "Quickly!"

As the taxi rolled into traffic, Alex heard frustrated shouts behind them. Once again, the Chameleon had disappeared.

The taxi shot through traffic and rounded the first curve, nearly rolling up onto two wheels in the process. Alex had two lockers waiting—one at each end of the airport. Depending on what he saw when he arrived, he'd go to one or the other, change again, take his tickets and board a flight for the United States. He wanted a hot meal and a long nap. Maybe something stronger to drink than a cheap Mexican beer.

In his lap, his hand trembled, and he frowned, staring out into the growing darkness.

2

Three weeks later, Alex sat in the doctor's office, trying to remain calm. He'd have better luck staring into the business end of a gun than staring at that damned clock. The door popped open, nearly sending him off his seat. The groan of new leather betrayed him, and he fought to relax his muscles, to sink casually back into the chair.

Under normal circumstances, Alex would be utilizing one of the doctors who had been specially selected to serve the agents of Room 59. But this wasn't a normal circumstance and Alex wanted his situation to be private—at least until he could figure out what was going on and what to do about it. His mandatory time off after a mission was almost over, and he'd soon be sent out again. He needed to know what was wrong before that happened.

Alex had chosen Dr. Britton because he had a reputation for being discreet, he was one of the top in his field and he was close to home. He was also blunt and to the point, which Alex appreciated. As Dr. Britton stepped through the door, Alex's eyes riveted on his face, he shifted the file folder from one hand to the other. That folder bore the fruits of a battery of tests. It held Alex's fate.

"Sorry it took me so long." Dr. Britton eased into his own chair; the wheels scraped across the plastic mat as he moved closer to the desk. "I had to take an emergency call."

"No worries, Doc. It's not like I have somewhere else more important to be." Alex dry swallowed and recrossed his legs.

"Let's see." Britton sighed, licking one finger and turning quickly through the various lab results until he came to the one he wanted. "I'll start with the good news. You'll be happy to know that you're in wonderful physical shape. Heart good, lungs good, muscle tone impressive. That's all going to be a help to you with the bad news."

Alex offered up a tight grin by way of reply and recrossed his legs. Patience eluded him.

"The bad news is that there is one problem and it's a big one," the doctor said.

He paused, Alex supposed, awaiting a response. Alex gave none.

Dr. Britton nodded. "I'll put this as simply as I

can, then. No sense fooling around with it. Your MRI showed extensive lesions—we call them plaque—on your brain and spinal cord, and the fluid we took from your spine has elevated protein markers. You have multiple sclerosis, and based on the history you've given me, it's very progressive."

Alex felt the small lunch he'd eaten earlier rise into his throat, and his head spun. "MS. Like Muhammad Ali?"

"Not quite. Ali has Parkinson's disease, which is also neurological, but has a different progression. MS causes lesions on the brain and affects different parts of the nervous system based on where the lesions are occurring. Most forms of MS progress slowly, or more commonly relapse and remit, with recovery between. The symptoms are mild, often unnoticed at first, then build to larger problems over time."

"Like, decades, right?" Maybe he had time. Time to live, to work, to find a cure. Room 59 had access to all sorts of classified things. For all he knew, some government agency already had a cure that hadn't been released to the public yet.

The doctor shook his head. "Not decades, Alex. That's not the form you have. Your tests indicate that you most probably have primary progressive MS. Its onset is much more dramatic and, I'm afraid, it doesn't afford you as much time before you get into some serious and often debilitating symptoms."

"How long?"

Dr. Britton scanned his chart, avoiding looking up at Alex.

"Come on, Doc. Just give me the worst case and we can work back from there."

"Alex, there's just no real way to predict how MS is going to progress. Sometimes it can take quite a while before you run into serious problems, and then one day you wake up and can't get out of bed. With the problems that you're having now and the location and size of the lesions it could be as little as a few months, maybe less, maybe more. It's not a predictable disease."

Alex's face betrayed him. He could dodge bullets without so much as a tic, but this had thrown him into a spin. His grip on the arm of the chair loosened and he felt the tremors start again.

"Months."

"I'm sorry, Alex. This disease isn't something that I can give you a shot for—we can't even predict with any accuracy the symptoms you'll experience from one day to the next. Muscles spasms, tremors, pain, blindness—there are so many neurological possibilities." He slid several prescriptions across his desk and sighed. "There are some medications that will help relieve some of the symptoms for a while. They will help lessen the spasms a bit, make the pain more tolerable. But the disease has a mind of its own. It'll take its own

course and have done with you when it damned
well pleases."

"What can I expect? I mean—" Alex didn't
know what he meant. He wanted the doctor to tell
him he had years before he went shopping for a
personalized license plate for his wheelchair. He
wanted the doctor to guarantee him a few years
before he became totally useless.

More paper slid across the desk, this time in the
form of fat pamphlets. Alex took them without
really looking at them.

"You can read these and they'll give you a better
idea of where you're headed. There are also plenty
of informative Web sites on the subject. Do some
digging and you'll get a handle on what's known
about the disease. We'll want to repeat several of
the tests in a month, especially the MRIs, and then
again in six months if you're still—"

Alex's head snapped up, eyes glaring daggers.
"Alive? If I'm still alive?"

The faint smile disappeared from Dr. Britton's
face. "No, nothing that severe. But given what
we're looking at, if you are still walking I admit I
would be surprised."

Alex stood shakily. "I know. Not your fault.
Sometimes, shit just happens, eh?" He turned
toward the door, the pamphlets clutched tightly in
his hand. "I'll be back in a month. Then again in six."

Dr. Britton stared after him, frowning. "Call me

if you have any concerns, Alex. And try to minimize your stress. There are many worse neurological diseases than MS. It's not fatal. I could have told you that your life is ending."

Alex laughed harshly. "You just did."

Britton slumped back into his chair. "I'm sorry, Alex," he said. "You'll want to take some time with this at first. Just remember that stress makes MS symptoms worse. Go easy for a bit and maybe the symptoms will settle down a little."

Alex nodded sharply, then left, stalking down the hall toward the elevator. His face was steady and he hadn't blinked since opening the door to Dr. Britton's office. The Muzak droned in the elevator, but he didn't hear it. He stared straight ahead, stoic and silent. He showed no reaction at all until he stepped out onto the sidewalk and the bright midday sun assaulted his eyes.

There he stood, Alex Tempest, master spy and assassin, husband, father and soon…useless. For the first time, he became aware of the pamphlets in his hand. That hand trembled as it brought the pages closer to his line of sight and he grimaced. Multiple sclerosis. Didn't that just beat the hell out of the band?

He realized he'd never really thought about walking. Everyone just takes for granted that they can. It might have been easier if it had been a death sentence. That would have been devastating to most people, but Alex Tempest was not most people. He had thought at length about the manner and time of his death. He'd always figured that he'd die in a blaze of glory, bullets raining down on him from every direction. He'd hoped he would die in brave, heroic fashion, maybe even in the process of saving someone's life. Death like that was something he could face.

But he'd never imagined something like this. A disease, wasting him away, helpless in the face of an enemy he couldn't see, couldn't fight. It wasn't even a good disease, the result of a life of excess or debauchery. If it were, he'd at least have something to show for it—some good memories.

Two blocks down the street was a dark little bar called Pete's. Alex headed in that direction, the pamphlets clutched in his trembling hand. The prescriptions were tucked neatly into his wallet, folded twice to ensure a good fit. His free hand gripped the door handle and pulled, allowing him entrance to a world inhabited solely by the lost.

Inside, the bar was dark and the air smelled like stale beer and smoke. The faintest scent of burned French fries wafted out of the kitchen and the phone rang shrilly against the soft hum of voices. Alex slipped onto a stool and flagged down the bartender. "Double Black Jack, neat."

The bartender nodded, and then reached for a glass. It was artfully filled and pressed into his hand.

Alex traded him a twenty for it. "Four more. Line 'em up." He downed the first one and tried to smile.

"Tough day?" The bartender was too young and too innocent to know anything about bad days.

"Last day." The hint of sadness in Alex's voice was unmistakable and it was enough to make the bartender leave him alone with his liquid friends.

Alex sipped at the second drink and spread the pamphlets out on the bar. Might as well know what he was up against. He flipped open the fat one, skimmed the opening details and gore, then cut straight to the dos and don'ts. He hoped that he'd find some secret remedy contained in those scant pages. Instead, he found bad news and more bad news.

Chief among the don'ts was drinking. "Fuck you!" he grumbled to the pamphlet, then slammed it shut and tossed back the third shot. The bartender stared at him for a moment, then turned away in silence.

There were few dos included. Not much advice and little or no hope. Apparently, nothing much helped, beyond doing none of the things you enjoyed up until you were left drooling in a wheelchair and then killed by something stupid, like a cold, when your immune system finally collapsed.

He thought about his wife, Brin, and his eyes welled with tears. He'd have to tell her, but he didn't know how he'd do it. She was strong and brilliant and amazingly self-sufficient, but this would devastate her. And he didn't want to think about what the news would do to their daughter, Savannah. She was Daddy's girl, tried and true. Alex smiled as he thought about her, her sweet face, her tiny hand in his. Then he frowned. She was a little over two. If the disease progressed quickly, she might not even remember him, or worse, she might only remember an incompetent in a wheelchair who could never help her or protect her.

Alex thought he would rather be dead in some hell hole than face his wife and daughter with this kind of news. Dead that way, he was making a difference. He was a warrior, and if he couldn't fight this disease, he could damned well go out fighting.

And who knew, he thought, maybe he was strong enough to beat it for a while. The power of the mind, his body was still in great shape, maybe he could will himself to overcome the disease. He shook his head and took another swallow of the burning liquor.

If not, what good could he do himself, his family or the world, with this damned disease?

He swallowed as the answer came to him.

None.

3

Denny Talbot heard the faint tone in his earpiece that indicated someone wanted to speak to him and he slipped on the wraparound-style sunglasses that allowed him to access the virtual world of Room 59. Using his avatar, he keyed in the codes that would transform the digital green lines of nothingness into what looked like a normal office in seconds. When it was done and his avatar was seated, he said, "Enter."

Kate Cochran, the director of Room 59, came through his virtual door at a good clip, her platinum-blond hair bouncing around her neck as she moved. She had one of those damnable red folders in her hand, which meant this was important—life-altering important.

Denny leaned back in his chair, which squeaked

in protest. Everything in the Room 59 virtual world could appear as real or unreal as the user desired. He preferred reality to the strangeness of a dream, so his office mirrored reality to the smallest detail. "A red folder," he said without preamble. "What do you have for me this time?" A smile played at the corners of his mouth.

"Something big," Kate said. "And very juicy." She tapped the folder and set it on his desk. "Rare-steak juicy."

Denny started to reach for the file but she pulled it back just in the nick of time. "Okay, why don't you fill me in, then?" He smiled, full on, and laced his fingers over his belly as he rocked slowly in the chair.

"Ever heard of a company called MRIS? Medical Robotic Imaging Systems, Inc.?"

"Can't say as I have."

"They're a high-tech medical-imaging firm, mostly working on the research-and-development side of diagnostic equipment. They've even developed a successful prototype of a nanobot camera—nanobots are tiny robots that can be injected into a person's body—eliminating the need for such things as endoscopic procedures and upper GIs. It still needs a lot more testing before they can go public with it, but it will happen soon enough. They're privately funded, very quiet and already making hundreds of millions of dollars a year," Kate said.

Denny nodded, wondering where this was heading.

"Last year, MRIS opened a facility in China, up in one of the northern provinces, specifically for the continued development of this nanobot imaging system."

"Where's the part where this concerns us?" Denny asked. Kate could be blunt, but she could also drive a man to distraction with too much detail.

"Apparently, that isn't all they're up to. Yesterday, we got a communiqué from one of our assets in China. Site intel and surveillance shows that MRIS isn't *just* working on the imaging systems. Seems they're also building some sort of related biological weapon. According to the Chinese, the biological end of it is complete. It's just the weapon part—the delivery system—that needs work."

Now his interest was piqued. He sat forward and leaned both elbows on the desk. "And they want us to eliminate the threat."

"Bingo." Finally, she tossed the file across the desk, watching it skid slowly into Denny's hands. She took a seat in a chair and crossed her long legs, watching his face as he accessed the information and read through the file and scanned the pictures.

When he was done, Denny slid the folder back and shook his head. What he'd read had made him sick, deep inside. The particular nerve gas MRIS had created was very spooky. They'd found a way to use the nanobots to deliver a payload specifically designed to kill slowly in order to maximize suffering and increase the contamination rate. "They're right," he said. "We need to stop this. Now."

"Pai Kun completely agrees," Kate said. "It was one of his who that initially got the intel. But he wants us to take the lead on it, rather than using a local asset."

"Why?" Denny asked.

"He thinks we'll have a better shot at keeping things quiet and suspicion away from any of his local assets," she said. "I think he's right."

Denny stared at the folder for a long moment, and then glanced up, another question in his eyes. "Who do you want to send?" he asked.

"I was thinking of Alex Tempest. This is right up his alley. He'd be perfect for it."

Denny shook his head. "He's great at blending in, but even he might have trouble looking Chinese."

A crease formed down the middle of Kate's forehead and she frowned. "He pulled off that mission in Korea just last year," she countered. "I think he can do it."

"Maybe," Denny admitted. "But he's only been back from that mission in Mexico a few weeks or so. And things didn't go very well down there. I

was thinking of giving him some extended downtime."

Kate nodded thoughtfully and studied her shoes
for a moment. "There's nobody better suited for it,"
she said. "And we can't afford a failure here. Who
else has his level of experience, let alone his
training?"

"I can think of a few—"

"Who else will get the job done or die trying?
Come on! You know damned well that nobody
else we've got right now is capable of taking this
on with any kind of certainty of success. There's
only Alex." Kate paused for a moment and studied
his face with the trained eye of an interrogator.
"We mandate three weeks minimum between
missions, Denny. He's had that and is probably
sitting on his hands waiting for something else to
do by now. Maybe sending him back out is what
he needs, more than extra time off."

Denny thought for a moment. He knew Kate.
She had all the tenacity of a bull terrier. He could
tell her no until the cows came home and still not
win the argument. "All right. But you have to
promise not to try and influence his answer in any
way. Not to pressure him into it. I'm still waiting
for his full report on what happened down in
Mexico, but I've got a bad feeling right now where
he's concerned. If he says no, then we'll find
someone else, okay?"

Kate nodded her head slowly. "You know I would never, ever try to push an agent into taking on a detail he wasn't ready for."

Denny stood his ground, frowning. "Promise me."

When several beats passed without an answer from Kate, he glared at her, staring daggers. "Promise or you can ask him yourself."

She held up her hands to ward off the heat of his eyes. "Okay, okay! I promise I will not try to influence his decision in any way. Happy now?"

"Yes."

"Okay, then. Good luck chatting with Alex." Kate rose, tucking the folder under one arm and pushing open the door. Once outside, she shoved the door shut and Denny sighed, then disconnected from his virtual office.

They both knew it was as good as decided.

Alex would take the job. He was too white-hat not to.

4

Alex was folded over a cup of coffee, his gaze turned inward, when Brin joined him. She was dressed for work, not a hair out of place, her brown eyes bright and dazzling. He was the opposite— careless hair, unshaved, vision murky. When he wasn't on a job, he was unkempt and relaxed. He kept it casual. He loved that Brin could roll out of bed looking perfect. Her gorgeous blond hair always looked sexy, either smooth and perfect or playful and tussled, his favorite, the way she looked after sex. Or was it just that his love affected his vision?

Brin eased into the chair opposite his and rubbed his hand for a moment. "Sleep well?"

He looked up at her with a smile and a wink. "Always do, first night home." He hadn't told her that he'd been back for almost a month, staying in a nearby hotel until the doctors had finished working him over. It had been incredibly hard not to race right home, to see her and their daughter, but he wanted to know what was going on before he allowed himself the luxury of the feelings his family aroused in him.

"Me, too." She let loose an uncharacteristically girlish giggle.

Alex took a long sip of his coffee, studying her face over the rim of the cup. He held it in both hands, just in case the tremors returned. So far, they had only affected one hand at a time. He could always steady one hand with the other.

"Things went okay in Mexico, then?" She fiddled with her briefcase latch. "You were gone longer than I thought you'd be."

"Took longer than I thought," Alex said. "They don't have a lot of the resources we do here, but it turned out all right. No worries." Brin had no idea what Alex really did for a living. She thought he was some sort of security expert, doing contract work all over the world. He wasn't sure if she'd have been able to handle all the alone time if she'd really known what he was doing in those faraway places. But he couldn't tell her anything without putting her in danger and he liked the image that she had of him now. Besides, she might actually take exception to his killing people for a living.

Quite a few people seemed to think that it wasn't the most honorable line of work.

"Glad to hear it." She turned a bit in her chair, so that she was facing him, and cupped her chin in one hand. "So, how long do we have you for this time?"

"Right up to the moment you get tired of me. There's nothing on the radar, so I guess I've been gifted with some major downtime."

"Good. Savannah will be happy to hear that, too. She misses her big old daddy bear when he's gone."

If there was anything sexier than Brin talking baby talk, Alex couldn't imagine what it was. "I miss her, too. Like I'd miss the air." He reached for his coffee and a sigh slipped out before he could cut it short.

"Alex, are you all right?"

Confused, his arm paused halfway to his mouth and he frowned at her across the table. "Fine. Why?"

Her arms were folded and crossed on the table. She nodded toward his hand in a quick jerk of her head and the frown deepened.

Alex looked at his hand, holding the coffee cup almost to his lips, and his breath caught in his chest. It was shaking, and not just a little, but a lot. Coffee sloshed gently against the sides of the cup. Quickly, he transferred the cup to his left hand and put it back on the table.

"I'm fine, really. I'm just still a little tired from

the trip and all the excitement. Guess I just didn't realize how tired I was."

Brin's face was etched in worry, strained.

"Are you sure? Maybe you should see a doctor or something. I don't think I've ever seen your hands shake like that."

Her tone changed from concerned wife to scientist. He knew that he needed to move on to something else or she would sit and analyze until she uncovered the truth. Part of the problem with being married to a Ph.D. was that sometimes she was too observant for his own good.

"I'm sure. Now, come here, wife!" He held out his arms to her and she rose instantly, slipping around the table.

Alex grabbed her by the hips and swept her into his lap in one easy movement. His lips found hers from experience, resting there as they had done a thousand times before. When he released her, his eyes sparkled.

"If I were sick, could I still do that?" Another wink and a smile.

Brin giggled again and nuzzled his neck. "I guess not. Now, you have to let me go before I'm late for work. You get some rest today. Promise me?"

"Yes, Mother." He swatted her on the backside, a little too roughly perhaps, but with good humor and great results. "Love you."

5

With Brin safely off to work and Savannah hugged, kissed and off to day care, Alex was alone with his misery. He tried to focus, to find a positive he could cling to that would help him map out the next few months or weeks. Days? Nothing worked. He finished his coffee, then puttered aimlessly about the kitchen before pouring another cup.

He tried thinking about the house, his family and planning for the future, but it was hopeless. In many ways, they were fortunate—far more so than many of the people he'd seen in other countries. The house was paid for and a college fund for Savannah was already in place, accruing interest. He had more money tucked away than the family would ever need, and, in all reality, Brin didn't actually need it. The research lab she ran was on the cutting edge of the hunt to cure a dozen or more degenerative diseases. She made plenty of money on her own.

Sometimes he thought it was marriage to him that held her back from a Nobel Prize or more. And she was a wonder with Savannah. It was true that the girl loved her Daddy, but it was Brin who got the call when knees were scraped or a stuffy nose kept the girl from sleeping.

He couldn't shake the feeling of frustration that he wasn't going to be part of building their family, their life—-he was going to be a burden on it.

One thing was certain. He couldn't put off telling Denny Talbot that he was done as a Room 59 agent. They would have to replace him, and quickly. His personal life might have gone into a slide, but he knew the world wouldn't pay a bit of attention to that. He might even have saved it once or twice—it was all the same to Mother Earth.

Alex stalked to his desk. The computer monitor was dark. He punched the power button and brought the machine to life. As it booted up, he plopped into the leather chair and stared at the screen.

He didn't even know what he'd say when he logged in. He had his final report on the Mexican operation to upload, but they already knew the details. He'd given Denny a quick debrief when he'd returned. Nothing was really news to Kate or

Denny. They probably also knew that he'd nearly screwed up, though they wouldn't say anything about it. If he'd failed or the mission hadn't been completed, he'd be hearing about it in spades. His mistake this time had no lasting repercussions, so he was sure that was okay.

The computer screen filled with the smiling faces of Brin and Savannah, and Alex stared at them. He didn't want to touch the keyboard or the mouse. He didn't want to disrupt the image. With a long sigh, he leaned forward and typed in the coded keystrokes he'd memorized so long ago. While the commands ran, he removed his virtual reality glasses from a hidden slot beneath his desk and put them on. The image on the screen shifted, dissolving to a slowly spinning number 59 in the center of the screen, followed by a login prompt. This was the first of a multiple-stage process for logging into the ultrasecure Room 59 reporting center.

As he followed the familiar electronic trail, he considered what he'd say once he was in. He knew he'd have to resign. There was no way to continue under the circumstances. It was likely he wouldn't be in any condition to deliver for much longer.

He passed the final security level and his personal portal opened. To the right were icons for a variety of contacts and resources. Down the left side were alerts, memos and communications. The center icon sent a direct chat request to Denny.

Despite using the Room 59 technology on a regular basis, there was still a feel of science fiction to it all as far as Alex was concerned. Virtual offices, avatars, conference and briefing rooms. Anybody could look like anyone, though he'd noticed that humor was not highly appreciated. His initial avatar of choice had been Yoda, the Jedi master from the *Star Wars* movies. The frowns alone told him to choose something more mundane and now he appeared as a somewhat altered version of himself.

Alex started to open the link, and then stopped. One of the communications icons was blinking. He had an urgent message waiting for him. He frowned. These were usually reserved for assignments or emergencies. He hadn't even been home a full month, and they'd never contacted him for his next mission so quickly.

Yet there it was. Alex touched the icon with his virtual hand, and immediately a series of folders opened in front of him. The files were from Denny Talbot and Kate Cochran, including a note that he should review them before checking in for his assignment. A final document opened without prompting, and, curious, he began to read.

It was an intelligence report from one of their Chinese operatives, interspersed with notes from Chinese intelligence, as well as the conclusions of Denny and Kate and Pai Kun, the Room 59 leader for China. Alex's frown deepened. This intelligence represented a serious threat to the security of the world, but all it had taken was the name of the company, MRIS, to get his full attention. He quickly skimmed the rest of the materials.

He closed the document, minimized the files, reached out and launched the chat icon. The scene in front of him shifted and he was standing outside the door to Denny's virtual office. Denny had been waiting for him, and when he rapped on the door he heard "Enter," just as though they were in the real world.

Alex stepped through the doorway. Though he had never met the man in person, Alex suspected that Denny's avatar was exact in almost every detail. He had a heavy build and his hair was graying at the temples. Still, he looked strong, and his eyes were sharp. Denny didn't miss too many tricks, despite the fact that he wasn't a field man anymore.

"What do you have?" Alex asked without hesitation. "What the hell is this file, Denny?"

"Big stuff, cowboy," Denny replied. "The Chinese are pretty worried over this one, and if they don't like it, you know it's got to be bad. They don't play well with others, as a general rule."

"I just got home a few weeks ago," Alex said. "I was sort of planning on some downtime." He knew it didn't mean a thing; he was buying time and running what he'd read through his mind. He knew he should be telling Denny what the doctor had said. This one was hot, and there wasn't going to be a lot of time to find someone else to handle it. If there was someone else.

"I know, Alex, and I hate it, especially considering that things didn't go great for you in Mexico, but I told Kate I'd at least present it to you. We don't send out operatives this soon unless it's mission critical, and I like to give my men at least a month or more off between assignments."

"That's why I'm surprised," Alex said. "I've always had at least that long—usually closer to six weeks or more—between missions."

"This is going to be a tough one, Alex. Security is tight, and the schedule is half a gnat's ass short of insane. We're under the gun, and you may be our only field agent who can pull it off. You have experience with the Chinese, and you speak the language."

It was true. Alex had completed two missions in the east in the past ten years. As an Army Ranger he'd been specially trained for Chinese operations—he spoke several dialects, and with some work he could pass for a tall Asian if he had to. Of course, given the right opportunity, he could pass for almost anything.

"The file said MRIS was involved," Alex said. "You know Brin works for them. It's pretty close to home."

"As far as we know, her work isn't a part of this," Denny said, "but it's a safe bet that they're using every resource they have in one way or another, even if the people don't know it themselves. I doubt there's any part of the company not involved in this one way or another. I'm sure she's clean— we checked and rechecked to make sure—but I don't know what it will mean for her if they bring this all together. Hell, I don't know what it will mean for China, or the world, but it won't be good. Chemical attacks are bad enough—if they manage to infect someone over here with those damned nanobuggers of theirs, it could get out of control pretty fast. We can't let that happen."

"Of course not," Alex agreed. "Do we have an in? They're going to be looking for trouble, especially if they're as close as you say. You sure we have time for this? Might be better to turn one like this over to more standard channels and get them shut down."

"Can't risk it," Denny said so quickly that he must have anticipated the question. He was like that. "Relations between China and the U.S. are already too strained. Our sources on this are in deep—they can't be the ones to bring this forward. If we tried it, it would just be seen as us taking another shot at their culture. They'd tighten up, shut us out, and by the time they'd realized their mistake, it would be over. We have to go in—hard, fast and right now."

Alex didn't reply. Denny didn't wait long.

"You want it, cowboy?"

Alex glanced down at his hand. For the moment, it was steady. He thought of Brin, smiling at him and hurrying Savannah out the door. There was such trust in that smile, such love. How could he leave her alone to face—what? A company that wasn't really trying to cure diseases, but intent on spreading new ones? Would she be safe? Would they come after her, others like her, to force them into creating bigger, better diseases instead of curing the ones they had now? How long before Savannah was in danger?

He sighed. Maybe he wasn't one hundred percent, but even at ninety he was better than most. This might be his last shot at doing something that really meant something. Maybe he could beat the MS and still do what he loved.

"I'm in," he said. "Give me what you've got."

"Timetable transferring to your calendar," Denny replied. "You have the files. There are photos, a database of personnel, instructions on contacts and credentials. You know the drill. Once it's all transferred, and you're airborne, we're out."

"The assignment?" Alex asked. He knew the information would be in the file, but he wanted a few seconds more to back out if he thought of a way to get clear. Nothing came to mind, and this wasn't a drug lord making things nasty on the border—this was a huge global threat.

"We need the research either retrieved or wiped out," Denny replied. "It has to be removed from all their systems and backups. We want it utterly gone. There is also a list of key personnel, the people we have established with certainty are behind this. They have to be taken out of the equation so they don't just recreate the work. There has to be a message sent with this, Alex. It must be made clear that this kind of thing won't be tolerated. If we hit too hard, we'll get too much attention—but if we don't hit them hard enough, they'll—"

"Just come back like bad pennies," Alex finished. "Where do we stand right now for field support?"

"You'll have a local asset in Beijing who will supply any and all needs beyond your departure. You have, of course, full run of equipment, data and assistance on this end. That ends the minute you hit the ground over there, so take advantage while you have the chance."

"Will do," Alex replied. "Damn. And I was looking forward to weeding the garden this week."

"You'll get to it, cowboy," Denny said.

"Yeah," Alex replied. "I guess. I'm out. I have a lot of reading to do, and then I have to explain to Brin and Savannah why I won't be taking them camping this weekend."

"Alex, one other thing," Denny said. "I tried to talk Kate out of calling you on this one. I know you could use a break—if for no other reason than to finish that report on Mexico."

"It's okay," Alex replied. "I have to do this—you know I do. It's too close for me to ignore. I'll get in, do the job and get out as quickly as I can. Plenty of time left for gardening when it's done." He grinned. "And I'll upload the report on my last mission to you before I leave."

"That's the spirit," Denny replied. "Catch you soon."

Alex left Denny's office, then brought up the icons again, choosing the one for home. His view shifted and once more he was in his own virtual office. He flipped open the first file. He wouldn't be able to download or print any of the data, so he had to make the most of the time he had to read and memorize everything they knew. His life might depend on it. What he could safely carry would be waiting for him at the equipment drop—names, photos and false identification.

"Damn," he muttered. "Holy five-flaming hell."

He cursed, and he read, and he drank black coffee. When his hand twitched and then began to tremble, he told himself it was just the caffeine.

Alex had meant to offer his resignation. To call it quits and spend his last good days with his wife and daughter. If Denny or Kate or anyone in Room 59 found out about the MS, the mission would be aborted. They might even take him out to keep

him from snapping. He couldn't let that happen—
he needed this one. It was his chance at the blaze
of glory—a final shot at being a hero. This was a
mission that could make a difference, and he
wasn't about to turn it down. A warrior without a
war to fight wasn't much of anything.

As far as missions went, it was a good one. Chal-
lenging and making the world a safer place. At the
least it beat holy hell out of a pile of useless pamphlets and a race to oblivion. It would have to be
enough.

As Alex read, memorizing names and places
and facts, the sun slipped toward the horizon. The
sad little lamp on his desk—considered a treasure
when they'd found it at the garage sale years ago—
was an inadequate soldier against the shadows that
had filled the room. He was just about to take a
break, make some more coffee, when he heard
sounds of talk and laughter in the driveway. Brin
and Savannah, returning from their day out in the
world. How many times had Brin come home to
an empty house since they'd been married? Too
many, he guessed. Still, that would be ending soon
enough.

Alex disconnected from his office, and put the
glasses back beneath the desk, then stood and
walked toward the front door. For now, his body
seemed to be obeying all commands, but he wasn't
sure just how long that would last. The door swung

open, and there was Brin, looking every bit as prim as she had that morning, one hand full of mail, the other clutching her briefcase.

"Hey, you." Alex chuckled. He leaned on the wall, this time because he wanted to, not because he needed the support.

"Daddy!" Savannah rocket launched across the room and left the ground in one last glorious leap, knowing that her daddy would catch her in midair.

Catch her he did, smothering her little cheeks and neck with kisses and growling his big bear hug into her hair. God but he'd missed that! "How was your day, princess?"

"Good day, Daddy." Savannah smiled, eyes sparkling, giggling as she patted him down for presents.

"Sorry, kiddo. Daddy hasn't even left the house."

She sighed and squirmed, wanting to be put down.

"How about you, Mommy?" Alex asked. "How was your day?"

He set Savannah on the floor and turned to sweep Brin into his arms. She was ready with a kiss and a smile, and most anything else he needed. He hoped she was ready with understanding, too.

"You know, gene splicing, curing diseases, saving the world. Blah, blah, blah!" She tossed the mail and her keys onto the hall table and tucked her hair behind her ears. "Give me a minute to change and I'll start dinner."

Alex wondered if her company was also working on a cure for MS, and if they were, would they find anything in time to save him. None of the pamphlets he'd read sounded promising, but a lot of medical advances were kept quiet until they were ready for a public unveiling. Maybe when he got back from this mission, when he could tell her the truth about his condition, he'd ask her about it.

She was halfway to the bedroom before Alex thought to call after her. "No need. I ordered pizza and it should be here any minute."

She spun on him, a silly, crooked grin stuck to her face. "I'm that predictable that you can order food to be delivered the moment I walk in the door?"

"Yep! You're the predictable one. I'm the irrational, flighty one. Good system." The doorbell rang and he reached for his wallet. "Hurry up and change. I'll get the pizza and get Miss Savannah seated."

He swung open the door and thrust out the twenty in one easy movement. The pizza guy was young and his face looked a lot like the pizza he delivered. Outside, there was a small blue Toyota, built sometime back when Carter was still in office.

Alex smiled. "Keep the change." He shut the door and turned the lock.

When he reached the kitchen, Savannah turned and smiled at him from where she sat, legs swinging, in the high chair. "Pizza! Yay!"

Alex stopped abruptly and frowned, then grinned to himself. "Did you get up there all by yourself?" Of course she did. Who else would have helped her?

Savannah mumbled something incoherent but nodded her agreement.

"You're a very smart girl. But please—" He stooped to fasten the strap and put on the tray. Then he leaned in close and whispered, "Please don't grow up so fast. Daddy will miss his little girl."

He pecked her cheek and slid her close to the table, stopping then to study her face. It changed daily, growing, maturing. A week away brought him home to find all her expressions morphed somehow. A month, and he could hardly recognize her.

"Did you remember the pineapple? I love pineapple." Brin swept into the room, still buttoning the buttons on her blouse.

Alex caught sight of her and smiled, thinking how nice it would be to pop each and every button right off. "Pineapple present and accounted for, ma'am!"

She smacked him as he saluted.

There was lots of pizza, chitchat, a sundae for

Savannah. The normality of it almost made Alex think that things might end up fine. It was all part of the dance. They both knew what they were working toward…later…after Savannah had gone to bed.

The nightly ritual was followed to the letter. The table was cleared, Savannah bathed, her story read and her little covers pulled tightly under her chin. Just the way she liked it. Her poodle night-light softly glowed from across the room, and Alex blew kisses as he shut the door.

His body had behaved quite nicely all evening. He was thankful for that much. Brin waited for him in the kitchen, a glass of wine in each hand. She pressed one into his right hand and turned him toward the door with a kiss, then pushed him in the direction of the sofa.

Alex took up his place, all territories having been decided on long ago. Brin slid into his arms and sipped her wine, pulling his arm around her and kissing the back of his hand.

"I missed you so much." She sighed. "I always do."

For a moment, he thought he would cry. He took a sip of his wine, against doctor's orders, and swallowed hard. "I missed you, too. I just don't feel right when I'm away from my girls. Which is why I don't want to leave you again. But I have—"

He got no further. Brin spun in his arms,

crushing her lips to his, shaking a bit as she kissed him. When she pulled back, there were tears in her eyes and her lip quivered.

"Wow! What was that all about?"

"I didn't want you to tell me that you're leaving again. Not so soon. Please, not so soon. You just got home."

He drew the back of one hand over her soft cheek, found a tear there and wiped it away. "I wouldn't go if it weren't important, Brin. It's my job. I have to go."

"I know." Her voice quavered. It broke his heart. "When do you leave?"

"Tomorrow."

"No. Please."

She hesitated, then dropped her eyes in resignation. "Where to?"

"The Middle East," he said, hating to tell her yet another lie, but knowing that he could never tell her the truth. "I can't be any more specific. This is huge. Really huge. I couldn't say no." She nodded and he continued. "After this one, no more for a long time. I swear. I'll take an *extended* downtime. Maybe we'll even take a vacation."

"Promise?"

He nodded. "I promise."

She slid along his body, pushing with her toes and letting her lips reach for his. One hand found his glass, pulled it free and set it on the table. She kissed him again, then whispered, her breath washing hot over his cheek, "Make love to me. Please."

He slid his fingers into her hair, pulled her down on top of him, and the world faded to soft flesh and whispered kisses.

For a while, it was almost enough to make him forget.

6

It was still dark when Alex woke. He lay very still, not wanting to disturb Brin, who was curled tightly against his side. Sunrise was still more than an hour away, and he dreaded its arrival. The new day would mean the beginning of the end, the start of his last mission before the disease took its inevitable toll.

Even after reading through the pamphlets and scouring the Web, all Alex really knew was that his prognosis was grim. Primary progressive MS, when it moved quickly, often robbed a person of mobility, eyesight…even sex could become too painful or impossible due to mobility impairments. He didn't want to go out that way—useless, hopeless, miserable.

Too many things he cared for would begin to

unravel when the night ran down, and he could hear it ticking away like a giant clock—or a bomb. He would do this last mission and go out a hero.

Brin stirred, rolling toward him, and he slid his arm around her, pulling her close. She turned a sleepy-eyed smile up to him, and he brushed her eyelids with his lips. He was shocked at the sudden heat the contact brought. She sensed it and pressed closer, running her lips up his chest. He shivered as her hair tickled his throat.

Alex rolled onto his side, slid his arm across Brin's body and rose to stare down at her. His arm trembled and his heart raced.

"No," he whispered.

"What?" Brin raised her head, but he dropped over her fiercely, covering her lips and sliding his hips up to mesh with hers. She gasped, but as his palm pressed her thigh, she parted her legs and he drove forward, pinning her to the mattress, pressing so tightly the friction burned. She cried out, but not in pain. Her legs curled around him, drawing him deeper still, and he dropped into the sensation. He ground his hips, and she met each motion. He slid over her, felt her breasts press into him, nipples hard and rough. Sweat lubricated their motion and they fell into a rough rhythm.

The room blurred and Alex closed his eyes. He wrapped his arms around Brin's taut, muscled body and moved with her, chasing the sounds of her pleasure with his motion. He closed his eyes and clutched the sheets, digging his fingers into the mattress and fighting for control. She sensed his urgency and bucked up into him with a soft cry. It was more than he could stand.

Tears flowed down his cheeks and blended with the sweat of their coupling as they climaxed. His body tightened, shuddered and grew still, but he didn't move off of her. He lay there, limp, drained and gasping for breath as she kissed his cheeks, ran her fingers through his hair and brushed his shoulders with long, sharp nails. Slowly his mind, heart and lungs dropped back through levels of sensation. He felt her heartbeat against his chest. He lowered his head and managed to brush his eyes on the sheet in his hand in a pretense of wiping away sweat. He didn't want her to see his tears.

Brin stroked his hair in silence for a few moments.

"What was that?" she asked.

"You didn't enjoy it?" He stiffened at the thought it might have all been for himself, that he might have stolen their final moments of intimacy in selfish lust.

"I didn't say that. It was wonderful. It *is* wonderful. But it was so intense. It was like you were trying to pull me into you, or through you. I—"

Before she could go on, a soft thump sounded beyond the door. They both glanced up sharply. The sound repeated and Alex couldn't stifle a chuckle. He rolled slowly off Brin, wrapping her in his arms. She reached down quickly and drew the sheet and comforter farther up the bed.

"Savannah?" Alex called. "Are you out there?"

They lay in silence for a moment longer. The bump repeated and a soft voice called out.

"No."

They both laughed, and moments later, childish giggles sounded in the hall.

"Go lay down, baby," Brin called out. "We'll be out in a minute."

"I want to come in," Savannah called petulantly. "I want to wake you up."

Brin started to speak again, but Alex stopped her. His hand shook as he gripped her arm, and he released her as if he'd been bitten. He let his voice break a little to help explain away the tremor.

"Let's get dressed and let her in," he said softly. "I miss both my girls, you know? I don't want to miss a moment with either of you."

She watched him. He saw her glance at his hand, and he willed it to be steady, just this one time. It remained rock solid, and she stroked his cheek, then laughed.

"Okay, hotshot. I'll get dressed first, then you. I have to get out and make breakfast. I have a big day. I have a meeting with Rand this morning, something new—and big. He wants me to go over some new research."

"Big brains and nice breasts." Alex laughed. He lunged for her, but she was too quick, slipping off the edge of the bed. He watched her, and a lump filled his throat. He didn't try to speak, and moments later she had her nightgown on and stood, waiting on him.

"Rise and shine, hero," she said, smiling brightly. "I get the shower, you get the child. I'll trade you in twenty minutes."

He grinned at her, rolled out of the bed and fumbled in the dresser until he found a pair of pajama pants and a T-shirt. He turned just in time to see Brin disappear into the hall, and Savannah's bright, inquisitive face peering back in through the door. Growling like a bear, he charged.

His daughter squealed, spun and scampered off down the hallway. Alex pursued, but not too quickly. Some races are better if you come in last, and he knew where she was headed. A soft couch pillow to hide behind and screams for cartoons would come next. He smiled and dived after her, sliding onto the couch, spinning and curling her in close. Before she could even ask, he'd clicked the remote and brought the big-screen TV to life. Alex buried his nose in his daughter's soft hair and closed his eyes as she giggled, squirmed and laughed at the prancing animated nonsense on the screen.

He squeezed her tight, enjoying the contentment he felt at that moment. If only it could always be that way.

THE REST OF THE MORNING passed far too quickly. He nearly broke down hugging Savannah goodbye, and she wasn't happy to hear he was leaving again. Alex watched from the doorway as Brin bustled the girl into the SUV, and didn't turn away until the two of them were down the road and out of sight.

He packed lightly. There was no way to know what he was getting into—not exactly. It was better to choose his gear after he knew. His magic was camouflage, but it was a subtle art. He couldn't carry too much, or too little. It wasn't enough to take on the appearance of a new persona. It was absolutely inadequate to simulate change. He had to disappear. He had to melt into another reality where Alex Tempest didn't exist at all—or if he did, he was disconnected. He had very little time.

Too many things could go wrong. If the doctor mentioned his condition to anyone connected to Room 59, the mission would be aborted. If there was any incident indicating he was less than one hundred percent, he'd never leave the country. Funding would dry up, and very likely his access to Room 59 would cease to exist, as well. There was nothing he could do to expose them, not that he would. They might contact him, but somehow he didn't believe that they would. They were a tight, close-knit group, for all their independent operations, but there was one truth binding them all. The mission came first. The greater good overshadowed personal glory, needs and safety.

In less than an hour, he was out the door. Before he left, he went to the small garden he and Brin had planted behind the house. Very carefully, he clipped a single rose and a small violet. He carried them inside and sat at the table in the kitchen to write.

He started several notes to Brin. He wanted to tell her everything. Their love had always been based on trust, and not sharing—particularly at this moment—felt like a betrayal. In the end, he carefully shredded his first four attempts and wrote simply, "I love you," on a card. He drew a heart and carefully slit the paper, sliding the stem of the rose through it like an arrow.

Then, with equal care, he drew a cartoon bear on a second sheet of paper. He laid the violet across it and wrote carefully, "I can't bear to be without you. See you soon. Love, Daddy."

He couldn't remember ever tearing up so many times in the space of a single day. It seemed as though even the ability to control his emotions was being taken from him. He brushed it away, grabbed his things and slipped out the door, locking it behind him. He looked back only once, staring at the small, comfortable home wistfully. Then he turned and walked into another life as if he'd never existed.

7

Brin spent the first hour in her office, filing corre-
spondence, answering e-mail and fuming over lost
time. Meetings were a big part of her life as
director of the lab, but they infuriated her. Every
moment she spent schmoozing board members,
entertaining investors and planning for the future
of the company was time away from her research.

A lot of very talented men and women were
involved in the same sort of research she conducted,
searching for clues to the nature of degenerative
diseases, testing and retesting possible cures. She
knew most of the best and brightest by name, the
rest by reputation. In a few she recognized kindred
souls, minds and hearts dedicated to healing and
life. In too many others, though, she found only
greed, pride and the bickering nature of academia.

This time it felt different. She'd had an odd sense of impending accomplishment since the call from her CEO, Hershel Rand. He very seldom involved himself in the nuts and bolts of the company. He was a high-energy, high-efficiency administrator. He knew the worlds of money and corporate warfare as well as Brin knew her cultures and petri dishes, and the two rarely crossed paths. Other than annual budget talks and occasional pep talks, he let her run things the way she saw fit.

Now he said he had something she had to see, something he didn't trust anyone else to handle. He knew how she worked, and more importantly, she thought he knew why she worked. He said researchers in China had presented some brilliant work—something that could shift the entire paradigm of genetic research. These weren't the sorts of things he would say in idle conversation. Nothing was insignificant in his world; no moment was wasted. As Brin's fingers slipped and she nearly spilled a file folder's contents onto the floor in her haste to clear her desk, she smiled. She hadn't been so excited about a meeting since her initial job interview years in the past.

She only wished Alex would be there to share it with. He didn't fully understand her work, but he supported it—and her—and she knew he'd listen. When he was away, she felt isolated and kept things bottled up. He really was a vital part of her life, and she felt—too often—that she was operating under a painful handicap.

Brin swept the rest of the mess off her desk and into a large box. She could file it later, when there was idle time. Her hand whipped up in a nervous gesture that displayed the watch Alex had given her for her first Mother's Day—the year she got pregnant with Savannah. Five minutes. She'd better go upstairs to Hershel's office.

She made the elevator just as the doors began to close, slipped inside and sighed with relief. The ninth-floor button was already lit and she smiled. She didn't usually get this worked up, but Hershel had been excited and her mood had fed off his ever since.

Elaine, Rand's executive assistant, was at her appointed place, the phone tucked under her ear and her glasses halfway down her nose. She waved Brin past, into the CEO's office. The door was open.

The office was empty, another odd fact. Hershel never left his door open, especially not when he was out of the office. Brin slipped inside and eased into a leather chair. She bit her lip and wondered if she'd have long to wait. Nothing about this day, or this meeting, was normal—why expect the normally punctual Rand to be the exception? She had just fixed her gaze on the skyline beyond the great window when her boss popped up from behind the desk, scaring her half to death.

"God! You just about gave me a heart attack!" She laughed then, but there was little humor in it.

"Sorry. I had some new equipment installed this morning and the cords keep tangling around my chair wheels." He offered up a feeble smile, stood and crossed the room in quick strides. "Let's get down to it, shall we?" He stuck his head out the door. "Elaine, turn on my voice mail and go get yourself a latte. Don't come back until I call you." He shut the door to his office firmly.

Brin frowned. She had never known Elaine to leave her desk without someone to fill in, and she had never known Rand to let her. She studied his face as he slid back into his chair, rolled forward and regarded the plasma monitor set into the top of his desk. Whatever he saw there made him smile and he relaxed a bit.

"Everything okay?" Her voice sounded weak, even to her.

"Fine. Just making sure we're really alone, if you know what I mean. Now, as I said, we have some research material coming in from China. You'll be impressed—I guarantee it."

"All right. But why not have it sent electronically? We've got the best network security in the business."

"You don't understand. This is huge. World-changing huge. I couldn't risk having it sent electronically, no matter how impressive security is. It will be arriving late this afternoon, and after I review it, you'll get a chance to have a go at it."

"What type of research is it?"

"Sorry, Brin, not just yet. All I want you to do right now is clear your schedule. This project is going to be your number-one priority for a while anyway. And I have to insist that you not discuss this. Not with anyone on your team, not with Alex. No one. Do you understand?"

She paused for a moment, the crease in her forehead deepening. This was so out of character for Rand that it scared her. "I understand. And I don't discuss my work, except in the vaguest of terms, with anyone. I doubt they'd understand anyway. But my team—"

"Is out of the loop on this one. Totally out. It's you and me. I need your help on this one, but it has to be our secret," Rand said.

"Understood. I don't have a problem with that, but any serious research is going to require assistance."

"I knew you'd understand. Once things get past the initial stages, we'll find ways to compartmentalize the research. Now, I have another meeting. I'll let you know when it arrives." He gestured in the direction of the door, dismissing her. His face, which had shown traces of humor when he popped up from behind the desk, now lacked any humor at all. In fact, it seemed almost pressed in on itself, creased and tight with stress.

Brin nodded slowly and made for the door. Whatever was going on was huge—that was certain. And it made her nervous as hell. It also irritated her that Rand was so nervous he'd called a meeting with her to not tell her what was going on. He could have had her meet him after whatever the big deal was arrived. Every move he'd made on this one was out of character. There was only one thing that would make her feel better—Alex. She only hoped that she wasn't too late to catch him.

Cell phones were prohibited inside the building. Not only did they lead to slacking off, but they also interfered with a lot of the equipment they used and could be a security risk. Brin made for the roof of D-wing. It was only five stories high and there was a small lounge out there for those people who liked to escape the sterile air of the lab. In that small area, the cell phone dead zone was lifted. She hurried out the door, smiling as five pairs of eyes met hers and looked askance of her.

Alex's cell phone was first on her speed dial, permanently recorded in every contact log she had. "Alex," she said quickly and the phone dialed. There was a dead-air pause and then it rang. And rang. Suddenly, Brin felt as though she might cry. Her call was forwarded to voice mail and she stomped her foot, cursing her luck for having been too late.

"I just wanted to call and let you know that I

miss you already." She swallowed hard, fighting back tears at the thought of how empty the house would be that night. "I love you."

She slapped the phone shut and sighed, staring at the clouds for a moment before she shuffled through the door, back into the carefully sterilized and conditioned air. Now she wished that research would hurry up and arrive. At least then, she would have something to focus on other than Alex's absence.

8

Alex stepped out onto the tarmac and heaved a sigh of relief. It had been a long flight to Seoul and his back ached. He couldn't be sure whether the pains and twitches were from exhaustion or a byproduct of the MS, and just that uncertainty alone was enough to keep his nerves on edge and disrupt his rhythm. He stretched, yawned and headed toward the south side of the airport. He'd arrived in a private Room 59 jet that traveled under a counterfeit corporate name. If someone checked, the phones would be answered, but the address was nothing more than an abandoned warehouse near the docks in New York.

His contact in Seoul would provide his gear and take him into China. There was nothing like running around the fence to get to the barn to eat at a man's nerves.

About three hundred yards away from where the plane he'd come in on was parked, another plane waited. This one was smaller and not anywhere as close to being well-maintained. A small Asian man puttered about beneath it, checking the landing gear and whistling. Alex recognized him immediately as Yoo Jin-Ho, a contact he had used before in both Korea and Southeast Asia. Jin had the typical dark hair and eyes of his native Korea, and his skin was still ageless and smooth. It was a small relief to see a familiar face, but something was off and it took Alex a moment to place it.

What was unrecognizable was the bright smile on Jin's face. The last time Alex had seen him, he'd been beating the hell out of a South Vietnamese asset who'd turned double agent. Jin's smile widened, and he climbed to his feet, wiping his hands on his gray coveralls and then extending one in a handshake.

"Good to see you again, my friend. I trust you are well?"

"Fine as frog's hair. It's good to see you, too, Jin," Alex replied.

Jin nodded. "Your jumper is in the plane with the rest of your things. We're flying a load of televisions to Beijing today. I hope you are up to some heavy lifting."

"I'll go change," Alex said, "and check my gear."

He turned and marched up the short stairway into the plane. It was a small cargo plane and, judging from the smears of oil on each side, the engines had failed more than once. When not assisting the agents of Room 59, Jin ran a small freight service out of Seoul. He had a couple of planes, one other employee—his son—and a boatload of guts. Alex had liked him at first sight and he welcomed the opportunity to see the man again.

His hands had begun to tremble, and he made a conscious effort to remember to keep them out of sight. Jin was no fool, and if he caught a whiff of something, anything, wrong, he'd bow out. Jin wasn't a coward, but he didn't like taking stupid chances. There was no way to complete the mission without him.

The tremors were very slight this time, but enough to remind Alex that he wasn't one hundred percent. He had to lean on the cargo netting in order to pull on his jumper, and it made him want to hit something. Already he felt exhausted and wrung out, even though all he'd done so far was sit on the long, boring flight from the U.S. to Seoul and review the mission parameters.

Jin had placed a large duffel bag in the back of the plane. It contained everything Alex needed for the mission except the explosives. It wouldn't do to be caught entering China with those. Aside from that, he was well equipped. Jin had come through for him yet again. Alex settled in, lost in thought.

When Jin's face popped back over the pilot's

seat a few moments later, the sound of his voice startled Alex, and he sat up, shaking his head.

"I've filed the flight plan and almost finished the checklist. We should be able to take off in about twenty minutes."

Alex hadn't even heard the pilot return. "Good. I'm ready to get started," he said. "The sooner I can get this over with, the better." He checked the cargo netting over his duffel, and glanced dubiously at the boxed televisions lining the cargo bay.

"So, all of those are boxes are TVs?" Alex asked, raising an eyebrow.

"That's what my invoice says. You know what a law-abiding man I am," Jin said.

"Do you know anything about the local asset I'll be utilizing in Beijing?"

"I don't know him personally," Jin said. "He has a good reputation, gets the job done at all costs. Very John Wayne. Reminds me of someone else I know, eh?"

Alex chuckled and looked down at his boots. "You *do* know me too well. Usually I kill anyone who does."

"I'll take my chances. Now, I have to finish the last three things on this checklist and then we'll take off. You might as well strap in."

Alex slipped the harness over his waist and clipped the buckle together. No matter how many times he rode in one, he would never get used to the touch-and-go ride of these little puddle jumpers. He sighed and for a moment his mind was pulled back to Brin and Savannah. It made his heart ache. He was anxious to get this flight under way. The sooner he got started on this mission, the sooner he could be on his way back to them. The longer he was away, the less precious time he'd be able to offer them. He knew he had to tell Brin everything, and the thought of it filled him with dread.

Alex closed his eyes and pictured his two girls curled up together on the big bed, and he fell asleep with that image filling his thoughts.

9

Brin awoke the next morning to Savannah's sweet face. Somehow, she had crawled into bed with her mommy, laying her head on the pillow where Alex usually slept and staring at her mother until she woke up—another thing Alex did. Brin's eyes snapped open and a small gasp escaped her lips. That first glimpse of Savannah's eyes made her think, just for a second, that Alex had somehow returned to her. Stupid. He was never gone less than five days, and quite often it was several weeks or more.

"Good morning, baby." She kissed the tip of the girl's nose. "And what are you doing out of your bed?"

"I have to go potty."

There was urgency in that last, a little fear, as well.

"Let's go, then."

Brin threw back the covers and grabbed the girl, hurrying down the hall toward the bathroom. No telling how long it had been since that urge first hit. No telling how long the girl could hold out. She tugged her daughter's pants down and placed her gently on the potty seat, then turned to take care of her own needs. Before she could even get the lid up, the phone rang, echoing down the hall and making Brin's head hurt a bit.

"Who the hell would call at this hour?" She glanced at the clock in the living room and realized that it was past nine.

"Hello?" she mumbled, the phone halfway to her ear.

"This is Woodard's Pharmacy. We have a prescription ready for Alex Tempest."

Brin spent a long moment furrowing her brow instead of speaking. "Uh, okay. I didn't know he needed a prescription filled. As far as I was aware—never mind. I'll be down in a few hours to pick it up for him, if that's all right."

"That'll be fine, Mrs. Tempest. Thank you."

"Goodbye."

Down the hall, Savannah had sounded the "I'm done" alarm. Brin hurried down the hall to help her.

"You go sit in the living room. Mommy will be there in a minute to get your juice. I just have to go potty first." She pecked the top of Savannah's head and shooed her out the door.

Was Alex sick? She didn't remember his mentioning anything about a doctor or medicine. She wasn't even aware that he hadn't been feeling well. Suddenly, she felt like the worst wife in the world.

Savannah's juice chant made her finish in a hurry. The next hour would be filled with getting ready and feeding Savannah her breakfast. No time to wonder what, if anything, was wrong with Alex. Savannah was cute and sweet and it truly was a blessing to be her mom. At the moment, the girl was a godsend. If not for her daughter, Brin would just sit around and worry all weekend.

After they finished breakfast, cleaned up the kitchen and went through the complex rituals involved in dressing Savannah for the day, Brin threw on her own clothes and they piled into the SUV. She had the usual shopping to do for the week. But first she had to stop at the pharmacy.

When Alex and Brin had first moved to the neighborhood, Woodard's Pharmacy was the only one for ten miles. There were several more now, of course. But they continued to use Woodard's out of loyalty and comfort. There were things in that pharmacy that you couldn't find anywhere else, like a dollar ice cream cone and a pharmacist who kept track of all your medicines and knew when not to give you one pill with another. They also

sent cards on your birthday. That kind of dedica-
tion and caring just couldn't be bought.

They were no sooner through the front door of
Woodard's than Savannah was running full-tilt
toward the ice cream counter. They also had
squished cheese sandwiches there, which made
Savannah squeal with delight.

"Savannah, no, honey. We'll have ice cream
after I get Daddy's medicine, okay?" The day was
hot and the ice cream would taste so good, but
first things first.

"Aaaawwww!" There was a tiny foot stamp to
punctuate her disappointment, but no tantrum
followed. Her terrible twos hadn't been too
terrible—so far. Brin took her daughter's hand and
led her to the prescription counter, where she was
met by a young woman with a head full of thick
red hair and the brightest green eyes Brin had ever
seen. As many times as she'd been in the place,
she'd never seen the girl before. For some reason
the change in personnel felt like a betrayal.

"Hello, I'm Mrs. Tempest. You called earlier about
my husband's prescription?" She felt Savannah lean
against her leg and knew that all was well.

"Please give me your husband's full name and
address."

"Alex Tempest. One-thirty-four Brickle Lane."

"Thank you, Mrs. Tempest." The young lady
sorted through the waiting prescriptions and pulled

out the proper bag. She held the bag out to Brin with one hand and worked the cash register with the other. "That'll be thirty-eight dollars, please."

Brin swiped her debit card and keyed in her PIN number. Once the transaction had gone through, the young lady handed her the receipt with a smile. "Thank you for shopping at Woodard's and come again."

Brin turned and walked toward the ice cream counter, Savannah hurrying to run around her and get there first. Brin bought them each an ice cream—Brin's in a cone, Savannah's in a cup. Then they sat down in their favorite booth, right next to the candy counter, and dug in.

Brin took the amber pill bottle out of the bag and squinted at the label. Klonopin. It was used to treat seizures; that much she knew. What she didn't know was why Alex would be taking it. The doctor's name didn't ring a bell, either. For as long as she had known him, Alex had never had a regular physician, nor had he gone to a doctor unless he was genuinely in pain. There was just that one time, when he had had pneumonia so bad that walking across the room brought on a five-minute coughing fit.

"Savannah, baby, you sit right here for a sec, okay? Mommy has to go back and talk to the medicine lady again."

Brin slid out of the seat and hurried back to the

prescription counter. "Excuse me," she said to the young woman behind the counter. "I was wondering if you knew anything about the doctor who prescribed this?"

The woman took the bottle and read the label. "Just a moment, please." She went back into the pharmacy and typed something into the computer, then returned with a piece of paper. "I'm afraid this is the only prescription we've ever filled for this particular doctor."

"Well, what kind of doctor is he? I mean, is his office nearby?" Brin frowned and then bit into her lower lip.

"According to the physicians' database, he's a neurologist. Here. I've written down his address and phone number in case you need to contact him about your husband's medication."

Brin took the piece of paper and studied the address written on it. It was only a mile away from her lab, but she couldn't picture the building it was in. "And you're sure he's a neurologist?"

"Yes, ma'am. That's what his license says."

"Okay. Thank you."

Brin turned and walked slowly back to Savannah, the paper clutched in one hand and a dripping ice cream cone in the other. Savannah was coated in ice cream, and Brin took a moment to clean the girl's face, still distracted by the medicine bag next to her on the seat. Why the hell was Alex seeing a neurologist? More importantly, why was he keeping it from her?

Whatever was going on, she was damned sure going to talk to this doctor first thing Monday morning. As soon as Alex came home, she was going to have a little chat with him, too.

10

Alex gritted his teeth as the small plane touched down at the airport in Beijing. Jin was a terrific pilot, but Alex's legs ached all the way to the bone and his head had begun to throb. The flight had been uneventful and smooth, but he still longed to stretch his legs. There was simply no way to get comfortable in the small space of his seat.

Smaller aircraft landed in the back of the airport, where most of the freight lines came in. There was a customs office right there, and each plane was inspected before anyone or anything was released. Jin unbuckled and grabbed his clipboard. He stretched for a moment, and then opened the hatch.

"We must stay on board until the customs officer has signed off on the cargo." Jin sat down at the edge of the gangway and let his legs swing.

"What about my bag?" Alex asked.

"They won't look. They are only interested in inspecting the cargo. Your bag is in the middle of all those boxes. They will test a few boxes from the front, a few from the rear, and then they will sign off and move on. I have an excellent reputation."

"How long does it usually take?" Alex stood and stretched a bit, then paced from side to side, trying to walk off the pain in his legs.

"Not so long. There are only a few planes here today."

The gangway creaked and Alex's eyes turned toward the hatch. A heavyset Chinese man stood in the doorway, a clipboard in one hand and his hat in the other. He and Jin exchanged words and clipboards and then the customs officer began slitting open boxes.

Once he had inspected four boxes, he paused at a fifth, going so far as to remove the back from the television, checking inside for something. He nodded, satisfied, and then wrote something on his clipboard. Alex stayed casual. Jin knew to expect this and how to handle it so there should be nothing to worry about.

More words were exchanged and Jin turned to Alex and said, "He needs to see your passport."

"Oh! Sure!" Alex whipped out his passport and presented it to the officer. Of course, his real name wasn't on the form. For this trip, he was Donald

Vance, living in South Korea on a work and education visa.

The officer stamped the passport and handed it back to Alex. "Thank you, Mr. Vance," he said in heavily accented English.

A small truck drove up and a large man jumped out, walking purposefully toward the plane. Jin stepped toward Alex, but kept his eyes on the new arrival. "We must be very cautious now," he hissed. "Don't do anything unless I tell you."

He spoke rapidly to the customs inspector, but his voice only carried far enough for Alex to catch a couple of words. Alex eyed his bag in the middle of the larger boxes, knowing that it would take him precious time to get to it and make some use of it if the situation turned violent.

"That's Yau Sin," Jin whispered. "Chinese Mafia. They run the inspection ports. You can get most anything in or out if you pay their fee."

Yau pulled a semiautomatic pistol from a holster beneath his suit and pointed it at the inspection officer, directing him toward one of the televisions.

"If you don't pay their fee," Jin added, his voice hushed, "then very bad things happen to you."

The inspector walked over to the TV he'd examined. He nodded to the back and Yau looked inside. He looked back up and without another word shot the inspection officer point-blank in the chest.

He raised the pistol and pointed it toward Jin and Alex. Alex knew he could never reach a weapon in time. Yau walked closer and pushed the pistol into Jin's side.

"Leave the box, get rid of the body," he said in Mandarin.

Jin nodded his understanding, never saying a word.

Yau slipped the gun back into its holster, crossed over to his truck, got in and drove off of the tarmac.

Alex looked at Jin and said, "What the hell was that all about?"

"The inspector hasn't been paying them their fees. Nothing crosses the border without their okay."

"Nothing?"

"Nothing," Jin said. "As soon as the truck gets here, we will have to unload the televisions. You will go with the driver when we are done. He is your asset for this trip and he knows far more about the facility than I do."

"Is that the truck we're waiting for?"

Jin looked past Alex to the tarmac beyond. "That is the truck, yes. It will only take us a few moments to load the boxes. Then you can be off." He nodded curtly and waved at the truck.

A man climbed out of the truck and met Alex and Jin at the bottom of the gangway, walking past the body with barely a glance. He shook Jin's hand

and smiled. "This is Donald Vance," Jin said, stepping to the side. "He'll be leaving with you when we're done."

"Pleased to meet you," the man said, giving a slight bow at the waist. "I am called Liang."

"Thank you for your help, Liang." Alex sized the man up quickly. He was much larger than Jin and appeared to be only part Asian. He was well muscled and had an economy of motion that reminded Alex of Brin and the way she moved about the lab when she was working. There was something else in his movements, too. Liang moved like a trained martial artist, and Alex knew that he would be a dangerous man in a fight. And yet there was something in the man's eyes that appeared gentle. His gaze made Alex trust him instantly.

True to his word, it didn't take any longer than twenty minutes for the three of them to move the boxes into the large panel truck. Alex tossed his duffel bag into the truck and offered a handshake to Jin.

"Thanks for the ride, my friend. I'll see you again soon, I hope."

"Godspeed, Mr. Vance." Jin bowed and Alex mirrored the motion, though it hurt his hips to do so.

"Ready to go, Liang." He climbed into the truck and waved once more to Jin.

Liang started the truck and headed off across the

tarmac. "We'll have to drop the televisions at the warehouse. I'll take you to the facility after that. Tonight, you'll stay at my house."

"Is the facility far?" Alex asked.

"Halfway to the Mongolian border. It shouldn't take any more than two or three hours to get there, depending on traffic. We'll go tonight, after it gets dark."

"Good deal."

"In the meantime, we will deliver the televisions then enjoy my wife's fine cooking. I think you will approve. My wife is head chef at one of the finest restaurants in Beijing."

"You're a lucky man, Liang."

"Tell me about it." He patted his belly and chuckled.

11

Denny stared at the document in his hand and frowned. It was a single page of a few precisely typed lines and an attached medical report. The report itself was a poor copy, printed from a tiny digital camera. It wasn't the method by which the report had been obtained—in an organization like Room 59, even the watchers had to be watched. The information in the report was disturbing on a much deeper level.

"Christ," he muttered, tossing the document on his desk in frustration. "What the hell was he thinking?" He sat down heavily in his chair. The report had come in from one of his field watchers less than ten minutes earlier.

Room 59 was comprised of concentric rings of secrecy. In order for there to be control, checks and balances, most of those who worked for the organization were watched by others to whom they had no connection. Quiet surveillance of field agents was necessary to ensure the safety and security of the organization. It was, as Kate liked to say, important to back up your backups. And in case that failed, one should always have a way in through a back door or window.

The report was short and to the point. While only trusted doctors were consulted for Room 59 assets, it never paid to trust too much. Routine checks were made on the records and activities of all medical professionals within a hundred-mile radius of any of his field agents. The report on his desk was the result of just such a routine sweep.

The message itself was simple, and the report appeared to back it up.

Alex Tempest diagnosed with primary progressive MS. Medical testing and MRI scans reveal extensive medical problems related to disease. Recommend immediate removal from active missions and debrief for termination of fieldwork.

The report, photographed from the private files of a neurologist named Britton, confirmed what was written in the memo. Not just MS, either, but the bad stuff…the crippling kind.

Denny grabbed his glasses and immediately launched himself through the security protocols that would send an urgent message to Kate Cochran.

Kate appeared almost immediately and activated a secure room for them to talk. It looked like a prison conference room. "Denny?" she asked. "Why the urgency?"

"We have to talk," he said. "It's Alex Tempest. I think we may have to consider some sort of recall on the mission."

She was silent for a moment, and even though her avatar was unchanged, Denny imagined the frown creasing Kate's brow in real time.

"What the hell are you telling me, Denny? Recall? We *can't* recall. He dropped into the black zone yesterday. You know our rules. *We* don't even have contact from here out. By now, he's already inside China and working with the local asset. What could be so bad that we'd have to risk everything to get him back?"

It was Denny's turn to be silent. It was possible that Kate would consider this his fault, but he didn't think it likely. It just looked bad all the way around, and Denny hated the feeling that produced.

"It's bad, Kate. Really bad. I don't know what our wonder boy was thinking, but we've got to do something. I've got a report here from an agent who did a routine sweep on a Dr. Britton's office.

He found a record of a recent appointment with Alex." He took a deep breath. "Kate, he's got multiple sclerosis. The worst kind."

"You don't think he'll be able to complete the mission?"

"I don't know, but I do know that what I'm seeing here explains a lot about the errors that happened during his mission to Mexico. And this is a mission that cannot have errors," Denny replied. "A critical failure here and they'll be warned but without any real threat. They won't stop."

"You're not kidding." It wasn't a question, and Denny didn't answer.

"What the hell was he thinking, Denny?" Kate asked, slamming her hand onto the table for emphasis. "He's risking a hell of a lot of lives."

Denny glanced at his feet. He had some ideas on that, at least. He'd seen the expression on Alex's face at the mention of MRIS. Denny was well aware of how close Alex was to Brin. If he believed that there was only one mission left in him, Alex would want to spend it protecting his family.

"He seemed fine," he said at last. "When I talked to him, there was no hint of this—no mention of a problem."

"We did receive those intelligence reports out of Mexico," Kate reminded him. "He got the job done, but it wasn't clean. Not by a long shot.

They're still combing the streets for him over there, and it took some work to cover his tracks. It's not like him to be sloppy but then again maybe he wasn't. Maybe he did the best that he could—and unfortunately, his best just isn't good enough anymore."

They were both quiet for a moment after that.

"He's already in Beijing," Denny repeated, almost to himself, then directed his gaze to Kate. "You're right. There's no good way to contact him without breaking his cover and our silence. I hate to leave him out there, but this is way too important for that."

"Not to mention that it's too sensitive to let go," Kate growled. "I hope to God he knows what the hell he's getting into, because if he blows this, there won't be another chance. This kind of crap gives me the creeps. I don't mind an enemy I can see and kill, but this—"

"I know," Denny replied.

"Get hold of his wife," Kate said. "*Quietly.* Find out what you can about how sick he is. And have someone talk with that doctor, Britton, as well. We need to know as much as possible, as soon as possible." She paused, considering, then added, "And let's see if we can get someone else in the field. We have got to keep an eye on this—and that means we're going to take some chances. I'll make some calls and see if I can think of a way to back him up."

"Are you sure?" Denny spoke quickly. "Really sure? It's your decision, but that's opening the floodgates to a lot of trouble."

"What do I always tell you?" she asked. "Back up your backups."

"Yeah," Denny said, grinning. "And what do I tell you? We aren't IBM and we don't *do* backups. Ever. You said it yourself, Kate. Alex is in the black zone as of yesterday. Anything we do now risks the mission, Alex and our local asset there. That kind of risk is not acceptable to us—it never is."

"You sound like a damned brochure," Kate growled. "Get on that doctor, and get Brin on the phone if you can. Find a way to get what she knows without being too obvious. We don't want to spook her, but we need to know what we're up against."

"Yeah, right, no problem," Denny grumbled sarcastically. "Excuse me, ma'am, I work with your husband down at the security company. We were just going through some confidential doctor-patient files, and we wondered if you could tell us the status of Alex's health. We found some disturbing things, and we're worried about him. He's on a difficult assignment that we, of course, can't tell you about—you understand?"

"Actually, yes," Kate said. "His cover story has held up just fine with his family. Tell her that a required physical turned up some irregularities or whatever." She stared hard at Denny for a moment longer, then said, "Just get it done." She severed her connection to the room and vanished, leaving Denny to stare at the empty virtual space and shake his head.

"Alex," he said to himself, "you are a class-A bastard."

He returned to his virtual office and illuminated the keyboard, punching keys rapidly. He had a lot of information to gather in a very short amount of time, and he needed to call in some favors to get it done. He'd get in touch with Brin himself, and he'd find a way to keep things calm. If he was careful, and played his cards right, maybe he could even gather a little intel on what was going on at MRIS.

12

By the time Brin reached her office, she was in high temper. The delay at the pharmacy had led to a small tantrum when she'd dropped Savannah at her babysitter's. From there she'd hit the freeway, and it had been much like hitting a brick wall. By the time she'd worked her way through the various security measures the company kept in place, her mood had gone from bad to worse, and being greeted by a curt note from Hershel Rand didn't help things a bit. He wanted to see her immediately, and the word was in all caps, which came off like shouting.

MRIS had courted her for this position. She was the top of her field, and the research she managed was vital to the company's future. She came in on Saturdays because her lab ran 24/7 and she wanted to stay on top of things. She wasn't Rand's personal assistant, and she ignored the urgency of his note, knowing that she needed to compose herself.

First, she pulled out the small brown pill bottle and placed it on her desk by the phone. Beside it she placed Dr. Britton's phone number. Then, carefully and deliberately, she went through her routine. She plugged her cell phone into the docking station, logged on to the network and brought up her e-mail, then carefully returned the files she'd worked on the night before to their proper places and pulled a few new ones that required attention. She knew she would not be likely to get to them, but it was the act of keeping Rand waiting that mattered.

She was worried. She knew it was irrational, but Alex had never kept anything from her—not big secrets or small. The Klonopin wasn't a simple painkiller, or even an antidepressant. She thought about dropping into her chair and bringing up the online *Physician's Desk Reference,* but she didn't want to push it. It was one thing to remind Rand that she wasn't an office girl—quite another to actually disrupt company business. Besides, despite her bad mood, what Rand had told her the previous afternoon had intrigued her. She'd half hoped to hear from him later that afternoon, or even at home, but he hadn't called, and despite all the concerns pulling her in different directions, she wanted to know what he had.

When her office was in order, she stepped out into the hallway and walked to the elevator. As she went, her steps speeded slightly, despite her efforts at control. By the time the elevator door closed, she was almost sorry she'd fooled around.

WHEN BRIN ENTERED Rand's office, he was pacing like a caged beast. She caught him staring out the window at the parking lot below. When he heard her he spun, his hair wild, and she'd have sworn she saw sweat fly.

"Where the hell have you been?" he snapped.

"Calm down, Hershel," she replied. "I know what you have here is big, but I have a job to do. I have an entire department dependent on me, and I can't just get up and run every time you call. Besides, it is Saturday."

He stared at her, as if deciding whether to scream at her or laugh, and then he turned to his desk and waved his arm.

"It's here," he said.

Brin stepped up to the desk and examined the object that sat in the center of it. It was a climate-controlled package. There were several layers of insulation. The package was cooled by a small, battery-operated refrigeration unit. It was impossible to see what might be contained within the unit, but there were only so many likely possibilities. Chemicals, cultures, viral specimens, antibodies. Brin received a dozen similar packages any given week, though arguably less well contained. The labels on the box were covered in Chinese script. She understood none of it.

"What is it?" she asked, reaching out to touch the box.

Rand flinched as he saw her draw close to it, and in that instant she saw how, as excited as he was, he didn't let his hand slide too close.

"Not now," he said, calming himself. "Not here. We need to get this to one of your labs. Clear one—a small one, fully equipped—right away. We'll need it for the rest of the month, maybe longer, and I can't risk anyone but you having access. I'll have a locksmith in to upgrade the security."

Brin turned away from the case to stare at Rand. The man was clearly not himself.

"Have you lost your mind?" she asked. "What did you bring in here, some new form of plague? What are you afraid of?"

Rand frowned and Brin pushed the case an inch closer to his hand. He yanked his hand back and cursed under his breath. Brin would have laughed if it hadn't been such an unexpected reaction.

"What have you done?" she asked.

"Just get that lab ready," he snapped. "This is

big and could means hundreds of millions of dollars to our company. I'm counting on you for this. It isn't what you obviously think, but it is, I will admit, disturbing in other ways. This may well be the break you've been looking for your entire career—not exactly related to your work, but very, very close—and with implications that could change your whole approach."

Despite herself, Brin laughed. She looked at the package again and her scientific curiosity won out over any misgivings she had. "Okay. I can clear the corner lab on my wing. We have some cultures in there, but they aren't under any critical environmental restriction, and there's room for them in other spaces. It will take a couple of hours to remove what's in there. I assume you have a list of specifics—equipment I should requisition, supplies I might need? And while you're at it, if we're going to be doing any serious research I'm going to need a laptop for the data—I get the feeling you don't want me taking this work home with me."

"If I had my way, you'd sleep in the lab until this was over with." Rand's tone finally lightened up a little, and he chuckled ruefully. "I'm sorry for the attitude, Brin—and my paranoia. This development took me a bit by surprise. I knew we were working on it, but I didn't expect this level of success so soon, and the pressure from up top is huge."

"I thought you were *up top,*" Brin replied.

"There's always someone further up the chain—that's how chains work. You know that our research-and-development side is largely funded by foreign interests. Our own government would rather spend its money elsewhere, and we couldn't do the work we do, the work *you* do, without foreign investors. That's where the push is coming from on this. Those shareholders want results and want them right now. There are other parts of the company working on different aspects of this project, as well, but we were chosen as the only U.S. branch. I guess it's an honor, but at the moment it's starting to feel more like one giant pain in the ass."

Brin turned back to the case. She ran her hand over the labels and wished for a universal translator.

"I'll get right on it," she said, turning away. "I'll give you a call when the lab is ready, then I'll bring up a transport cart and we can move it down ourselves. I'm not sure it's going to help security if the CEO and a department head cart a sealed climate-controlled case off into a sealed lab, but I'll do as you ask. You have me curious—I want to crack this thing open and see what's inside."

"When you get the lab cleared, I'll send down the laptop you requested. I anticipated it, so I had it preloaded, and I've already personally transferred the files that came in with this case. The reading should keep you busy while the security is upgraded and the equipment is installed. There are cover stories in place for all of this, and they are included in the files. The first and best answer to any questions is that you don't know, and that it's something coming down from the top. Hopefully you'll have time to catch up on the back story while you figure out what the hell is in there—and what we're in for when we let it loose."

Brin took a last look at the case, shrugged and turned to the door. "I'll get Steph and Billy in there to clean up the cultures. I can keep the curiosity level down for a while, but once the dark forces descend on that lab, all bets are off. I'll keep my mouth shut, but I hope you have a good plan. Otherwise the rumors on this one are going to span the gap from terrorism to genetic tampering, and there won't be anything we can do to stop them."

"We'll deal with that when the time comes. For now, we need to get moving on this and keep moving. They're expecting the first report in a week—that doesn't leave much time, even for someone as brilliant as you."

BRIN RODE the elevator alone and stopped by the coffee mess for a strong black cup of concentration. When she entered her office for the second time that day, she stopped cold. In the excitement she'd forgotten all about the pharmacy. She hadn't even been thinking about Alex, and while that was usually a good thing when he was on the road, it still upset her to think how easily she'd been distracted.

She sat down, picked up her phone and dialed her lab assistant's extension. Stephanie Peters picked up on the second ring.

"What's up, boss?" she asked.

"Nothing too important," Brin lied. "I need you to find Billy and get over to the corner lab. Rand has a special project in, and we need a place to isolate some samples. Those cultures we have going can be moved easily enough. Stick them over in the back of 7C, okay?"

"Sure thing. I'll get right on it. I was just finishing up some slides, and I don't have anything pending this afternoon. Is the new project something I can help you on?"

Brin smiled. "Not this time. It's a security clearance issue. I know you're cleared to secret, but this one is in from the top—probably some new form of fungus that makes golf balls fly farther. I'll let you know what's going on as soon as I can, okay?"

"Sure. I'll give you a call when the lab's cleared."

"Thanks."

Brin hung up and reached for the brown bottle of pills and the phone number. She had some time, and until she had the laptop from Rand, there wasn't anything she could do to prepare for the work to come. It was time to get to the bottom of the mysterious neurologist and the unexpected prescription. Maybe the doctor had a weekend clinic or emergency contact number.

If Alex called, she intended to give him holy hell about it—for keeping secrets and for scaring her. He almost never called when he was on assignment, though, and she assumed this time would be no different. She really didn't have a clear idea of what kind of work he did. Security consulting covered a lot of ground, but when he'd gently told her he couldn't explain fully, she'd understood. Now she wished she'd been more insistent. She didn't even have a good contact at his company to check in with—just an emergency number in case she or Savannah was hurt.

The separation had always bothered her, but this time was different. This time it left a dull ache in her chest, and she needed to make it go away.

She glanced at the number, picked up her phone and dialed.

13

Liang and Alex left the airport without incident. Liang guided the truck through the bustling streets of Beijing as Alex watched out the window. His legs still ached a bit and his eyes were dry and itchy, almost as though he had allergies or something nagging at them. He thought Beijing was part industrial city, part sociology experiment. There was noise everywhere, bright splashes of color and people packed so tightly together that you could topple them all just by shoving one down.

The airport was surrounded by the city itself, and huge, close buildings that seemed to lean on each other. The farther they drove, the farther apart the buildings became until Alex found himself looking out the window at far-flung warehouses and factories. The air grew heavy and gloomy with soot that assaulted his already itching eyes. Alex longed for the countryside and the quiet.

Finally, Liang backed the truck up to a loading bay at the rear of a desolate warehouse. According to the sign, the building belonged to the Wang-Soo Electronics Company. The loading bay door rolled up on its huge tracks, and three large men stepped from the concrete slab to the back gate of the truck. Liang stepped out, exchanged a few words with them and then flung open the truck's door. Alex wondered briefly if he should step outside and help, but thought better of it after a shift in his position sent warning cramps up his legs. He'd managed to keep the aches and pains to himself thus far, but he couldn't afford to have Liang lose confidence in him.

It took less than ten minutes for the four men, working together, to unload the truck. Alex glanced at them in the rearview mirror once or twice, but paid them no more mind than that. He caught sight of Liang, proffering the bill of lading for a signature, and then lost sight of him as he crossed to the driver's side and stepped back into the cab.

"All's well?" Alex studied the man for a moment. Hauling all those TVs hadn't caused him to even break a sweat. It occurred to Alex, just then, that aside from the illness, maybe he was getting too old for all this.

"It's all good, as you Americans say. We'll go to my apartment now and wait for the sun to set."

"What cover story do you give your wife?"

"I don't need a cover story. I import electronics from South Korea. I work hard. When I want to go out, I go out." He nodded curtly and smiled. "It's a cultural thing."

"My wife thinks I'm in security," Alex said. "A consultant."

"Ah." Liang pulled away from the loading dock and turned back toward the city. The truck bumped and lurched over the potholes in the road.

Twenty minutes later, Liang parked the truck at the back of a huge apartment complex. He pocketed the keys and locked the doors, then fished another set of keys from his pocket.

"We're home."

No matter how he craned his neck, Alex couldn't seem to see the top of the building. "I have just two questions—what floor do you live on? And do you have an elevator?"

"Twenty-second and yes."

"Thank God," Alex said, sighing with relief despite himself. The idea of climbing all those stairs had sent chills down his spine.

Alex let Liang lead the way, some of the road weariness sloughing off as he stepped into the air-conditioned back lobby. They rode the elevator to the twenty-second floor, stepped out and walked a short distance down the hall to Liang's apartment. The key wasn't even in the lock before Liang's wife threw open the door and launched herself into his arms. Liang caught her, looking slightly embarrassed.

"I missed you," she cooed, kissing him hard. Her face paled as she spotted Alex, standing off to one side and watching his shoes.

"This is Soo Lin, my wife. Soo Lin, this is Mr. Vance, an associate of mine."

Soo Lin half bowed and pressed her hand into his, the best of both worlds. "So pleased to meet you, Mr. Vance. Please, come inside."

"A pleasure to meet you, too. Liang brags about you constantly." He noticed her blush and smiled back at her. "He says you're quite the amazing chef."

"Well, I suppose I have a reputation to live up to, then." She shut the door behind them and stepped off to the side. "I will make tea. Dinner will be ready in half an hour. You should rest for a while."

Alex noticed the pile of shoes on the mat by the door and added his own to the collection. Liang was already in his stocking feet, padding quickly across the carpet toward the hallway.

"We'll take tea in a moment. First, I have something to show Mr. Vance. Come this way, please."

Alex followed him to the back bedroom, one of

only two in the apartment. It was all very sparse, but clean and neat. Alex felt comfortable at once. Liang stooped down, lifted a bit of the carpet and pulled it back. Beneath the carpet lay a wood floor panel, and once that was lifted, Alex could see Liang's small cache of tools.

"Whatever you don't have in that bag of yours, I have in here or can get at a moment's notice. I've taken the liberty of contacting a few of my associates, sources for those items that are harder to come by." He smiled at that, his eyes twinkling with a hint of menace.

"Good to know. We can better decide what we need to take that place out once we've had a look at it," Alex said.

"No need to worry here. I have security measures in place and, despite their appearance, these walls are quite soundproof. You can talk freely unless my wife is in the room."

"You're very thorough, aren't you?"

"I am."

"You have the explosives covered?"

"Yes. They aren't here, of course. I have access to what we need. We could start a war, if that was our desire."

Soo Lin called from the living room and Liang tugged at Alex's arm. "Time for tea and dinner. We have about two hours before the sun sets. The building usually clears out about an hour after that, so there's less traffic on the roads around it and less chance of us being seen."

"Two hours until we leave, then."

"Until then, we can stuff ourselves." Liang poked him in the stomach with his elbow and laughed.

ALL THE HYPE over Soo Lin's cooking had not been exaggerated. Not only did she also lay out a five course meal, but she did so as if the president of China himself were coming to dinner. They ate until they could hold no more and then they retired to the living room to rest while Soo Lin cleared away the mess.

Fifteen minutes after the sun was completely down and the darkness had stolen the shadows, Alex gathered his gear, changed into darker, more appropriate clothes and followed Liang back to the parking lot. This time, they took a small hybrid car out into the countryside. It was quieter and faster than Alex had anticipated. Like the plane he'd flown in from South Korea, it just wasn't much on legroom.

Liang drove them to the top of a hill just south of the lab building. The view from there was good and the woods offered cover. Alex lay flat on the ground, Liang at his side, and pulled the night-vision goggles from his duffel bag. The building was heavily guarded, more so than might be expected of a mere medical-research company. The entire compound was ringed with razor wire, and guards with large dogs at their sides patrolled the parking lot and surrounding landscape. Alex supposed that, somewhere inside that compound, there were more than a few men staring at the woods beyond that fence.

"There are cameras on each corner of the fence and the building itself," Liang whispered. "There are three sets of doors—front, back and a set with the loading-bay doors in the rear—and each has a camera and coded lock. All but the door cameras are programmed to sweep the entire area."

Alex nodded but did not speak. He was watching the cameras do their sweep and using the timer built into the goggles. "Every forty-five seconds," he said. "It's safe to assume those are being fed to recording devices, as well as monitors."

He did another visual sweep. "At least the advance reports I read were correct. The guards are heavily armed—rifles, pistols and Tasers."

"I did the advance report," Liang said, "so if it was incorrect, I would be to blame. But yes, they are well equipped and there are a great number more inside. They work in shifts, changing one third every twelve hours. These aren't the usual sort of guards we see out here. They are well trained and professional."

"PMC," Alex grunted, as he watched several

groups of men and women move in and out of the building. He scanned the parking lot, making mental notes of makes and models, checking the height of those he saw, hairstyles, manner of dress. Most of the workers he saw seemed to be Chinese, but there were a sprinkling of others.

"The staff-demographics report made it sound like a much broader range of ethnic backgrounds," he said. "Any Europeans? Latinos? Arabs? There have to be a lot of research-and-program development positions in there. I assume the Pakistanis and Indians have a presence?"

"It's an eclectic group," Liang replied. "The night crew is more heavily Chinese—for security purposes. During the day you'll see that they have brought in scientists, researchers and doctors from all over the world."

Liang glanced at Alex and grinned. "You won't stand out unless you don't know anything about drugs, research or biochemistry."

"My wife is in biomedical research," Alex said. "I can get through that part of it. If it's anything like the lab where she works, there will be plenty of drones—research assistants working on their own degrees and doing the drudge work. No one will care what they think or say."

Liang nodded. "Well, then, all that remains is finding the best way to get you in there—and a way to get the explosives in with you."

"I still have some reading to do," Alex said, handing back the night-vision goggles. "I need to be more familiar with the layout and with the particular project we're after."

"I have some files we managed to recover," Liang told him. "They're supposed to be shredded, but sometimes people get lazy, and if you're in the right place at the right time, you can find things."

"Like the loading dock?" Alex asked, grinning.

"Maybe so." Liang chuckled. "Let's go. We need to have a couple of drinks so Soo Lin will know we've been out behaving like men."

Alex nodded. He pressed off from the ground, felt his arm giving out on him and hesitated. His hand shook violently, and he closed his eyes for just a second. The tremor passed, and he managed to lever himself to his feet with reasonable grace. Luckily Liang had been turned away, putting the glasses into a bag. They returned to Liang's car and headed into town.

As they passed out of the industrial district, Alex saw bright lights ahead. Liang saw them, too, and grinned. He sped up, pulled down a side street, turned up an alley and moments later they emerged onto a wide, well-lit street. Colored neon rippled over the doors. Men and women flooded the streets, moving from club to club in an ocean of color and sound. The contrast was incredible.

Liang pulled onto another side street and found

a place to park. It was easy to see why he preferred the small vehicle.

"We got lucky." Liang grinned. "Most nights we'd have had to go half a mile from the action for a parking space."

Alex eyed the streets and shook his head. The brilliant colored lights irritated his eyes, and he fought to keep his sight clear. His legs ached, but he thought they'd support him. He didn't want to have any drinks. The last thing he wanted was anything that might fuel the erosion of his motor control, but he couldn't do anything to make Liang suspicious. Once he was inside—once he was on his own—he could worry less about the MS and more about the job, but up to that point he needed Liang. The big man had the explosives, the key to the doors of the MRIS plant and the files.

"Have you had a chance to go through the files?" he asked, turning quickly to exit the vehicle and pulling his hand in close to his chest. It was shaking again, and he was afraid if the spasm became more violent he wouldn't be able to conceal it.

"I've been through them," Liang said. "We'll get to that in the morning. Have you ever been to Beijing, Mr. Vance?"

Alex shook his head. "I've been in China several times, but never the city."

Liang nodded. "Good. I like it when I can show

a man something he's never seen before." They locked the car and headed back to the main drag, stepping into the ocean of bodies. Liang had to shout to be heard over the laughing, babbling throng.

Alex was taller than most of those around him, but he spotted a few non-Asian faces in the crowd. Music blared from several doorways. Young couples, teenagers and groups of older men and women who he assumed were businessmen, rolled in and out. Each time one of the doors opened wide, the music from that particular club rose, blotting out the others, and then faded back into the general roar of sound.

"What would Confucius have thought of this?" Alex wondered out loud.

Liang stopped, as though considering the question seriously, and then he laughed. "It's a whole new world," he said. "The West leaks in through all the cracks, across the Internet, through television and popular music. Everything about your culture is popular with the youth of China, and even the rest of us are catching the fever a little. It's too close for me to what came before."

The big man's face darkened. "I remember students being shot for their beliefs. I remember days when you didn't dare write or say a thing that wasn't programmed into you from birth. We've been fighting a very long war with ourselves, our ancestors and our culture. We always hope it will get better." Liang considered his words for a moment, then added, "Confucius would probably say too much of anything is bad for everything."

Alex nodded. They stepped up to the doors of a club outlined in bright blue neon. He focused on the sign, but they passed under it before he could fully translate. His spoken Chinese was fluent, but accented. He'd worked on it carefully. American accents were recognizable, and more likely to draw attention. His Chinese had been learned from a woman with a thick British accent. The combination of her influence on his pronunciation and his own slight accent gave his voice an odd European inflection. It had served him well in the past because its very ambiguity made it forgettable. In a company where Arab doctors worked side by side with Hindu researchers, it wouldn't even register on the scale of oddity.

The interior of the club throbbed with sound. There were three dance floors, all brightly lit with fluorescent borders and colored spotlights. Disco balls dangled from the ceiling and spun slowly. Lights flickered off the walls, the floor, the faces, and behind it all was the music. There was never a break in the sound. The conglomeration of dance tracks and techno beats stretched from the 1970s into some future world of sound Alex had never experienced.

"Loud, huh?" Liang cupped a hand over his mouth and directed his hoarse yell into Alex's ear.

"What?" Alex grinned as he answered, and Liang laughed. He led Alex through a beaded curtain and into a hallway where the sound was muffled. A few yards farther they stepped through into a shadowy bar. Soft music played— so soft that after the cacophony of the main dance area, it was a few moments before Alex even heard it.

They stepped up to a cherrywood bar and leaned on it. Alex was grateful for the support. He was also grateful for the dim lights. His legs shook, and the pain, which had been no more than a steady ache during the drive into the city, had evolved into something like bags of broken glass shifting under the muscles.

Liang spoke to the bartender and a moment later two tall brown bottles of beer appeared. Alex didn't even glance at the label. He picked his up and took a long drink. The beer stung a little going down, and the faint tang of formaldehyde burned his tongue, but he ignored it. He'd drunk worse, and the cool liquid soothed him. He drained half of the oversize bottle in a single long gulp.

"Thirsty?" Liang asked. He was watching Alex with cool curiosity. His smile was genuine, but Alex knew when he was being sized up.

"It's been a long day. The flight in was rough,

and I didn't sleep too well the night before. I guess I'm more tired than I thought."

"We'll have just one more," Liang said. "I was going to show you some of the city, but maybe we better concentrate on this one and get through it."

Alex nodded. He glanced around the room.

"From the street you'd never guess this room was here. I thought for a minute you were going to try and get me out on a dance floor."

Liang laughed again and took a swig of his beer. "I'm not much of a dancer. I come here because the beer is cold, and with the sound out there, this is a good place to talk. Not many know it's here, and those that do have business of their own. It works out well."

Alex's respect for the big man jumped another notch. It was easy to see why he'd gotten the nod from Room 59. It was almost always easy to see. There was something about the men and women who were capable of doing what Alex did that shone through, if you knew how to look. Their eyes were a little brighter—they moved with a certain grace—and invariably they saw through everything you thought they shouldn't. It was going to be harder to conceal anything from Liang than it was to get into MRIS. Maybe it would be impossible.

"You *do* look tired," Liang said abruptly. "We'll go back and have that second beer at my place, and then you can get some rest. Tomorrow you can hole up in a place I know and hit those files. We have a short fuse on this one."

"When don't we?" Alex asked, lifting his beer and holding it out.

Liang tapped his bottle against Alex's and grinned.

They downed the last of the beer and turned away from the bar, disappearing back into the dancing crowd and the wall of sound. Liang took the lead, and Alex, his hand shaking like a leaf in a heavy breeze, followed.

14

The lab was cleared in less than an hour, just in time for Rand's people to start rolling in with their equipment. Steph and Billy tried their best to hang around at first, pestering Brin with questions and trying to peek at the equipment as it rolled in, but she chased them away with a promise that she would tell them whatever she was authorized to soon. The laptop arrived in a sealed case. Brin took this in herself, setting it up on a small desk in the rear of the lab.

She was anxious to know what was in the files, but she knew she couldn't begin reading until the room was clear and secured. She made herself ignore the machine and concentrated on supervising the equipment setup. She grinned when she saw that Rand had included a small espresso machine. Apparently even her coffee breaks would be private for a while.

The windows were blocked and sealed, inside and out, and the locks on the door had been drilled out and replaced with several high-security coded devices.

"Ma'am?" the technician installing the lock called her over. "We're going to need you to key in a code for this when we're done. Our orders are that only you will know the access code—and Mr. Rand, of course. The code needs to include numbers, letters, upper- and lower-case. The longer the better."

Brin nodded. She thought for a few moments. "Where do I enter it?"

The young man handed her a keyboard that was wired into the lock. He stepped away, leaving her alone.

She typed her code quickly, then repeated it to verify.

"S@VanNah60024220."

She knew she'd never forget. It was Savannah's name and her birthdate backward. She knew, also, that it made the password less secure, but the insertion of the @ symbol and random caps should make up for her lack of attention to protocol. A series of lights flashed on the keyboard, and the small digital screen went blank. Only a single green light remained.

Brin handed back the keyboard, and the tech glanced at it, then smiled. "It accepted the code. Usually we have to have people give it three or four tries to find something complex enough."

"I'm a complex person," she replied.

He held out a second keypad. "This one is a print analyzer," he said. "Please place your right thumb on the pad."

Brin did so, and a thin beam of light scanned her thumbprint. The tech went back to work for several more minutes, installing the print analyzer next to the door, then he turned back to her. "In order to enter the lab, you'll need to key in your code, then place your thumb on the analyzer for a scan, okay, ma'am?"

She nodded, thinking that of all the labs in the building, this was the only one she knew of that had both a coded lock and a thumbprint lock to get in. Curious, she asked, "What happens if either the code or the print isn't correct?"

The tech shook his head. "The whole lab will go into lockdown," he said. "Short of someone blowing this steel door off the frame, no one will go in or out unless the system is reset by us." He grinned at her, then added, "Try not to do that, ma'am. I hate being called out in the middle of the night for a lost password."

"Got it," she said.

Within fifteen minutes, the techs were cleared,

the equipment was set up and only two things remained. Whatever was in the case she'd seen on Rand's desk would have to arrive, and she would have to figure out what the hell it was.

She closed the door, started up the coffee machine and booted up the laptop. Four hours and so many pages of data later that they blurred in her mind, she sat back and stared at the machine in disbelief. Her coffee sat cold and forgotten beside her. She glanced at her watch, noting the time, and gasped. She closed the files, stood and turned to stare at the sample case, which was still sealed. Cables ran from the case to an outlet on the wall, and to a UPS backup in case the building power failed. Now she understood the caution and the secrecy. She reached out and touched the case gently—almost reverently.

Despite the mountains of data, what she had in her lab was relatively simple, at least in principle. It was an answer, and the question was as familiar to Brin as her own heartbeat.

Degenerative diseases could be attached in a number of ways, but in too many cases all that medical science had done was find ways to slow them down. When the body quit fighting on its own, or began eating itself from within because some cell or protein mutated, or changed or blended incorrectly with another, it was difficult to reverse the process. In fact, for all practical purposes, it was impossible.

But this case held an answer. In fact, it held an army. It was a very small army, but potent. What the Chinese branch had sent for verification and further study was nothing short of the miracle she'd worked her entire career encounter.

They called them nanoagents—small manufactured structures capable of performing work on the cellular and subcellular level. They represented the smallest machines ever created, biological in nature and programmable to a purpose. That purpose was the restructuring of cells. She ran the data through her mind, searching for flaws and somehow unable to concentrate because she was lost in the possibilities.

In China, they'd taken healthy cells and used them to program the agents. Using tiny electrical signals, they'd brought their tiny machines into harmony with those cells, and then they'd released them into the biosystems of diseased cells. The nanoagents served a single purpose. Once programmed, they worked to bring their host into harmony with their programming. They'd been used to slow, halt and even reverse viral attacks and cellular dysfunction.

The claims made in the report on her laptop were pretty outrageous, but the research seemed solid. It hadn't been slapped together or hurried, and somehow they'd managed to keep it under wraps. That alone was amazing, because just the possible discovery of something this big—some-

thing this overpoweringly wonderful—would have
sent waves of reaction through several scientific
communities.

She turned off the coffeemaker, checked the
equipment and shut off the lights, slipping out into
the hall. The building was down to a skeleton
staff—she was nearly half an hour beyond her
normally scheduled departure time. It wasn't like
her to forget time, even less like her to risk being
late picking up Savannah. She had just enough
time if she pushed the speed limit on the way.

A FEW HOURS LATER, Brin sat on the sofa, chewing
her thumbnail and forcing herself to watch television. She wasn't even sure what program was on.
She'd reached Dr. Britton's call service and left a
message, as well as a numeric page. There had
been no return call, despite her use of the word
"emergency."

Now her eyes flitted between the TV screen and
Alex's computer. It sat idle on the desk in the
corner, mocking her—tempting her. There might
be something in one of the files that would clue her
in as to what was happening with him. As much
as she needed to know the truth, she also hated vio-
lating his privacy. He'd never forbidden her access
to the machine, but he'd mentioned it was work—
and that there were security issues. She'd always
felt that was enough reason to leave it alone.

"Screw it!" she growled at last, slamming one fist on the sofa as she rose, stalking to the computer as though it might run away from her at any moment.

She hit the power button and watched the machine hum to life. She knew he had the system password protected. She was also pretty sure she knew what the password was, or at least a variation of it. The security login screen opened and she stared at it, frowning.

Savannah. She typed it in with the caps at first. When it didn't take, she dropped the caps. Met with that failed attempt, the furrow on her brow deepened and she sighed as she sank back in the chair and folded her arms around herself. Then she sat up, and she smiled. She reached for the keyboard and typed.

"Savannah02242006."

The computer screen went blue, and then the desktop popped into view, icons all in their neat rows along the left side.

"Bingo!"

Brin started sifting through files in the documents section. Chances were the document she was looking for would be a word processor or database document. She tried e-mail briefly, but the password was different and she couldn't manage to break it. She even tried Alex's old standby from their early days, but it was a no-go.

Then she found a document titled "Resignation." Her finger paused over the mouse button for a second, and then dropped on it with some urgency.

It was a letter of resignation to someone named Denny, dated just two days before Alex's departure. She had just begun to read it when an odd thing happened. A chat window popped open in front of her, obscuring the letter and flashing an annoying orange bar.

"Hello, Mrs. Tempest."

Brin gasped and yanked back her hands. The top of the window said "Room 59" but she had no idea what that was. That aside, how had the person on the other end known she was on Alex's computer?

"Who are you?" she typed in, and then minimized the window and popped open the search bar. She searched for Room 59, but received no results. She closed the search and maximized the chat window.

"My name is Denny. I think we need to talk about your husband, don't you?"

"I've got a better idea. You talk, I'll listen. How do you know my husband, and what is it you think we need to talk about? Is he in trouble? Is he hurt?"

"Alex and I work together, and as far as I know, he's fine. But we can't chat here. Follow this link and it will lead to a secure chat location. At the bottom of the screen is a small Easter egg—a hot spot on the screen that only activates when you mouse over it. You'll have to search around the bottom left corner until you find it."

Brin hesitated for a minute, but then searched and found the login. A voice suddenly began speaking through the computer's speaker. It recited a password. When it repeated, she typed. It took her a moment to realize what it was.

"I'm in," she typed in the window that opened.

The password had been a shared secret. Alex had once shown her a code called Caesar's Cipher. They'd played with it, encoding first his name, then hers and finally Savannah's. She hadn't realized it at the time, but he'd been leaving her an emergency message. She noticed that when the new chat window opened, nothing else on the computer reacted. She couldn't close the window or open any others.

"This chat program isn't just secure, it's paranoid," she whispered to herself, as though someone else could actually hear her.

"Now," she typed in carefully, "why don't you tell me just who the hell you are, and what you know about Alex?"

"To start with, I know what's wrong with him. I assume that you do, too. This morning, I received a report claiming that Alex has multiple sclerosis. Can you confirm this?"

Brin stared at the screen. She read over the words several times, trying to find a way that they could mean something else. How could Alex have MS?

"No," she typed at last. "I can't confirm it. He hasn't told me a thing. I knew he was, well, I didn't think he... Alex said he was fine, but..."

"How did you know? Did he say something?"

"No, he didn't say a thing. I got a call from the pharmacy this morning about a prescription that had been called in for him. He didn't pick it up before he left. I've been trying all day to figure out why he'd be taking this particular medication, and now it makes sense—it's an antiseizure medication."

"Does Alex ever check in with you when he's away?" Denny typed. "Is there any chance you could deliver a message to him?"

"He works with you and you can't get hold of him?" It made her suspicious. She didn't want to give anything away to this anonymous person. Hell, she couldn't be sure that he wasn't someone who might hurt Alex. The secrecy of the chat room was starting to make her feel the paranoia she'd assigned to the room only moments before.

"Our field agents are often in places where communication is difficult, if not impossible. Do you have any idea how sick he was when he left? The information that we have indicates that he has primary progressive MS. It could take him fast and hard."

Brin shuddered and forced back tears as though she were face-to-face with Denny and needed to conceal her feelings from him. "There were a few tremors. Mostly in his hands. I don't think it's gone very far, actually, but I don't know for sure. He was hiding it from me, though. I don't know how much you know about me, but I understand this disease. There is a very real risk that it will escalate and I have no idea whether he's begun taking the meds or not. He didn't pick up the prescription he was given before he left."

"We have to get in touch with him if it is at all possible. Given his location, he isn't likely to contact you—no more than he would contact us—but, please, if he checks in, can you give him a message from me?"

"Sure," Brin typed, not feeling sure at all.

"Just tell him, 'Personal Option Mission Recall.'"

She paused, held her breath and blinked. "If he checks in, I'll give him the message. But you still haven't really told me who you are or what this is about. I still don't understand why you can't reach him."

"That's all for now. Thank you, Mrs. Tempest." There was a long pause and Brin wondered if she should shut down the window. Then, "Once you shut down the chat window, don't open it again. I'll know if you do."

"How will you know?" she typed, half-smiling.

"You don't look good in red. You should have worn your blue pajamas."

Brin began to shake, her teeth rattling as her eyes darted about the room. The computer camera. It had to be on. She shut down the computer as quickly as she could and then shoved off from the desk hard enough to nearly topple the chair. Once she was up, she whipped off her robe and threw it over the computer and its small camera, just in case.

The weight of what she'd learned sat heavy on her chest. Alex had always seemed so healthy. She shook her head, knowing that thoughts like that were useless. She was a scientist, she knew that things like this struck without warning.

She tried to reason it and then realized there was no reasoning. It was what it was.

Brin started to cry.

15

"There's an advantage to being an electronics importer," Liang explained as he slipped out of the chair and let Alex slide in. "You get to know all sorts of electronics engineers, technicians, programmers—you know the type."

"I guess so," Alex said as he leaned forward.

After rising and having a quick meal, he'd started in on the MRIS files from Room 59. Liang had been out all morning and returned with a small jump drive full of files and data of his own. He was the local asset and it was his responsibility to gather as much intel on the target facility as possible. He'd come through admirably in very short order, and Alex appreciated it. He was on a shorter schedule than even his superiors knew, and all his plans were geared toward a quick hit and quicker exit.

Spread out on the computer screen was a series of documents. Each one, when maximized, was a blueprint, or a wiring diagram. The entire plan for the MRIS compound had been captured digitally.

"I don't suppose these plans for the building just happened to be on the Internet?" Alex commented drily. "I hope there's no trail back to the leak?"

"No trail. A friend of mine was kind enough to procure them for me. I must say, he had to go through quite a few less than standard channels to get them. You can view several different versions, calling up just the electronics plans, locations of the security components, all exits, et cetera."

Alex brought up the security blueprints, scanned the location of all the cameras, motion detectors. He nodded slowly. It seemed too easy, and this worried him a little. Room 59 operations usually targeted high-level security risks. One thing that was standard was the quality of the enemy. Alex never trusted anything that seemed easy, because he knew that taking anything for granted was the fastest way to mission failure— usually on a catastrophic level.

"It won't take me long to memorize these," he said after a couple of moments. "At least the portions I need to be familiar with. The sticky part will be identifying and allowing for any changes in the security clearances at the checkpoints. How recent are these?"

Out of Time   135

"As of six days ago," Liang said.

"I'd like to go take another look at the place in the daylight. Is that possible?"

"We'll go tomorrow morning. In the meantime, you can go over the files and these plans. We'll eat dinner here, and then you can get some rest. This could get tricky. You'll let me know if there is anything else you need?"

Alex thought for a moment. He considered asking for a pain pill, but decided against it. He wished he'd remembered the damned medication that Britton had prescribed, but on a deeper level he was glad he hadn't. There was no way to know ahead of time how it might affect his performance or his mind. He could overcome some physical handicaps, but if his brain went fuzzy, he was finished.

"I think I'm all set. Thanks."

Liang exited quietly, and Alex got to work.

The file on MRIS was thick. A lot of what had been provided wasn't necessary to his operation, but everyone involved had been thorough, as usual. On a public level, MRIS was involved in biomedical research, mostly diagnostics. Alex knew that from Brin's work. They specifically targeted degenerative diseases. The irony of this was not lost on him as his hands trembled over the keys of the laptop. The world looked to MRIS as a leader in the war against disease. Room 59 had uncovered a secondary arm of the corporation. It was unlikely that the stockholders were aware of this particular side. Unlike the main holdings of the company, this entity had a less than stellar rating in international protocols, which was a polite way of saying that several key figures had been suspected at one time or another of terrorism. Everything has a negative side, and the negative side of biomedical research was that often the technology developed to cure could also infect.

As he read, he was drawn in, fascinated by the technology, and at the same time sickened by the use it was planned for. He thought of Brin. Her name came up more than once on records in the research on this project, but he knew she would never have participated if she'd read what he was reading. He wondered briefly if Hershel Rand was involved, or if he, like Brin, was just being fooled by the benevolent mask behind which his company operated. If he did know—if he was aware of what was coming—then Alex thought he might have to add a personal element to the end of this mission.

The concept read like something out of a science fiction novel. The actual biological research was conducted in labs across the globe, in Beijing, the United States, France and several other locations. Breakthroughs had been made, but, as Brin had patiently explained to him, understanding the breakdown in a cell and finding a way to reverse-engineer the damage on a cellular level were two very different concepts. They knew what broke down in the body when it fell victim to degenerative disease, but not how to provide that same body with the ability to rebuild itself. Once the natural immune system broke down, it was a game of compensation and prolonging the battle, but very seldom was there victory.

In many ways, the human body was a machine and the immune system was what allowed all the other parts to function correctly. Without it, it was only a matter of time until the machine malfunctioned on a critical level.

Alex read about the nanoagents MRIS had developed. What was chilling was that, rather than rebuilding cellular structure, the nanoagents could be used to introduce a virus, or a biological contaminant, and speed the process of infection. At the same time, they would continue to battle against anything trying to reverse the effect they sought. It would be like setting loose a hive of bees in a sauna—the cellular structure of a human being could be destroyed in seconds, and the agents could be designed to transfer. Once they introduced a virus, they could also enhance the spread of that virus.

This was the process that Room 59 had discovered underlying the MRIS research. They had also uncovered evidence of a planned test of the process, and it was aimed at a target within the

United States. It would not be traceable back to the
company, of course. Terrorist groups all over the
world would leap at the chance to claim it, but a
weapon of this magnitude couldn't be allowed to
flourish in secret, or to be fully tested and put into
production. The only thing on Alex's side was that
the research was hidden behind deep security. The
scientific community wasn't even aware the break-
through had occurred, and if Alex had a say in it,
they never would be. He only hoped that the intel
he had on the scheduled test was accurate, and
that he would be quick enough to protect Brin.
The more he read, the more certain he was that if
the process was brought into the U.S., it would be
through her branch. If Room 59 found out that she
was involved, it wouldn't matter to them that she
was his wife. She and everyone there would be just
another target.

Finally he'd read and picked up all that he could
retain. He had a headache from his blurring
vision and sitting in front of the laptop for so
long had caused an uncharacteristic stiffness in
his limbs. He rose and performed a quick set of
simple calisthenics and waited for Liang to call
him to dinner. In the corner, a simple futon
waited, and he found that he was really looking
forward to making use of it. The next morning
he was going to need his wits about him. There
had to be more to the MRIS complex than

appeared in the schematics he'd gone over. There had to be a flaw, and he had to find it.

WHEN ALEX AWOKE the next morning, sunlight had crept in between the slats of the blinds and striped his face white and gray, making his eyes burn. He rolled to one side on the futon, trying to escape the light for a few moments before he was forced to face the day. It was no use. Thin bands of light fell from the wall to the center of the room, leaving him no safe haven.

He rolled to the edge and pushed himself into a sitting position. For the moment his legs and arms seemed still and pain free. A few blinks brought the room into focus and he risked standing.

Once he had finished his ablutions, he wandered into the living room, hoping there was coffee instead of tea for breakfast. Liang was seated at the dining-room table, smiling brightly and reading the newspaper.

Alex smiled. He was taken by how different Liang's household was from what he'd known on previous visits to China. The way Liang and Soo Lin interacted, the Western styling of the table, the disco clubs lining the streets downtown—such things would not have been possible a decade before.

"Good morning, my friend," Liang said, a smile lighting his face. "I hope you slept well."

"Well but briefly."

"There's some coffee in the kitchen, if you care for some."

Alex almost let loose a cry of joy. He walked at once to the kitchen, to find a very familiar coffeemaker, several cups, a sugar bowl and creamer all laid out. Soo Lin was thorough, and Alex laughed as he realized the coffeemaker was probably another benefit of being an electronics importer. Liang was a man of many talents, and good taste, it seemed.

Alex poured himself a steaming cup of black coffee and took a sip, grimacing at the heat as he walked back to the dining room.

"Where's Soo Lin this morning? Still sleeping?"

"She has already left for work. She doesn't have to work, of course, but it helps us to maintain appearances. It also keeps her busy, and prevents awkward situations when my work is of a less mundane nature. When she is home, she watches over that kitchen like a tiger. Nothing gets done there without her supervision."

Alex smiled. "She's quite a lady. If we're alone, then, we can talk. Your plans were most helpful. I think I've memorized the highlights. I'll go over them again if I get a chance, but it's a pretty straightforward setup."

"Excellent. We can leave in about an hour. Perhaps the daylight will reveal more of the lab's secrets, eh?"

"Hopefully," Alex said.

He was actually hoping for a little divine inspiration. So far, it had not been forthcoming. Part of being a chameleon was having a grasp of the environment that went beyond the physical world; it was understanding deep down what other people saw when they looked around.

Liang and Alex drove the small car out to the lab site once again. They approached from the opposite side this time, circling through the woods and stopping at the top of the hill. From the facility, all that was visible of the woods was a small patch near the top. No one down there could even see their car as it drove along the dirt road.

Alex stared down at the parking lot and frowned.

"Does anything about that parking lot strike you as odd?" he asked. "You've seen the shifts change, people coming and going."

Liang followed Alex's gaze, then mirrored his frown. "The cars. There are too many cars. Only about half that many people come or go at any given time."

Alex squinted through the binoculars at the fenced-in parking lot, scanning the area for other differences that hadn't been reported.

"Exactly. There is something going on here that isn't in those plans."

"The entire facility isn't large enough to house

that many workers," Liang commented. "Perhaps there is more here than meets the eye. Could there be more underground?"

Alex spotted something at the far edge of his field of vision and he focused the binoculars in on that one object. He'd been looking for someone of a particular physical type, an American or European who had basically the same build and coloring as himself, and just to the side of the main building, he'd spotted him. Alex studied the man as he crossed the parking lot to the security area. There were six men there, standing at attention. His target was apparently a squad leader of some sort. That was good—his clearance would be higher.

"Those guards are PMC," he told Liang. "Private military contractors of some sort. There are six per squad, two squads, a leader for each. That's on the exterior. I'm tracking the squad leader of the team on the right. See if you recognize him."

Liang took the binoculars from Alex and studied the man. "He does not look familiar."

"He looks enough like me that I can pass for him. It won't fool his men, especially up close, but for our needs, he's perfect. We'll come back for him tonight. If the schedule is correct, he'll change shifts around eight."

Liang looked at him briefly. "You have a plan?"

"I do." Alex nodded. Best to have a plan, he thought.

A field agent quickly learned that it was far too easy to improvise yourself right into an early grave.

"I'LL FLASH A LIGHT through the back window twice. Then you follow." Alex zipped up his flak jacket and shoved his gun into its holster. The many pockets of the jacket were filled with his tools of the trade, weighing it down.

Liang nodded and slipped his own gun into its holster. "Good luck, Mr. Vance."

Alex nodded and made his way down the hillside. The perimeter of the facility was well lit, especially at the fence line. But there was one spot that was dark enough to serve his purposes. He watched the two roving external squads carefully to gauge his moment. His target was a small, lonely stretch of fence running between the parking lot and the maintenance shed.

He moved quietly through the brush, nearing the fence at the center of that dark patch. One hand flipped open a pocket tool and pulled out a pair of wire cutters. He snipped the fence in a straight line upward, just large enough for him to enter. He would not be leaving the same way and didn't want to call attention to the hole in the fence. Another pocket produced a handful of small metal clips, which Alex used to fasten the sections of wire together again. Unless someone walked right up to the fence and stared, the damage would never be noticed.

Keeping low, he hurried off to the side of the maintenance shed. He could see both of the huge lights and all three cameras from where he crouched. He was in a small dead spot as long as he remained stationary. He'd noted the sweep of the cameras and the angle, and calculated the field of vision on each sweep.

A sudden noise rose from the back of the maintenance shed. Someone had turned on a pump of some sort, and once the shock of the sudden sound released its clamped grip on his heart, he realized it would work to his advantage, shielding any noise he produced. When the lights shifted just right, and the squad currently covering the lot had turned the corner at the far end, Alex made his move.

He ran at a crouch, covering the ground very quickly. He gained the back of the parking lot, slid beneath a small parked truck and paused, waiting for the camera to finish its eastward sweep, and begin scanning west again. Once he was clear, he began a carefully timed passage, using the vehicles as shields. At one point, the security squad passed within a few yards of him as he clung to the underside of a large sport utility vehicle. He moved cautiously and methodically, not allowing himself to think about consequences, only about timing.

His legs had begun to hurt again and the rush of adrenaline had only drawn attention to that fact. He was keenly aware of every inch of his body, how badly it ached, and that he had lost some strength in his legs. No matter. He had come too far to go back.

Liang had taken a long-range digital photo of their target. While they waited for the evening shift to change, he'd visited his contact with the photo in hand, and acquired the information they needed. Roy Boswell was a mercenary captain. He'd been brought in as part of the private military outfit and commanded a squad of twelve. Six of his men patrolled the exterior of the complex, and six were on internal duty. He drove a midsized black sedan, license number OB 0702. Liang had been able to spot the correct vehicle, and Alex had mentally marked its location.

Unfortunately, the car he sought was in the next-to-last row of the parking lot. Alex had to pass through four rows of cars and dodge three cameras in order to reach it. He watched the cameras, counting as they made three sweeps. The lights were fixed, able to be moved only when there was an emergency, and then only with a great deal of effort. Again it struck him how average the security precautions seemed to be. It made no sense, and it worried him.

Alex watched that first camera shift to the east,

and then made his final move. He slipped in
between his target and another car and flattened
himself against the driver's door as he pulled out
a small lock pick. The car might well be unlocked,
but if it was locked and the alarm had been set, he
could easily set it off by trying the door handle. He
pulled another small object from yet another
pocket and smiled.

He aimed the remote at the car, pressing and
holding the only button on the thing. It was
designed to continually fire an encoded signal at
the car, until it reached the proper frequency and
shut down the alarm and unlocked the doors. Not
even the horn would let off the usual telltale beep.
The device would have been useless to him
without that—the noise would most likely bring an
entire squad down on his head. There were few acceptable risks on this kind of mission.

He peered in through the window and watched
the dashboard. No blinking red light, no alarm.
He shoved the remote back into its pocket and
went to work on the lock. Within seconds, he had
the door open and was inside the car, stretched out
flat on the backseat. There was a good deal of
debris on the floor, including a large newspaper
and various food wrappers. He memorized the
position of each one, then picked them up and
piled them on the seat. Once he had stretched out
on the floor, he placed the debris on top of himself,

in roughly the same position it had been. It wasn't perfect, but unless someone was looking, they were unlikely to notice his presence. It was a large car, and he curled up as close to the backs of the driver and passenger seats as possible.

Then, he waited.

The light that fell into the car was yellow and dim. It certainly wasn't good enough to allow someone to see Alex's black clothing on the dark carpet inside the car. The guard jingled his keys as he approached, unlocking his door quickly and slipping into the driver's seat. Alex remained still, waiting.

All he could see from the floor of the car was scenery that passed by and the back of the guard's head. If he had any hope of signaling Liang, he would have to place the light against the window to avoid letting light flash across the glass. He reached up, the small flashlight clutched tightly in his right hand. For a moment, he feared he would drop it as his hand began to tremble. Then the trembling stopped as quickly as it had started and he placed the lens against the glass, flashing it twice. He hoped that Liang was paying attention. He had never worked with this asset before, so he had no idea how detail oriented the man was. If the situations had been reversed, Alex would have had the binoculars trained on Liang every single moment he had been inside that fence.

The car made several turns and then drove deeper and deeper into the city. Alex prayed that the guard would make no stops along the way, and his prayers were answered. From his vantage point on the floor, Alex could make out a tall building, probably an apartment complex. The car stopped. Alex tensed. The parking brake groaned as the guard engaged it.

Alex leaped up off the floor. He held a length of very thin piano wire stretched taunt between his gloved hands. He let his mind blank—no room for hesitation or compassion. Before the guard could cry out, the garrote bit deep, and Alex flexed his muscled arms, yanking hard.

Legs flailed and hands clawed at Alex's face, but the struggle was brief and feeble. A small band of blood marked the man's neck most of the way around, and during it all, Alex was aware of Liang's car pulling in next to them.

The guard went limp and Alex felt for a pulse while keeping the wire taut around his neck. Finding no sign of life, he released the wire and balled it up, ready to shove it back into his pocket once he had wiped it clean. Then he flashed the light twice at Liang and pushed open the back door.

16

Alex stumbled out of the backseat of the sedan. He still gripped the garrote tightly, and he realized that though he'd released his grip with his left hand, his right still clutched the wire. Searing pain lanced through his palm, and no matter how he concentrated, he could not force his fingers free of the wire. He stood, staring dumbly at the dangling wire, and Liang stepped up beside him.

"You all right?" the big man asked.

Alex nodded. He turned toward the car, trying to shield his clawed hand by the motion, and in that moment his grip released. His hand fluttered, beyond his control, but at least he was able to release the garrote. Liang watched him closely.

"We can take some time, if you need it," he said.

"No, there isn't time," Alex said. "I'm fine."

Liang looked unconvinced, and suddenly Alex grew angry. He was angry with his body, angry at his hand, angry at Denny and MRIS and the world. He wasn't angry at Liang, but the big man took the brunt of it anyway.

"We need to get this car safely moved near your place, and we need to make this body disappear. I have more planning to do, and the one thing I don't have is time," he snapped.

Liang's usually jovial face closed down a notch, but he nodded.

"Whatever you say, Mr. Vance."

Alex felt stricken, and despite the cultural divide, he laid a hand on the big man's shoulder. Liang glanced at it, noticed the trembling and met Alex's gaze steadily.

"I'll be okay," he said, softening his voice, "and I'm sorry."

Liang nodded. "You are not inexperienced at this, Mr. Vance, so you will understand my concern. If you are unwell, perhaps it would be best—"

"No!" Alex said. "The mission must be completed. It's just stress, Liang. I'll manage."

Liang stared at him for another long moment, then nodded. "Let's wrap Mr. Boswell's neck so he doesn't get too messy and get him into the back of my car. You drive his and follow me. I'll show you where to leave it—safe and out of sight. I'm going to have some people go over it, make sure you have a secure way to get what you need through the main gates without detection."

Alex nodded gratefully. His hands were almost numb, but functional. He rolled the garrote and slipped it back into its pouch. Then the two of them slid the guard's body from the sedan and stuffed it into Liang's vehicle.

"I'll take care of our friend here, too," Liang said. "I'm going to get you back and you're going to rest. I'm not asking you this time."

Alex nodded.

Liang slipped in behind the wheel of his car, and Alex took the sedan's wheel. Thankfully no one else had appeared. A wife or girlfriend coming out to greet the guard would have been disastrous—at least for her. The records Liang had found showed him as single, but things like that tended to shift often and rapidly. The fact he lived alone simplified things considerably.

Liang led Alex on a slow, winding route. They avoided main streets and ended up on another long industrial lane similar to the one where Liang's warehouse had been located. At the far end of a strip of squat, gray buildings, Liang stopped and stepped out of his car. A door opened, and a smaller man appeared. Alex held back until the two separated. Liang waved him forward.

"Chen will handle cleanup," he said. "I'm

leaving our friend with him. The clothing the man is wearing will be removed and cleaned. It will be ready for you by tomorrow night. As you know, Boswell was scheduled for night shifts beginning tomorrow, so he won't be missed in the morning."

"Perfect," Alex said.

"We'll leave the car here, as well," Liang explained. "They're going to go over it, make sure there isn't anything we've missed—some security feature—a transponder signal that requires an updated key, or anything that would give you away before you get inside the gate. They are also going to work on modeling his face more carefully. You might pass for him physically, but only at a distance. We need to make sure you do better than that."

Alex grinned. This, at least, was something he could handle without concern. "Don't worry about that," he said. "I have my own equipment. It's a specialty of mine."

Liang nodded.

"Let's get this thing inside," Alex said.

Liang gave a signal to unseen others near the doors, and a larger garage door opened in the side of the building where Chen had disappeared. Several dark forms emerged, and one waved Alex forward. He nosed the sedan through the door and into a dimly lit interior. Liang and one other man followed with the bundled body of the security guard. The garage door closed, and large fluorescent lights came to life, bathing the room in light. Workbenches lined the walls. There were welding kits, a small paint booth, machining tools and engine blocks, as well as racks of parts, tools and cables.

Alex stepped out of the car and whistled softly. Liang joined him, grinning again.

"This is quite the operation," Alex commented.

"Sometimes it is necessary to modify things before they are perfect for today's market."

"Stolen things?" Alex asked, raising an eyebrow.

"We prefer to believe that they are assets poorly employed by an overbearing political machine that are being reallocated to a more suitable and just purpose."

"Very diplomatic." Alex chuckled.

The large work bay bustled with activity. Alex saw that the body disappeared through a rear exit. He asked no questions.

"We should be getting back," Liang said. "Soo Lin will be waiting with dinner, and I'm hungry. It's already been a very long day."

Alex nodded, and they left the others to their work.

"They are thorough," Liang said softly as the two exited and returned to his vehicle. "If there is anything in that car to be worried about, they will find it, and when you drive it back into the parking lot, they will suspect nothing. There is only so much I can do though. When you are inside—"

"I'm on my own," Alex completed the sentence. "Believe me, Liang, it won't be the first time."

"Let us hope it is not the last," the big man replied. "Even the Chameleon knows that his enemies watch for him all the time, waiting for the day he fails to change color and disguise himself in time."

He started the engine and drove back toward the city.

THE NEXT MORNING Liang and Alex returned to the garage early. They entered through the smaller door, and found the building all but vacant. Only a very few lights remained lit, and it was Chen alone who greeted them.

The little man was all business. He led them straight to where the black sedan was parked and began chattering at Liang in rapid-fire Chinese that Alex could follow, but barely. He gave a quick rundown of the precautions they'd taken. Nothing out of the ordinary had been found. They had installed a removable false floor in the rear. It was shielded against every form of scanning they were familiar with, and a couple that even Alex didn't recognize. It was easy to access from the driver's seat without drawing unwarranted attention. It would hold everything Alex needed that he couldn't carry on his person.

Boswell's uniform had come equipped with a utility belt with adequate pockets for a wide array of equipment. A little rearranging had provided room for Alex's special tools that he preferred to carry on a mission like this. The uniform was bulky and allowed plenty of room to conceal packets, and he carried a deep-pocketed clipboard organizer. The only thing that would have been better would have been if he could enter the building carrying a bulky duffel bag.

When the brief was complete, they ushered Alex into a separate room, where he dressed and they outfitted him. All the time they worked, Chen chattered. When they had a moment alone, Alex asked Liang about this.

"I hope he manages to talk less when he's not here," he said. "I'd hate to see you in trouble because someone couldn't stay quiet."

Liang laughed.

"When Chen is not in this building, he might as well be a mute. You would see him, and you would not believe it is the same man. He is what Americans believe all Asians to be—inscrutable."

As if sensing he was being discussed, Chen turned and grinned at them, then he winked. Alex buckled on the utility belt and shook his head with a short laugh.

"It is almost time," Liang told him.

"This last part will take a few minutes," Alex said. He stepped over to a mirrored bench where he'd laid out his equipment. There was a blowup photo of Boswell on the bench, taken from his security badge. Alex studied it, tracing the lines of the man's face with his index finger, which was thankfully steady for the moment, then using the digital image, he transferred the data into a rectangular metal container. He tapped several buttons, then waited as the small machine hummed to life.

When it was finished, he opened the case, and removed a human face—a re-creation of Boswell's image in a special type of formfitting latex. He placed it over his own face, and set to work, ensuring that it fit properly around his eyes, nose and mouth, and using small touches of makeup to blend it in with his own skin. He moved quickly, having gone through this many times in the past.

It was ironic, in a way, that while he could appear to become someone else, he could not escape who he was, the disease that would forever change *him* into something else, as well.

Fifteen minutes later he took a last glance at the mirror, and then closed his eyes. He sent his thoughts back over the hours to when he'd first observed Boswell crossing the parking lot to his men. He pictured the set of the guard's shoulders, the way he held his chin and the way he moved. He brought his mind slowly into synch with that image, sensing how the man's gait would feel, watching himself through the other man's eyes.

This was the hard part. The mask was only the

most basic part of the disguise. To become someone else, he had to mimic the way they moved, held their body, even how they walked and talked.

To that effect, he took out a small recorder that had a brief sampling of Boswell's voice on it, obtained from his apartment phone. He sent that data into a different device that analyzed the sounds, then created a biodegradable chip. While it worked, he continued to practice his facial expressions and movement. When the chip was completed, he swallowed it, where it lodged against his vocal cords.

When he turned away from the bench and faced Liang and Chen, the two men took a step back.

"My God," Liang murmured.

Alex smiled. "Gentlemen," he said in Boswell's voice, "I believe it's time to go."

Chen started chattering under his breath.

"You're him!" Liang exclaimed.

"Just like Halloween," Alex said. "Only with better costuming." He walked past them and into the main bay of the garage. As he went, he clipped Boswell's ID to his chest. Liang watched him, not moving. A dead man navigated the benches and test equipment, opened the driver's door of the black sedan and slid in behind the wheel. The transformation was nothing short of eerie.

As Alex settled in and rolled down the passenger window, Liang stepped up close. Chen kept his distance.

"Now I know," Liang said softly.

"Know what?" Alex asked, grinning up at him.

"Who you are," he replied. "It has been said that our organization employs someone they call the Chameleon. That is you, yes?"

Alex laughed and started the engine. "If I said no, would you believe me?" he asked.

Liang shook his head, and Chen finally got moving and opened the outer bay door to the garage.

"You've got enough explosive to take out that entire complex, as it shows on the plans," Liang said. "If you're right, though—if they have another facility below?"

"That's what I have to make sure of before I act," Alex replied. "If it's there, and if it's protected against just such an attack, as I suspect it must be, then what I have isn't enough to do the entire job. I have to target the source of the research and take out the computers, laboratories and, with a little luck, the brains behind this entire crazed program. If there is a lower level, I'll penetrate as deeply as I can before I set the charges."

"Raises your risk," Liang said. "It's likely to have tighter security and we don't have any schematics for it. Now that we've killed a guard, waiting for more information is out of the question, yes?"

"If we don't stop this, the risk is raised for everyone. I don't know what I'm going to find when I get inside that building, but I know I have this one shot, and it's time to take it."

"Be safe, then," Liang said, holding out a meaty hand.

Alex thought about not shaking it. The slight tremor shook his fingers, and he wasn't sure what would happen if he applied full pressure. Then he met Liang's gaze, and he shook. The hand was fine, though the grip left a light tingle.

"Take care of Soo Lin," he said.

Without another word he rolled up the window, put the sedan in Reverse and backed out of the garage. He knew the route back to the parking lot and the MRIS complex, but he drove slowly. They had started very early that morning, and he didn't want to arrive uncharacteristically early for Boswell. The most important thing was to act absolutely calm. If he passed the guard at the gate and got parked, he knew he'd make it at least as far as the building. It wasn't until he got inside that it was likely to get interesting.

He knew the security checkpoints, unless they'd changed in the past week. He knew that each squad had six interior and six exterior components. What he didn't know, exactly, was the routine of the interior guard. He knew standard military and paramilitary procedure, and he could extrapolate somewhat from the patterns of the exterior guard, but there was more guesswork involved than he cared for. He also had the problem of trying to evade those directly involved with Boswell. Even with his careful disguise, his men might be fooled for a few minutes, but any prolonged involvement or contact would lead to his being exposed, and if that happened he might not even have time to set off his charges in one place and score an indirect hit.

As he drove, he reviewed the plans to the complex in his mind. He used the concentration to distract him from his right leg, which had begun to tremble. The muscles of his thigh felt as if they were contracting, pulling in on themselves painfully. When he tried to relax them, they fluttered and pulled tighter still, and the tension this brought tightened the limb further. He gritted his teeth and pictured diagrams of the security checkpoints in his mind.

He knew where the main stairwells were located, as well as the maintenance stairs, elevators and even a dumbwaiter that led down to the cafeteria. The complex was self-sustained. Once workers arrived for their shift, they remained within the confines of the building until it was time for their relief to arrive. There were services built in to facilitate this, break rooms, the cafeteria and even a small laundry. He tried to picture where the break in security to a secondary level would appear. Power and water had to break the plane of any such enclosure. The same types of maintenance that existed on the upper level would be required to support the lower, so the maintenance stairs were a good bet. The dumbwaiter shaft might actually extend downward, as well. It was even possible, he mused, that since everyone was aware of the heightened security, and everyone was apparently aware that there were too many cars in the lot, that there was no attempt at extra security.

If the latter was true, he might not have the same level of problems ahead of him. If the entrance to the lower level was open and secured electronically, he might be able to get in. If it was coded to access badges, he only needed to get one with a high enough level to get him through, if Boswell's proved inadequate.

At precisely 7:30 he rolled into sight of the parking lot. He was still slightly early, but he hoped he was correct in assuming that supervisors generally arrived first. That was the case in most military organizations he'd had contact with, and he assumed it would not raise an eyebrow here, even if it wasn't a requirement. He needed to be a little ahead of his "men" because he intended to be inside and on the move downward before they arrived. The timing was crucial. If he arrived too soon they might hold him or question him. For all he knew it was forbidden to be on site when you weren't on duty. It was equally important that he arrive first for his shift. Again, more luck was involved than he was generally comfortable trusting.

He put on the olive drab cap they'd taken from the dead man, and slipped the man's shades on to cover his eyes. It might look a little odd, but the sun was still out, and fairly bright, and it was possible he could just have forgotten to take them off. Anything that could remove a chance at detection was important. He could remove the glasses when he reached the building, possibly as an excuse to avert his gaze from someone inside.

He took a deep breath as he followed the circular drive to the main gate. He rolled to a stop beside the guard's shack. He handed Boswell's badge to the man in the guard shack and waited for all hell to break loose. If he'd made a mistake, or they had some way of knowing that there was a problem with Boswell, then he was finished before he began.

The guard glanced at the ID, glanced back up at Alex, who nodded, and then back to the ID.

"Go," the man said, nodding curtly into the compound. Alex took his badge back, affixed it carefully to the front of the dead man's shirt and drove forward into the lot, scanning for open spaces.

Another thing he didn't know was whether particular areas of the parking lot were assigned to particular groups, or individuals. Instead of making this an issue, he drove on to the rear of the lot and found the space where Boswell had parked the night before. There were places closer in, but somehow it felt right to put the sedan back where he'd originally found it. Again, it was a calculated risk, but it was a lower risk than taking an incorrect spot. He killed the engine and worked fast.

The false floorboard lifted easily and he slipped his hand under. Inside was the biggest risk he would take. He had to enter the compound with the explosives in hand. He'd left them secured as he entered in case there was any sort of routine search, but now he pulled out the utility belt, strung with black pouches filled with enough high explosive to remove the upper level of the building from the map. He snapped it around his waist, taking pains to move quickly and efficiently and to show none of the fear of motion the belt brought him.

As he'd done in the garage earlier, he closed his eyes and slipped back to the small snippets of Boswell that he'd recorded in his memory. He pictured the man crossing this very parking lot and then, without hesitation, he opened the door, stepped out, closed and locked the sedan and started off across the pavement.

At first he saw no one. He measured his breath

by the paces, remembering each time he moved that he was not Alex Tempest, but Roy Boswell. He wasn't breaking into a secret biomedical laboratory to try and save the world, he was a regular guy with a job to do, a few men to supervise and another shift to get through. He slowed his pace just slightly when the day shift guards rounded the corner of the maintenance shed and came into sight. They paid no attention to him, and when he hesitated to let the last of them pass, their captain nodded to him in recognition. Roy returned the nod, passed on by and headed for the main entrance of the complex.

No one gave him a second glance. He stepped through an arched, stainless-steel entrance and stood before a chrome-framed door of very thick glass. To the left of the door hung a magnetic-strip-card reader. He slipped the badge in and swiped it down. Two small green lights appeared, one below and one above the lock. There was a hum and a heavy click. He grabbed the door, pulled it open and stepped inside.

Almost miraculously, the foyer was empty. It was tiled with smooth, reflective stone. Doorways led to the right, left and straight ahead. In the angles between two of the hallways were the main elevators. He walked to the one on the left, swiped his card again and waited. There was a hum deep in the guts of the building and lights came on, illuminating the upward-pointing arrow. Moments later there was another heavy clunking sound, then the door slid open. A tall, thin man stepped out, glanced at Alex with a harried, irritated expression, then turned and headed off down one of the hallways, a sheaf of papers half-crumpled in his grip.

The plans he'd memorized showed a main floor, a basement level, a maintenance level below that and three floors above the ground level. All of these were indicated by numbered buttons. There were also four buttons off to the side of the panel. They were not numbered, but each was emblazoned with a symbol in bold Chinese script, along with its counterpart in English, for which Alex was thankful.

Sometimes, it was better to be lucky than good, he thought.

He pressed the lowest of the numbered buttons, and the elevator came to life with a loud hum. The car began its descent, and he closed his eyes. He leaned on the wall of the elevator car to remove some of the pressure from his aching legs, and he brought up a mental image of the lower floor he was about to reach. He had to move quickly and avoid contact and, if discovered, he had to act without hesitation. He thought suddenly of Brin.

How many of those who were about to die would be like her? People coming to work every day, believing they were doing work that would help to improve the lives of those around them? How many innocents would be destroyed in the interest of saving millions more? When he was done here, if he succeeded, would they send him— or someone like him—to the MRIS office where Brin worked? Was the knowledge she possessed a danger to mankind—enough so that she'd become a liability? If she was considered a liability, he needed to find all of the evidence that might point to her and destroy it. He wasn't about to let a loose asset or piece of research destroy his wife and his family.

He shook the thoughts from his mind and growled out loud, just as the elevator door slid open. Luckily no one was there to hear.

17

The break room on the lowest level had a small doorway leading to the laundry access. Alex slipped past vending machines, pots of tea and coffee and into the darker room beyond. He had managed to enter the break room without being seen, but he knew his time was limited. He would be late for Boswell's shift in only a few moments, and someone was bound to report seeing him when he entered the main building. They would be looking for him, and before that happened, to give himself half a chance at escape, he had to get where he was going, set his charges and get out.

He walked straight to the dumbwaiter and opened the access panel. It was a simple device, as he'd hoped. It consisted of a single solid platform that rose and fell by the control of a pair of buttons that dangled from a cable attached to a basketlike frame. Luck was still with him—the car was at his level, and when he leaned in to peer downward, he saw that the shaft ran much farther down than where he currently stood. He reasoned no one would take it lower—why should they? It was probably not guarded, and he doubted there was even an alarm.

He glanced over his shoulder to be certain the break room was still clear, and then swung up onto the little platform, regretting instantly putting so much of his weight on the grip of a single arm. His hand cramped and he almost cried out. He felt the dumbwaiter bounce under his weight and grabbed the control in his other hand. He pressed a button, and the platform lurched upward. He cursed softly, regained his balance and pressed the other button. The dumbwaiter descended slowly, dropping him through a shaft of utter darkness toward whatever lay below.

He listened carefully for voices, or for any sort of alarm that might have sounded, but he heard nothing. He rode down for what seemed an inordinately long time, but at last he saw the dim outline of an access panel rising to meet him. He timed his descent roughly and stopped a couple of inches below the panel. He reached out and slid it open a crack. No one moved or made a sound. Alex reached down to the holster on his belt and pulled out his porcelain-framed 9 mm Glock pistol. It was a special piece of weaponry, equipped with a laser sight, a silencer and loaded with Glaser rounds. Very carefully he pulled the panel open the rest of the way and stepped out into a dark room.

It took a moment to orient himself, but when his eyesight adjusted slightly he found he was in a large chamber with a low ceiling. Pipes and ductwork ran in all directions, and it was warmer than it had been on the upper floors. He moved away from the dumbwaiter access carefully and began a circuit of the wall. He found power panels, circuit breakers with huge snaking ropes of cable stretching up through the ceiling above him, and eventually he came to what he assumed was the central furnace of the building.

He tried to estimate how far down he'd come and cursed himself for not preparing well enough to have had string or rope—anything to measure that distance more accurately. He was nearly certain that there was another floor above him, and if the chamber he stood in was a measure of it, that hidden floor ran the entire length of the building. Alex followed the cables quickly. It didn't take him long to pinpoint where a large number of data cables extended into the ceiling, and he started there, planting the first of his charges. He placed another on the ventilation tubing he believed was intended for environmental control. If the floor above was comprised of computer banks and laboratories, as he expected, then the two largest repositories of data and danger would be the labs themselves, and the computers.

He was assuming that computers on the main floors were isolated from the hidden banks below. The very paranoia that hid the labs in the first place would drive the separation. If he was careful enough setting his charges, and if he managed to get back to the floor where he'd entered the dumbwaiter shaft and plant what remained, the point would be moot. The foundations of the building would be vaporized. Anything and anyone on the floors above would be wiped clean, and whatever secrets MRIS was keeping would be gone forever.

He planted a third charge at the base of the main furnace and took off at a run for the exit to the main hall. There was no reason to haul himself up using the dumbwaiter from here; he knew where the elevators would be located. The numbered floors would still be numbered, and since he was already on the lower floor, he knew where his next arrival point would be.

He saw no one in the hallway, but that didn't surprise him. This was a maintenance level, and though there were probably a few people with access, that would likely be when something needed to be adjusted, tested or repaired. He found the corner where the elevator shafts were located. There was no way to know if he had any time left at all. He opened a pouch on his belt and pulled out a small kit. He pressed the button to call the elevator.

While he waited he took a small moistened pad and modified the makeup he'd applied to his face and made minute adjustments to the musculature and shape of it. He worked quickly, and by the time the door to the elevator opened, he wore a thick mustache and his eyebrows had been darkened. He still wore the guard's uniform and had his ID tag, but he no longer looked like Roy Boswell. He no longer stood or held himself like Boswell. He stepped into the elevator and hit the button for the lower of the main floors.

"Going up," he breathed.

As he rode upward, noting that he'd been correct in assuming he would pass another floor, he unsnapped the flap on his holster and rested his hand on the butt of the 9 mm Glock. He had no way to know what to expect when the doors opened, and he didn't want to be taken by surprise. He had to be sure he gave the charges below enough time. They were set for three hours. He fully intended to be long gone by the time they went off, but if something went wrong, he needed to keep security focused on himself. The primary target was now below him, and if he was really lucky, what he'd already done would not only take that out, but would also collapse the upper floors. It was also possible the explosion would funnel up the heating vents. It could be spectacular.

The elevator halted and the door slid open. Alex stepped out into the hall and turned immediately to his right. He swept the hall as he turned, seeing no one on his left. Then he heard scuffling feet. A voice rose over the hiss of the elevator's door sliding closed behind him.

"Secure the elevators. He's on this floor."

The footsteps were approaching fast, and he saw a turn in the passageway ahead. Alex stepped slowly back toward the elevator, but he was too late. They rounded the corner. He knew he'd been spotted, but he didn't panic. They were looking for Boswell, or someone who looked like Boswell. He was a slightly taller man with a mustache. He wore the same uniform they wore.

Now was the time for one of those acceptable risks. There was a chance they would simply act if given a clue.

He stepped forward and called out, "The door just closed. I think he's headed up."

The two men who'd rounded the corner stopped. They stared at him for just a moment, then the guard in front nodded.

"Take the stairs," he ordered. Alex nodded. He turned and started back down the hall. He'd only gone a few steps when he heard the squawk of a radio, and he'd just rounded the corner toward the main stairwell when he heard the cry behind him and knew his cover was blown.

To either side of the main stairs were long corridors. He flipped through the memorized diagrams in his mind and veered to the right. The labs were on the left, but the computer mainframes were on the right. If the data had been copied, backed up or stored, it would reside in the drive arrays on those systems, so if he could take out only one more wing, that was the logical target.

Boots pounded on the stairs and he moved more quickly. He heard voices behind him and he ran for a large double door on his right.

"You!" someone called from behind him. "Stop!"

Alex ignored the command and lunged for the door. A shot fired suddenly and he moved instinctively, ducking left and reaching for the door to the computer lab. He twisted the handle and dived forward, shouldering through. He rolled, just as another shot ricocheted over his head. Then he was inside and moving. The computer banks were large. The room was air-conditioned, and fans hummed loudly. Banks of optical backup drives lined one wall. A glass-enclosed area housed more servers. As on the maintenance level, he saw no one standing or wandering around. Most of the computer management and would be handled from remote consoles. The machines themselves were kept in an environmentally controlled void. Alex scanned the room quickly and chose his spot.

The floor was made of removable deck plates that allowed access to the cabling below. He heard the doors burst open and knew he had only seconds. There were detachable suction-cup-tipped handles used to lift the deck plates, and he grabbed one, attaching it to the nearest plate. The plate lifted from its rails easily and, with a quick snakelike slide, Alex dropped into the cable trench beneath it. As he went, he released the suction on the handle so it would fall off to the side. He lowered the plate gently in place over his head and lay very still.

From beneath the deck plate, voices sounded muffled. He heard barked orders, and he heard booted feet moving slowly past the servers.

"You might as well come out," an amplified voice rose to a volume he could make out over the machinery. "Switch all internal cameras to thermal imaging."

Alex took stock of his position. The cable trench was wide. He could move relatively quickly. He grabbed one of the explosive packs from his belt and affixed it to the cable closest to him. He worked quickly, and then started crawling forward. The trenches followed the course of the passageway between servers. When he heard someone above him, he remained very still, and when they moved on, he followed. The same noise that muffled the voices of the team searching for him helped to conceal his movements. He worked his way back toward the door, and along the way he managed to get two more explosive devices placed.

At the door, he found that there was a narrow, oval opening that led through the wall and into the access beneath the floor beyond the door. The hallway flooring was solid, if he got beneath it; he might not have a way out. As he lay just inside the doorway deciding whether to chance the crawl space or make his break, the lights grew dim. The sound of the machines around him groaned as fans slowed, winding down to a deathly, echoing silence. He hadn't thought they could get the systems shut down so quickly, and he silently cursed himself for moving too slowly.

"You will never escape," a voice called to him. "You might as well come out now and save us all a lot of trouble." The voice was heavily accented with an Eastern European inflection. "You will not be hurt if you turn yourself in now."

Another voice crackled over a radio and Alex picked up the message clearly.

"Explosive devices detected on levels five and three."

"Find them," the first voice snapped. There was a squawk of static.

Alex crawled into the oval wall spacer and glanced up and down the outer hallway. There was no light at all, except a small square down the hall and across several runs of cables. It had to be another way out. He slid onto the snaking lengths of cable and crawled across. Pulling himself along with his hands, his fingers screamed in pain.

Halfway across his left hand locked, but Alex ignored it, using it like a claw and pushing with his booted toes, while simultaneously trying not to make any sound. It was less critical beneath the hall, but as soon as they figured out how he'd disappeared in the computer room, and where he'd gone, they'd be on him.

After what seemed far too long, he reached the gray-lit area on the far side of the hall. It was another oval passage between walls, and Alex slid through without hesitation. He immediately felt an increase in temperature. His mind flipped through floor plans, and he realized he was directly above the furnace area. It had to be a maintenance room, possibly leading to laboratories with access to the main passages.

Lifting the first deck plate he came to, Alex peered around the room. He saw duct work immediately ahead. He pulled himself up and out, lowering the plate back into place as quietly as possible. The space he stood in was a small, shadowed area. The room beyond consisted of several racks of operator panels, a long workbench that held equipment open for repair and a door that led out. He tried to think, but he couldn't seem to get his mind to focus. Between the pain in his body and the stress, it was as if someone had stirred his brains with a giant spoon. Sweat dripped into his eyes, and a sudden sharp stab of pain shot through his right thigh. He felt the trembling in his hand and willed it to stop.

"Not now," he whispered. "God, not now."

He heard footsteps again. In the distance he heard the amplified voice calling to him again.

"Give yourself up. You are surrounded, and there is no way out of this building."

He had nothing to lose by responding at this point. It would be only moments before they located him. All he could hope to do was to lead them on a slightly longer chase and delay the discovery of the explosives.

"Maybe I'll just kill you all and walk out," he called.

As soon as he spoke, he moved. He knew it would be difficult to pinpoint where sound originated, but they were going to know the general area. He wanted to get out of the maintenance room if possible and into one of the labs again. If technicians were present, he might use that to his advantage. If he moved quickly enough he might be able to assume a new disguise. There were possibilities, but none of them existed unless he got moving.

As he stepped through the doorway, he heard a shout from his right. He'd been spotted. Ahead to his left was the entrance to one of the main laboratories. He caught sight of frightened faces within. He lunged for the door, but this time the effort proved too much. His left leg suddenly gave out beneath him, and he tumbled to the side with a cry of pain. A shot rang out and something struck him hard in the shoulder, spinning him out of control.

Alex managed to get his Glock out of the holster. He turned and pulled the trigger. He heard cursing and shouts, but for some reason the words wouldn't register. He crashed into the wall by the door frame of the lab and pain shot through his shoulder, already soaked in blood from the gunshot. He gritted his teeth and tried to stand, but his legs would not support him. He turned and raised his gun, watching for movement.

Two men appeared, crouching low and moving down opposite sides of the passageway toward him. He took aim at the man on the left and fired, saw the Glaser round strike him midchest and blow him off his feet, leaving a splatter of blood on the wall next to him.

Alex tried to roll to his right, but somewhere between his brain and his legs, the signal went haywire. What was supposed to be a smooth roll turned into a flop, and he landed heavily on the floor as another searing lance of pain brushed his temple. He'd felt the bullet before he heard, as if from far away, the report of the gun.

Then everything went black.

18

The more Brin thought about Alex shutting her out of his world, the more it hurt. She wondered where he was, what he was doing—and if he was okay. She wondered if he'd found an alternate source of the medication he'd been prescribed, or if he'd just determined to "tough it out" and "work through the pain," as she'd heard him boast on so many other occasions. This was not a sore muscle or a bad cold. There was no way to "push through the pain" on this one. She needed to talk to him, to know how far it had progressed. The not knowing was the worst. That and the stupid, secret chat room where people knew things about her husband that she didn't.

The only thing keeping her sane was her work. What Rand had brought her was so miraculous that working with it took her away. She and Alex had always joked that when she was lost in an idea, the world didn't exist at all. To a point it was true. She took her research very seriously. It was important to her to make progress, to help people. With Alex itching at her thoughts, though, she considered calling Rand and asking for some time off. If the new project hadn't been on such a tight timeline, she probably would have—it wasn't fair to be distracted when she was working on something so important.

When he was on an assignment, Alex was usually completely out of touch. It had always bothered her, but when he told her it was important to his work, she'd never complained. Now she saw it for what it really was—a lie. He didn't tell her where he was because he had already built a lie that he couldn't dig his way out of, telling her he worked for a security company. No normal security company would be totally unable to reach one of its employees under these circumstances. She wondered if he had ever really been where he had told her he would be, or doing anything even remotely resembling what he told her he'd be doing. She wondered what else he'd lied about.

They had an emergency communication plan. She'd only used it twice, and Alex had only responded one of those times. They'd set up anonymous e-mail accounts on a Web server. The accounts were not associated with them by name, address, phone number or any account they shared. If they really needed to be in contact, they used the Web site to leave messages. Brin had logged into that site dozens of times in the past few hours. Each time she'd left him a note. Each time she'd checked her own inbox and found it empty. It grew compulsive, over time. She couldn't stop herself from opening the page, refreshing the inbox and sending messages.

Then it occurred to her that if the man in the Room 59 chat room had known what she was wearing, sitting in front of a computer in her own home, he would have a way to trace where she went on the Internet. She cursed and shut down the screen, aching to open it again. It was a portal to Alex, even if the other end of the portal appeared to be closed. If he showed up or contacted her, she wanted to know it the minute it happened. She felt helpless and it was terrible sensation.

To fill the hours when she should have been sleeping, once Savannah had been put down for the night, she turned to research. She had been to every major Web site on MS, and combed them all for useful information. She'd familiarized herself with symptoms, medications, treatments, and when those sources had been depleted, she'd moved on to the cellular level, her mind racing as she perused current research and development on cures, radical treatments, unapproved processes and theories on combating the disease. While MRIS hadn't spent a significant amount of time on this particular disease, there *were* applications within their research that might be relevant to MS.

At the least, it was something familiar, something she knew she was good at. She knew she wasn't going to suddenly stumble into a cure, but the scientist in her saw the implied challenge and she accepted compulsively.

Her calls to Dr. Britton had remained unanswered. She'd gone as far as to check with other businesses with offices in the same building where he was listed. There was a door there, it seemed, and his name was tacked onto a sign above it, but no one had seen him—not recently, maybe not ever. Brin called three separate businesses in the same building and all of them gave a similar answer.

No, they did not know if Dr. Britton was open.

No, they did not know if he had been open recently.

No, they'd never been in his office, and for that matter, only one person she spoke to could even remember seeing him.

The whole experience reminded Brin of the Room 59 chat room, and it made her angry all over again. Was Dr. Britton just another part of the lie? Did he exist at all or had he been arrested or taken away somewhere? Were they really asking what she knew about Alex's condition, or were they sending her on wild-goose chases after non-existent doctors and dead-end research to distract her from where Alex was and what he was doing? If Dr. Britton worked for them, why had they needed a second source to confirm Alex's condition?

She *needed* information, and all she had for the time being was her anger and a lot of bad guess-work. It was an infuriating situation.

She glanced at the clock. It was very late—or actually—very early. She glanced at the computer monitor, decided it didn't matter and logged in to the e-mail account one last time. There was nothing from Alex, and she shut the machine down. She needed at least a couple of hours of rest, even if she couldn't sleep. She'd be alone soon in a laboratory with only a laptop, valuable research and Mr. Coffee for companions. There was no room for error in that environment, and she couldn't go in with her mind buzzing from lack of sleep. She rose and made her way to the bed she'd shared with Alex for so many years and slipped in between the sheets without un-dressing. She laid her head on his pillow, breathing in his scent, and closed her eyes, but she didn't sleep.

THE DARKNESS RECEDED slowly. Alex heard what seemed to be voices, but he couldn't make out what they were saying. He could barely differentiate one from another, and then he wasn't certain what he heard were voices at all. It might have been the hum of high-intensity lighting or the fans on the computer servers he'd crawled beneath— when? Days before? Hours? Minutes? His thoughts began to focused, but he didn't open his eyes immediately.

A quick assessment revealed that he was bound to some sort of straight-backed chair. He felt heat on his face and as his mind cleared, he knew it was bright light shining on his closed eyelids. His mouth was so dry that he wasn't certain he could pry his lips apart, and the pain in his arms and legs was excruciating. It was much more intense than it should have been, even though the bindings were tight. He heard shuffling footsteps and an occasional muttered comment, but there was no real conversation, so there was nothing to learn. At last, taking a long slow breath to calm himself, he opened his eyes.

The light was so bright it was painful. He blinked, furiously, trying to clear away the sudden tears so that he could make out his surroundings. There was a flurry of motion and sound, and he heard a voice call out in Chinese.

"He's waking up."

Alex's shoulder was throbbing. His shirt had dried and stick to the gunshot wound. When he was able to see a little, he glanced down and saw that there was a rough bandage wrapped around his clothing, but that the wound hadn't been treated. He was almost grateful for it. The throbbing muscle pain from the MS stabbed through his arms and legs, and he felt his left hand fluttering again, as if it might cramp. His head pounded, and he felt a numbness in his left temple. He wished there was a mirror. It felt as if his head might be loosely bandaged, but he couldn't be sure. The wound on his shoulder was an intense, more familiar pain, and he thought that maybe if he could concentrate on it he might find a way to release the tension in his afflicted limbs. He didn't expect to have an opportunity for escape, but he also didn't intend to blow it if one presented itself.

The man who had spoken wore a white lab coat. He stared down at Alex through the thick lenses of heavy, black-framed glasses. A stethoscope dangled from his neck. He held a clipboard in one hand. The man reached out and lifted Alex's eyelids one after the other. He reached out and poked the makeshift bandage on Alex's wounded shoulder. When Alex grimaced and let loose a short gasp of pain, the man smiled.

Footsteps sounded, and Alex heard voices approaching. A moment later there was the creak of a door opening. He turned, but could not quite see where the sound came from, or who had entered.

The doctor—at least he assumed the man was a doctor of some sort—left him and stepped out of sight.

"Is he coherent?" a voice demanded.

"He is in pain, and he has not spoken, but I believe he is awake, and he will not die soon. There is something wrong with his hand—I had no time to diagnose—but it does not matter. He can talk."

There was a grunt of assent or satisfaction. He heard footsteps, and then someone stepped past the blinding light, blocking it from Alex for a moment, and then allowing it to stream back into his face suddenly as the figure passed. Alex cursed under his breath and closed his eyes, turning away again and waiting for his sight to adjust.

When he was able to see again, he turned his gaze forward. Standing before him was a lean, dark-skinned man with dark, penetrating eyes. He wore fatigues with some sort of collar device. On his waist he wore a belt very similar to the one Alex had taken from Boswell. A black holster hung from one hip, the butt of a nasty-looking gun protruding from the rear. Behind this, Alex caught sight of a long, thin scabbard. He wasn't sure what kind of blade such a sheath would house, but it wasn't any kind of standard-issue military blade.

The man's expression was unreadable. His eyes gave away nothing, and his face might as well have been chiseled from stone. Alex glared back at him.

He wasn't about to be intimidated, and even if he had been his training would have kicked in. He wasn't exactly frightened, but adrenaline pumped through his system and his senses were heightened. This sent waves of pain through his hands, and his legs felt as if they were collapsing in on themselves. There was so much pain he had to wrap it into one huge ball and set his will against it to hold his gaze steady.

"I am Captain Dayne," the man said at last. "It is my duty to oversee the security of this facility."

That answered at least one question. However long he'd been out, and whatever they had planned for him, they hadn't removed him from the MRIS complex. Alex met the man's gaze, but said nothing.

"You have caused me quite a bit of difficulty," Dayne continued. "Not only am I now short a good man, but my superiors are not happy with me. They count on me to provide absolute security. As you can imagine, they were not pleased to find you inside their complex. They were even less pleased by the explosives you managed to plant."

Alex's mind whirled. Had they found all of the charges? How long had he been out? Would they hear an explosion any moment, or were all the packages safely detached and disarmed? There was no way to know, and he could think of no taunt or question that might lead Dayne to tell him that would not, in the asking, give away too much. He held his silence.

"What am I going to do with you?" Dayne asked. "I wonder who sent you? I wonder why? I wonder what it is you know about our work that would make you risk your life to destroy it?"

"You'll never know," Alex spoke through dry, chapping lips.

Dayne's expression changed for the first time. The man raised a single eyebrow and something sparkled in his eyes. Then it was gone, the eyebrow settled and Dayne broke eye contact. He brought his hand up and began examining his fingernails, pointedly avoiding looking at his prisoner. He turned to a short bench behind him and, as though seeing it for the first time, stepped over to examine its contents.

"I've learned a few things from years of leading men and asking questions," Dayne said. His voice had softened, but somehow the shift was sinister rather than comforting. "I have learned that there are never questions you can't get an answer to. I have learned, as well, that it isn't always necessary to get an answer in so many words to find out what you need to know. Do you know another thing I've learned?"

Dayne turned. His expression had darkened. His face was flushed, and his brows knotted like lightning bolts ready to strike. Dayne seemed to sway slightly, and the motion was mildly hypnotic. Alex didn't like breaking eye contact, but he did. He

glanced toward the wall, away from the bright
light.

Dayne stepped closer. He reached behind the
holster on his belt, and Alex heard a snap released.
A moment later, Dayne had pulled free a long,
slender blade. It gleamed where the light hit it.
Alex had used a similar blade before. He had used
it on fishing expeditions for filleting fish. The
blade could strip off very thin strips of flesh with
almost no effort. Such knives were razor sharp and
could reach bone with only a slight effort on the
part of the wielder. Very slowly he swallowed. He
had to clear the lump from his throat, but he was
still unwilling to give Dayne the reaction he
sought, despite the twitch that rippled through his
muscles at the sight of the cold, honed steel.

"You are suffering from a misunderstanding,"
Dayne said. "You are assuming that I need information that you possess, and that my purpose here
is to question you, grill you until you break and
hand over your secrets. I would imagine you
expect me to use drugs, torture, to pin your eyes
open and shine this light directly into them until
the retinas burn, and to employ other such tactics.

"I won't lie to you. I would enjoy all of those
things very much. I have spent a lot of hours
studying the use of various tools on the human
anatomy, but there are still breaks in my research,
and I'd like nothing better than to fill those in.

Still, though you denied me information before I even asked for it, showing your fear, I have no questions for you. Instead, I have lessons to teach.

"The first is, you never come into another man's house uninvited unless you are willing to pay the price. As you see, I am still employed, but you have caused me a great deal of anxiety and stress, and I intend to return these to you in kind. I will find out everything that I need to know about you, one way or another, but I find that any sort of conversation including questions and answers is best left until a much later point. It is better to establish guidelines up front, to put things in their proper context."

Alex tried not to listen to what the man was saying. He thought about Brin. He thought about Savannah. He felt the power in Dayne's soft, sibilant voice, and fought against its influence. He had to keep his mind clear. There were things that didn't make sense, and he knew he had a short amount of time to put them in order before whatever Dayne had planned was put into action.

It made no sense that the man wasn't more concerned about the explosives. It made no sense that he had made no attempt whatsoever to identify Alex, or to find out about the force behind him. Everything about this setup screamed at Alex to pay attention to some detail he couldn't quite put a finger on.

Dayne rolled the hilt of his blade slowly over the palm of his hand and into the other, then back, watching the glitter of the blade as it rolled. He seemed to be lost in thought, as if something more important had suddenly occupied his thoughts and he was considering it carefully. Alex felt sweat bead on his forehead and dampen his underarms. His pulse pounded through his poorly bandaged shoulder. He wanted to distract Dayne, to bring him back to the moment and ground the threat, but he could think of nothing to say that would not convey the wrong message, and he was fairly certain that Dayne was waiting for just such a chink in his armor.

"I'll be up front with you," Dayne explained. "I find it inefficient and a waste of my time to question a prisoner in the first session we spend together. There are levels of pain, and one can achieve results with a variety of threats, but the truth is that a threat is just that. Until there is understanding, it is possible to be brave in the face of a threat. I like to erase that inadequacy in the process up front."

He stepped forward and reached out. Alex felt a soft tear, and Dayne held a bloodied strip of bandage in his hand.

"You are a fortunate man," Dayne said. "The bullet only nicked your temple. It's a nasty cut, but I don't imagine that I have to explain to you what a 9 mm slug would have done to your brain had it been a more direct hit. It is fortunate for both of us that you survived. I know you don't believe this, but it is true."

Without warning, Dayne gripped Alex suddenly by his hair. The blade shot out, and Alex watched in horror as a thin slice of his scalp—a slice that showed a furrowed slot in the middle that could only have been the bullet wound, dropped past his eyes to the floor. Dayne's smile widened. He leaned and skewered the bit of flesh, holding it up to inspect it. Alex's stomach churned, but he bit back the bile. This new pain was sharp and hot. It sharpened his senses further and helped him focus.

"Now I see I have your attention," Dayne said, flicking the bit of scalp off of his blade with one finger. "It is time to begin." He sheathed the blade in a sudden, quick motion and turned back to the workbench. He rummaged through the tools, lifting some, examining them and replacing them, fondling others. When he turned back he held a large soldering iron in one hand. In the other he held the open end of an extension cord. Alex swallowed again and struggled to free himself. The pain that shot through his hands and his legs drove him near the edge, and he embraced the sensation. As Dayne approached slowly, testing the tip of the soldering iron with the tip of his finger, Alex twisted his wrists cruelly.

Pain shot up his arms. His stomach churned with nausea and he twisted harder. It was a crazy ploy to gain time, but it was all he had. There was a white-hot flash deep in his mind, and then, again, he dropped into blackness.

19

Brin glanced up, saw that it was time to close the lab and sighed with relief. Never one to watch the clock, she'd found herself glancing up compulsively every few minutes if she didn't check the urge. She couldn't access the e-mail site where Alex might reply to her through the firewalls and security of MRIS without setting off flags, and she didn't want to draw any attention to herself, or her problem, until she had a better handle on it.

Thankfully, the work she was preparing was tedious but not taxing. The research had been done, and it had been done well. Case studies lined up perfectly with the numbers and graphics. The reports on the results were spectacular. In fact, the one thing that kept dragging her back to it when she started worrying too much about Alex was the possibility that this technology—these nano-agents—might even lead her to a cure in time to help the man she loved.

The distractions made her feel guilty, because she knew they were counting on her—had in fact handpicked her from a great number of good, qualified candidates—to analyze this data, validate it and to shift it into the next stage of testing and research required to bring it to the world. It was an incredible trust that had been granted her, and she felt the weight of it keenly.

She shut down the laptop with a last glance at the page she was working on. It was a study involving a viral agent that had been introduced into control hosts. The host cells were mutated in two control sets by the viral agent, and then the nano-agents, programmed to reverse the mutation, were introduced into one set. This gave three sets of data—control, mutated and those mutated and then treated with the nanoagents. The results looked more as if there were two control sets and one mutated set. The nanoagents had literally achieved a one hundred percent rate of repair. No anomalies. It was incredible. In other studies, data like that would have caused Brin to pause and consider whether the numbers might have been skewed, but she'd been through enough of the data from the Chinese branch of MRIS to know that if it had been skewed, then the entire study was a fiction.

The perfect score she'd just analyzed was the rule, not the exception. In all her years of research she'd never seen anything so absolutely conclusive.

She closed down the equipment and checked the cultures contained in the climate-controlled chamber. The cultures would become the last portion of her work on the project, as it stood. She would actually get to perform a series of experiments that paralleled what had been done. She would provide the final validation—repeating the results of her colleagues, and developing new tests on the specimens. She wondered if she could justify choosing MS degeneration on cells in those tests and, assuming Alex made it back safely from wherever the hell he'd gone, if she could find a way to get those nanoagents into his system. She shook her head to clear the unethical thoughts and turned off the lights. She still had to pick up Savannah, and she wanted to get home and check that e-mail site, even though she doubted she'd find anything waiting when she did.

AFTER DINNER, Savannah determined that she was going to draw pictures for Daddy. She had her art case and a pile of washable markers and was scribbling furiously on the floor in front of the television. Brin had dug out a DVD of Scooby Doo episodes for the girl to distract herself with, and was relieved at the momentary break. She took the opportunity to sit down at the computer and check for replies to her e-mails. The messages remained unread, and Brin slapped a hand violently on the desktop in frustration.

"What's wrong, Mommy?" Savannah asked.

The girl looked up with wide eyes. Brin doubted Savannah had ever seen such an outburst from her mother, and she wasn't sure how to explain herself. She decided on honesty.

"I just miss Daddy," she said.

Savannah nodded. "Me, too. I don't hit the table, though—I draw."

Savannah went back to her drawing, and Brin watched her, lost in thought, until the villain said, "You meddling kids," a final time. It was time for her daughter to close the art shop and head to bed. Brin's heart ached. She wondered how long it would be before she was raising the girl on her own. No matter the amount of time, it would be far too soon.

It was a long time before her tears cleared enough for another fruitless check of her e-mail. By the time she was back at the computer's main desktop, the tears had dried and she was growing angry again.

She didn't exactly know how to bring up the Room 59 chat room, and she'd been warned not to do it. She knew they might be watching her— might have been clued in to her presence the second she logged on to Alex's computer. The last time she'd been reading an e-mail addressed to them when the man who supposedly worked with her husband had appeared and the window had opened on its own. If that didn't happen pretty quickly, she intended to go searching until she found some trigger.

She'd gotten a clue from the method they used to hide the secure chat entrance. She took the mouse and very slowly began panning it over the screen. Alex's wallpaper was a picture of the family, taken on the beach a year earlier, Savannah holding up her plastic pail of sand tools and grinning widely, Alex tanned and strong with his arm around Brin's shoulders. Brin tried to ignore the memories flooding her mind and concentrated on the motion of the cursor across the screen. She started at the bottom right, where the first Easter-egg entrance had been hidden, and she slid her pointer slowly across the bottom of the monitor screen, then back, moving it only a fraction of an inch higher. It would take a while, but she had the feeling she was on the right track. When the cursor reached the point on the screen directly over her own heart, a small circle appeared around the arrow point. It took her by surprise, and she didn't stop moving her hand in time to catch it on the first pass, but when she brought it back, the circle returned. Brin clicked the mouse button, and the initial chat room window she'd seen during her first visit to Room 59 appeared.

She waited a moment to see if anyone would make first contact, but the cursor blinked in the room, unanswered. Brin moved the cursor to the input window and typed.

"Is there anyone there? This is Brin Tempest."

There was no answer. She thought about repeating her question, and then decided against it. She was wasting time. She dragged the cursor down to the point at the bottom of the screen where she knew the hidden entrance link was located, and when it appeared, she clicked it. She entered Alex's encrypted password and waited. She had been afraid it might be changed or locked out after they allowed her access the first time, but apparently they didn't really want to keep her out. The password was accepted, and the secure window opened. Again, she was alone in a chat room, but she was in.

She repeated her message.

"Is there anyone there? This is Brin Tempest."

She clicked on the send button, watched her message appear in the empty screen of the chat room and sat back to wait. It didn't matter how long it took, she decided; she was going to remain logged in to the site until someone noticed. Every few moments she repeated her message to make sure the system didn't lock her out for inactivity. The blinking cursor continued to mock her, but her mind was set. This was her husband and her life and she wasn't giving any of it up without a fight.

20

Denny stepped into the doorway of Kate's virtual office and waited patiently for her to join him. Finally she appeared and said, "Denny, you wanted to see me?"

"We've got a problem," he said.

"You have no idea how tired I am of that statement," she replied. There was no trace of a smile on her face. She had a folder open on her desk, and Denny knew it was the MRIS operation report.

"It's part of the same problem, I think. Mrs. Tempest has found her way back into the Room 59 chat. So far we've ignored her, but we're going to have to figure out how to deal with this. She may have information we don't have—Alex may have found a way to contact her. We need to make contact."

"You warned her not to contact us," Kate said.

"You ordered me not to change the access," Denny shot back.

Kate almost smiled. "I did, didn't I? Get in there and see what she knows. If she's heard he's been captured, all hell could break loose, and we'll need a plan for damage control. This one is already running way outside safety parameters."

"You don't have to tell me that," Denny grunted. "We're on the verge of needing a total scrub, and with the initial threat still intact. I don't want to have to send another asset out on this one. The risk of exposure is too great, even if the threat is nullified."

"Yeah," Kate said, turning back to her file, "it's bad. Do what you can. Report back when she's out of the system."

Denny nodded, but Kate never saw it. She was already immersed in a copy of the plans for the MRIS complex in Beijing. Denny left her to the work, and returned to his own office and the console where he was currently logged in to Room 59.

He sat down and began to type.

21

When the words appeared on the screen, Brin nearly jumped out of her skin. She'd been sitting alone for nearly an hour. Every two minutes she'd reentered her message to keep the screen active. She'd considered giving up but then the words appeared from nowhere.

"Hello, Brin."

"Who is this?" she typed at last. "Is this the same person I spoke to before?"

"Yes, Mrs. Tempest, this is the same person. You were warned not to return to this chat room."

"Yes, and I was asked to contact my husband," she returned quickly, typing furiously. "How did you expect I would reach you with that information without coming here? I don't have a business card for you, do I?"

There was nothing for a moment, then a new message popped up.

"Has Alex been in contact?" he asked.

"No," Brin typed immediately. She decided that at this point she had no other allies in this, so there was no sense holding anything back. "He and I have a private, anonymous e-mail drop," she typed, thinking quickly and trying to word the message as clearly as possible. "I've left dozens of messages for him, but there has been no response. He usually doesn't respond or leave messages there. We only created it for emergencies. I always thought he was at least checking it, but now I'm not sure."

"I'm sure he checks it if he can," he replied.

"What the hell is that supposed to mean? Why couldn't he? What kind of security job keeps you from being able to use a phone or check e-mail?"

"I'm not at liberty to discuss the nature of your husband's work," he typed. "There are security concerns, and I hope you'll believe me when I tell you that lives could be at stake. One of those lives belongs to Alex. I'm not surprised he hasn't contacted you."

"Where is he?" Brin typed. She didn't really expect an answer, and for a moment after she received one, she stared at it dumbly.

"All I can say is he's operating in the Far East. Even that is more than you should know."

"The Far East?" She typed the words before she thought about it, then added, "Not the Middle East?"

There was a hesitation at the other end, and Brin's anger bubbled over again. She slammed the computer desk for the second time that day and pushed away from the screen. Was anything she'd been told true? Had Alex lied to her about every aspect of his work, down to the location? If he'd been able to do that without giving himself away through guilt or tripping himself on a lie, how much else had he lied about? What kind of man had she married, and who was he? Really.

"Brin?" The word appeared on the screen and floated unanswered for a long moment, and she stared at it. Finally, whoever it was continued typing.

"I don't know what Alex told you when he left—this time, or any other time. I assume he told you he was going to the Middle East and you are angry with him for lying. Let me tell you a few things very quickly that I do know about your husband that are important, and we'll see where it leaves us."

Brin slid no closer to the screen, but she watched.

"Alex Tempest is one of the good guys. He's trained to a level that I suspect even you don't understand, and the work he does is the sort that actually makes a difference in the world. I can't tell you what that work is because there are overarching issues involved that I can't ignore. There are jobs that overshadow the men and women who accomplish them. What Alex has done, he has done because it was necessary to protect you from the danger he faces on a regular basis.

"I'm sure he'll be home to you soon. I imagine at that point the two of you will have a lot to talk about. Right now, I'd say he needs you in ways he never has before, and I'd hate to see that clouded over by actions he meant as protection."

Tears rolled down Brin's cheeks, and she shook her head angrily. She knew this person, whoever he was, had to be right. If he was not, then the things that did matter, the love she and Alex shared, their life and dreams together, their time with Savannah—all of it would be a lie. She knew in her heart it was not, and so she had to find a way to get through this anger. She had to find and fight for her husband.

She slid back to the computer.

"Whoever you are—whatever you are—I know my husband is a good man. Right now, I want only one thing from you. You sent him out there, somewhere far from home. You sent him out there, and he isn't back. You wouldn't be contacting me if you thought everything was okay. He's sick and I want you to get out there and bring him home to me. Am I clear?"

"We are doing all that we can. I'm going to ask you again not to come back to this room. If you access the system again, I'll be forced to lock out Alex's account, and if he can't access it, he can't get in touch with us. Believe me, I'm really hoping he'll be back and logging in personally soon. I also hope he contacts you, Mrs. Tempest, and I hope that he's home soon."

Brin reached for the keyboard, ready to pound out an angry reply, but the window closed and she was returned to the outer chat room, filled with her own message repeated over and over. She closed the program and sat back, lost in thought.

Oddly, her mind returned to the lab and the work she'd been immersed in. Something was tugging at her mind, and she couldn't quite locate it. Then it hit her. The Far East. The research had come from the MRIS complex near Beijing. It was a long shot, but if Hershel Rand had connections in the Beijing office, and if she could think of a way to ask for his help without giving away anything important—not too much of a stretch since she had no idea where Alex was or what he was doing—she might be able to enlist his help in finding Alex. At least it was a starting point. Maybe she could even request a business visit to China to consult with the original research team.

She suddenly felt worlds better. She was thinking and planning, and she knew that, whether or not they were useful in the end, there were things she could be doing. At least she'd be geographically closer to him than she was now. Alex had always said that if she had a plan and an open road, she could do anything.

22

Alex opened his eyes and his first thought was that that bastard Dayne had cut out both of his eyes. He couldn't see. Then he blinked, and felt no pain, and calmed slightly. He did his best not to move. It was very hard to concentrate through the pain. Every twitch brought a new spasm to his thighs and his hands. He was so cramped he wasn't certain he could move at all, should he decide to do so.

Then there were the more natural pains. His shoulder ached. It was numb, but the pain had begun to spread down his arm and back. It didn't feel infected, not yet, but he was certain no care had been taken in applying his dressing. His head throbbed, as well, sending a ringing through his ears when he coughed drily.

He took stock of his body, bit by bit. He had no

way to know how much more "fun" Dayne might have had with him after he passed out. For his body, unconsciousness was a simple escape mechanism. He'd hoped that they would believe he'd lost too much blood from the gunshot wounds and just passed out. They didn't know much about him, so they wouldn't be surprised to see him display a sign of weakness. Apparently, his ruse had worked.

Moving first one foot and then the other, he tested his legs, which, while sore and cramped, seemed to be functional for the moment. He had no specific pain in his back or sides. As he worked his way up his body, checking for new damage and assessing the impact of the old, he listened. He heard the distant hum of machinery. The sound echoed, as if down a metal-decked passage, but there was nothing else. He heard no footsteps, no murmur of voices. Wherever they'd taken him, they'd left him alone.

Still, he tried not to move noticeably. If they were watching him, waiting for him to regain consciousness, he didn't want to tip them off by any sudden movement. He needed time to regroup. He slowly tried to move his hands, and realized that they were bound together with a length of plastic cording, but not tied to anything else. The floor was cool, metallic, he thought, and he assumed he was on one of the two lower levels. It wasn't a deck plate, so he wouldn't be sliding out through any cable troughs, but if he could find a way to get free, he was still in the portion of the complex most crucial to his mission.

At this thought, he nearly laughed, and had to bite back the sudden rush of emotion.

"At any cost," he mumbled.

He had never felt as much pain as he did at that moment. He felt a bit short of breath, but every time he took more than a tiny gulp of air into his lungs, a wave of nausea shot through his gut, and he bit it off. Slowly he moved his left leg, bending it at the knee and drawing it up. He tested the joints, found everything intact, returned it to its original position and did the same with his right leg. He listened for a while, heard nothing and began the same process with his arms. His joints ached like fire, but they moved, and he was able to bend and straighten both arms, then press himself gently up off the floor a few inches. He did this several times, using the simple push-up as a test of strength and agility. Despite his injuries, and the rush of blood to the wound in his temple every time he exerted himself, he was able to function. It was enough.

Finally, there was nothing to do but wait. He wanted to be certain that his motion hadn't been enough to trigger some alarm or bring the guards back down on him. Alex half expected Dayne to step out of a dark corner, cradling his blade, that sinister smile welcoming him back to the world of the conscious with more fun and games. But it didn't happen. For whatever reason, they'd stashed him and left him alone, and that meant he had a window, albeit a very small window, to put together a plan, if that was possible.

Alex sat up slowly, crossed his legs, despite the pain this brought him, and worked to relax. He needed to think. As he sat, he stretched, trying to bring his stiff muscles to life and get himself to whatever level of readiness was possible. He had no real way to assess his wounds, no way to know how haphazard the Chinese doctor's treatment had been and no idea when, or for what purpose, they might return to retrieve him.

He heard a sound in the distance and froze. He thought about returning to his prone position and feigning unconsciousness, but if they were coming for him now, it probably meant he'd been right and they knew he was awake. Prone on the floor would just put him in a more vulnerable position. He closed his eyes and waited, then opened them again, trying to get the proper pupil dilation to pierce the darkness. There was simply nothing to see. He might be in a tiny cell, or a huge, open room. He needed to know.

Even more slowly than he'd moved when sitting up, Alex got to his feet. He nearly toppled as vertigo hit, a combination of the utter darkness, the pounding pulse in his head and nausea. He wavered, then managed to crouch and balance, and began moving away from where he stood. He found a wall within three feet on his left, and began to follow this to the right. Then he stopped, bracing his hands against the wall for balance.

He'd heard another sound. The scrape of a shoe? Something dropped, but there was no curse, and there were no voices. Alex rested against the wall, thinking hard about his next move. If he attacked too quickly, or failed, he would surely be beaten, and then dragged back to whatever torture Dayne still had planned. If he waited too long, they'd notice he had moved, be on their guard and, in his weakened state, they'd probably get him without much of a struggle. He silently cursed the lack of light and began moving again, slowly, searching the floor by brushing his foot ahead of him, hoping he'd come across something he could use as a weapon.

The sounds drew closer together and nearer to Alex. He heard breathing and soft footsteps. Whoever it was wasn't in a hurry to reveal his or her presence. Alex wondered what that meant. Could it be Dayne? Might he be hoping to come back in private and finish up what he'd started?

He pressed against the wall as the steps drew nearer. He tried to gauge from the sound where the door might be, and he worked his way along one wall toward it. He came to a corner, and, after a quick shuffle along this second wall, his fingers brushed the frame of a doorway. It was a standard door frame, but when he reached around it, he found that the door itself was formed of a framework of welded metal bars.

A voice hissed through the darkness.

"Vance?"

He froze. The voice was familiar.

"Vance, where are you?"

Alex stepped to the barred door and peered out. A second later he detected motion in the utter darkness, heard a snap of sound, and a small lighter was lit. When his eyes recovered from the slash of light and adjusted, he saw Liang grinning at him in the small, flickering pool of light.

"Liang?" he said stupidly.

"Who else?" Liang asked.

"What the hell are you doing here?"

"Seems pretty obvious to me," Liang said, pulling a tool from his belt. "I'm here to save your sorry American ass. I was ordered to come and get you out."

"But how did you get in?" Alex asked.

"The back door." Liang chuckled. "I managed to get hold of the uniform of one of the maintenance support staff, and came in through the loading-bay doors."

"Can you get this door open?"

"I think so," Liang replied. "When I took out the guard, I got his keys."

The big man stepped forward and fumbled with the keys.

"Give me the lighter," Alex said. "I'll hold it while you find the key."

Liang passed the lighter through to him. It took three tries, but Alex managed to get it lit. Because Alex's hand was shaking the light flickered more than was normal. If Liang noticed, he made no mention of it. The third key fit the lock, and the door opened. Alex started forward immediately and lost his balance as his legs failed to react. He fell into Liang, who caught him easily.

"No time for resting," Liang said. He pulled a knife from a sheath at his belt and cut away the plastic ties that bound Alex's wrists together. "That guard is going to be missed. We have to get you up and out of here before they notice."

"Water," Alex said. "I need some water or I'll never make it."

Liang took back the lighter and started moving around the outer room quickly. There was a thud and a grunt as he fell across a desk. Then a quick laugh of satisfaction.

"Well, what do you know," he said.

A moment later he stepped up close to Alex again, holding something out. Alex reached for it, felt it and managed a weak grin of his own. It was a utility belt. After a moment he realized it was the one they'd taken from him when he was captured. He clumsily slung it around his waist and buckled it in place. The weight felt good. He searched it quickly. His Glock was gone, but most of the tools were still in place. He opened a pocket on the left and found the small canteen he'd brought with him. He opened the top and guzzled the contents greedily.

"Better?" Liang asked.

"Yes," he said.

"We have to get moving," Liang said. "We haven't got much of a window to get out of here safely."

"I'm not going," Alex replied. He continued to check his belt, and smiled as he found two particular compartments he'd packed carefully. One held a final explosive pack, small but very powerful. The other was his ace in the hole.

"What do you mean you're not going?" Liang snapped. "Why the hell did I risk my ass to save you if you aren't going?"

"I'm still alive," Alex replied, "and I still have a mission to complete."

"I'll be damned," Liang said. "They said you were crazy—they just didn't say *how* crazy."

"You go on," Alex said, thinking of Soo Lin. "Your wife will be waiting for you, and by the time they figure out how I escaped, you and your friends can be long gone. I can't leave this undone. Too much is at stake."

"That's not how it works, and you know it," Liang replied. "I was told to bring you out of here. If I can't do that until you're done here, then I'll stay and help. What do you have in mind?"

Alex was already thinking about that. The odds were that the charges he'd set were long since disarmed but still in the building. If the blast was close enough, it could set them off. If not, an electronic signal from his minitransmitter could rearm them and he could blow them from a distance. Either way, he had one good charge left, and he knew where it needed to be planted.

"What level are we on?" he asked quickly.

"The level just below the main complex," Liang replied. "Lots of labs, and a big computer room, clean and climate controlled."

"We need to get to those computers," Alex said. "I know a way up if we can pull it off."

Liang touched his arm in the dark, then poked him with something hard. It was a 9 mm pistol, similar to the one that Dayne's men had taken from him.

"I think you're probably going to need that," he said. "Don't waste shots—there are no more clips. When it's empty, drop it and go. It won't trace to anything that would do them any good if they manage to get their hands on it."

Alex took the gun and tucked it into his empty holster, leaving the flap loose.

"Thanks. I have one charge left—they didn't find it. If we can attach it to the main server banks in that computer room, we should be able to take out their data. After that—if luck is with us—the blast will detonate the other charges. Otherwise, I'll blow them separately once we're out of the blast radius. Something tells me they haven't removed anything, or this belt wouldn't still be here.

"How will you blow them if they're already disarmed?"

"Minitransmitter device," Alex said. "Either way, with a bit of luck, where this building is, there'll be a hole a city block wide and just as deep." He took a steadying breath, then said, "And I hope like hell that bastard Dayne is standing in the middle of it when it happens."

They slipped into the darkness. After they'd passed through the outer room and down a short hall, stepping over the fallen guard, they entered a dimly lit hall. It led to another door, and beyond that Alex saw the first real light he'd seen since the one Dayne shone in his face. Liang glanced both ways, then stepped into the hall. Gritting his teeth against a thousand pains, Alex followed.

Pain or not, MS or not, he would complete his mission and kill anyone who stood in his way.

23

They encountered no one on the short walk to the computer lab. Liang moved ahead, and Alex covered him, trying to focus through the pain and miss nothing. It was difficult to be stealthy with his legs and arms cramped and the pounding in his temple. His shoulder was swollen and nearly numb, so he had only one good arm. In a pinch he thought he could use the injured limb, and he knew that before things got better, the pinch was inevitable, but he didn't push it.

The computer lab door was securely locked, but a small window revealed two technicians working in the room. The door opened outward, so Liang gestured and Alex knelt on the floor next to the door. Liang tapped lightly on the door, ducking down to ensure that the technicians wouldn't see him through the window.

Alex could hear their voices, but not make out the words. Liang's simple tap had aroused their curiosity. One of the techs opened the door and popped his head out to look. The empty hallway was the last sight he ever beheld as Alex rose from his crouch and pushed his Glock to the man's temple, squeezing the trigger. The silenced round barely made a sound, but it was enough for the other tech to look up from his work. Alex didn't hesitate. He spun and put two rounds in the other technician's chest. The man fell against a bank of computers, looking surprised, then slumped to the ground dead.

Alex continued into the room, with Liang close behind, his hand on the butt of his own gun but not yet drawing it.

"Drag them out of sight," Alex told Liang, "just in case someone decides to take a look inside."

Liang went work, while Alex scanned the room quickly. His first visit had given him a very general idea of the layout, but now it was more critical that he understand where things were located. He located two large racks filled with blinking drives. A cursory glance around the room showed no other drive arrays, so he knew the majority of stored data would be located on the drives before him. Beside the racks he saw banks of optical drives he assumed were the backup system.

He moved in between the two racks and set to work. It was difficult to be precise with one hand, and it took a bit longer than he'd planned, but he set the charge so he believed it would take out both the data drives and the backups, even if his theory of the missing charges still being nearby proved false. Liang, meanwhile, had dragged the two dead technicians away, hiding their bodies behind a row of computer desks. For a fleeting moment Alex thought of the cold-blooded way he'd killed them. It was likely they knew at least a little of what was going on, and may have even known that he was being tortured nearby only a few short hours ago. He felt no sympathy for their deaths—it was an emotion he couldn't afford.

"Ready?" Liang asked, backing away from the prone bodies and stepping to the door to check the passageway beyond.

"Just about," Alex replied. He scanned the room quickly. On a desk he found folders and papers next to a high-speed laser printer. He glanced through them and stopped on the third folder down. He dropped the others and opened it.

"What are you doing?" Liang urged. "We have to get the hell out of here."

Alex ignored him and read. What had caught his eye was a scribbled note in English on the side of a folder. It read "Prototype transfer to U.S. facility."

He read as quickly as he could, and as he did the pain melted away to pure, adrenaline-fueled anger. A prototype of the nanoagent technology had been packaged and delivered to the MRIS offices states-side. To Brin's boss—Hershel Rand. Was Brin somehow involved in this? Did she know what she had? Had she been in on it from the start? Alex's heart pounded.

"What is it?" Liang asked, stepping closer. "Vance, we've got to *go*."

Alex slapped the folder shut, folded it, and tucked it into a long pocket in his pants.

"Let's go," he said.

Liang checked the hall, then slipped out. Alex followed. When the big man headed for the elevators, Alex called to him.

"No, this way." He led Liang to the break room and through to the chute in back. As he'd expected, there was an access panel in the wall. When he'd made his descent, he hadn't seen this one, so there was no way to be certain it existed. It was sealed, and the only way to open it was from the outside. He gripped the handle and tugged it free. The panel opened, and he reached inside, found the switches to call the dumbwaiter and set it in action.

"We don't have much time," Liang said. "Someone is going to notice you are gone, or call for those two in the lab."

"We have exactly fifteen minutes," Alex responded. "That's when the charge I set is going to blow those computers into the next galaxy. We need to be outside the building. I think they'll have plenty to worry about inside once the charge blows. We should be able to slip off in the chaos. The hole I cut the other day is still in the fence. Once we're out, they might try to follow, but I think it will take time to organize anything solid."

"If you get us out, I'll get us to safety," Liang assured him. "This is my city. When we are in the streets, I have a lot of places to turn for help."

The dumbwaiter clanged to a halt and the two men slid through the small gap. Liang pulled the access panel closed behind them. The cables groaned and creaked, and Alex prayed they were rated for this much of a burden. The two of them together weighed nearly four hundred pounds. When he hit the up button, the car swayed slightly, then righted itself and began the slow ascent.

"We're going all the way to the top," Alex whispered. "When this opens, we'll be coming out into the main break room. I don't know who might be there, or how they might be armed. They put on a good show of normalcy topside, so it will likely be just the regular guards—and they should be patrolling. If we are lucky, we'll hit the parking lot before they really spot us."

"Can you run?" Liang asked.

Alex started to say of course he could run. He'd

been pushing his body to the limit for so many years, it was difficult to keep his current situation in perspective. He knew that if the MS left him alone, he could run. He knew that if he hadn't lost too much blood, or pushed his adrenal glands beyond their limits, he could run. He knew there were a lot of ifs involved.

"I think so. I'll get by somehow," he said.

"You go first, then," Liang said. "I'll follow and that way if something goes wrong, I'll back you up however I can."

"If not, you get out," Alex said softly. "The folder I have is a transfer report. They sent some of this crap to an MRIS facility in the States. If it arrived safely, and if they sent files along with it, then we've only wiped out half of the threat. Once they know for sure we're after them, they'll guard that a lot more carefully."

"We're both getting out," Liang stated. "When the company says I'm supposed to get your sorry ass home, that's what I'm going to do."

Alex grinned tightly. He knew Denny wasn't going to be happy with him at all. He wouldn't be surprised if both he and Brin had become targets. He knew they'd work it out—they had to. He also knew, despite his momentary questioning of it, that Brin would never support something like what MRIS planned for those microbes. If she was involved in the research, she thought they were going to put it to beneficial use. That put her in even more danger. If she found out, he knew she wouldn't take it lying down.

They passed an access panel door for each level. As they neared the final door, Alex whispered, "Ready?"

He brought the car to a shuddering halt.

"On three," Alex said. He counted one and Liang kicked the access panel off its hinges, rolling forward and dropping out of the chute. He came up quickly. Alex followed.

The laundry room was empty.

"Wait a minute!" Alex said, before Liang could move on into the next room.

"What?" Liang said. "We've got to keep moving!"

Alex pointed to the corner of the ceiling, where a small strobe light was flashing in red. "They know I'm loose," he said. "Or that you're here." He shook his head. "Either way, that's got to be a security alert and if we continue to rely on timing and luck, we're both going to die. We need a new plan."

Liang nodded. "What have you got in mind?" he asked.

Alex's mind raced, then he moved across the room and climbed into an empty laundry cart. "Take some of those linens and pile them on top of me," he said. "They're most likely looking for me, and you've got on a maintenance uniform. Maybe we can make it to the doors before anyone thinks to question you."

Liang agreed and started piling uniforms and towels on top of Alex, who was kneeling at the bottom of the cart, his gun held at the ready. If the worst happened, he'd at least have the advantage of surprise springing out of the cart.

"Just keep calm and act like you should be here," Alex said. "There's no helping it, but the front doors are closer and we're running out of time."

"Got it," Liang said, adding the last of the laundry to the cart. "Now, if you please, shut up."

Alex felt the cart lurch into motion and heard the voices of men and women. He tried to control his ragged breathing and ignore the excruciating pain in his legs—his position in the cart was almost intolerable. He listened carefully and it sounded as if they were in a break room of some kind. By now, there were at least two interior squads on patrol, maybe more with the alert.

Over the faint squeak of the carts wheels, he heard several people talking. One of them said, "Another security problem? How long do you think we'll be locked down this time?"

Liang didn't hesitate, but kept right on going. In a barely audible whisper he stated, "We're in the lobby."

Alex looked at his watch. "Four minutes," he whispered.

"Uh-oh," he heard Liang say. "Get ready!"

"You!" a voice cried out. "You there! Stop!"

The cart lurched into motion as Liang shoved it forward, running for all he was worth. "They're on us!" he cried just before the cart slammed into the front doors, jarring Alex's shoulder hard enough to make him bite his lip to keep from crying out.

The sound of guns cocking echoed throughout the lobby and Alex whispered, "How many?"

"Five," Liang said. "The doors are locked."

"Stall them," Alex replied. "Get them closer."

He peered up through the linens to see Liang raise his hands. "Don't shoot," he said. "Please."

"What do you think you're doing?" one of the guards asked. "We're in lockdown."

"I'm new," Liang said. "I just work maintenance and they asked me to take this cart out."

Footsteps drew closer and Alex tensed, waiting to spring.

"Outside?" the guard asked. "Are you stupid or something?"

Alex jumped up. "No, but you are," he said, firing even as he spoke. The squad leader took two rounds in the chest, flying backward and knocking down a second man in his death throes.

The guards already had their weapons out. Alex lurched out of the cart and shoved it toward them, forcing them to pause, while Liang opened fire with his own weapon. Another guard went down, screaming as the bullet took him in the stomach.

"Get that door open!" Alex cried, diving and rolling over the hard marble floor. He came up shooting, taking down the fourth guard with a center-mass shot that knocked him on his heels. Liang went to work behind him, and Alex knew that it was him against the remaining two guards. In seconds, the whole lobby would be swarming with armed men and they would both be dead.

He picked himself up and dived forward again, smashing into the guard who'd been knocked down earlier. Alex drove his knees hard into the man's sternum and heard the ribs crack, even as more guards began swarming into the main lobby.

He picked up the fallen man's rifle, a standard-issue M-16, flicked the selector switch to full-auto and opened up. Guards dived in all directions, trying to avoid the spray of bullets.

"Get that damned door open!" Alex yelled, even as he fired a quick 3-round burst into the closest guard, dropping him like a ton of rock.

"I've got it!" Liang shouted.

"Go!" Alex said, firing another burst to keep the guards under cover and running for the doors as low as he could.

Bullets whined and screamed around them, shattering glass and sending splinters in all directions. He dumped the last few rounds from the clip and dropped it even as he burst through the doors, the impact jarring his good shoulder and sending waves of pain through his chest. Blood rushed to his head and the roaring nearly wiped out his vision. Then he staggered, righted himself and kept moving. Liang was right in front of him. A moment later his balance evened and he risked a glance back.

The guard units left inside were rushing toward the doors, firing as they ran. The exterior guard units were rushing across the parking lot, straight for them. Liang half turned and fired into the group. They scattered, diving behind parked cars. There was a shout from near the building, and Alex knew the second squad was joining the chase. He risked a quick glance at his watch.

"Liang!" he shouted, "Get down. Now!"

Alex dived toward the fence, covering his head and hitting hard. He felt skin scrape from his forearms and palms and his shoulder screamed in pain. He didn't want to risk anything, so he pulled the minitransmitter out of his utility belt and pulled himself to his knees, despite the pain shooting through his legs. Alex ignored it all. He waited for the telltale sound and a second later, the first blast sounded in the building. The building shook slightly and Alex triggered the transmitter, rolled to the fence and covered his face. A second later, the earth opened up with a huge flash of fire. The MRIS complex went up in a huge ball of flame, shooting debris into the air, shattering glass and stone. Alex stayed down, then, the moment he could move, he rose and hit the fence, looking for the break. Liang was beside him. All around them debris began to rain down. Dust choked them, and they were in danger from rocks and falling glass.

"Here!" Liang called out. He kicked loose the clips Alex had left holding the wire tight, and they rolled through. Then they were up and running, making their way up the hill to where they'd first watched the parking lot through the binoculars days before.

The crest of the hill was nearly a hundred yards away. Alex's legs were burning, his shoulder had gone numb, but still managed to pour liquid fire down his arm every time he tried to use it. Branches lashed out at his face and he managed to fend them off with his good arm, but still he thought he could hear fast footsteps behind him.

He had no idea what Liang intended to do at the top of the hill. They had mere minutes before Dayne and his men, whatever was left of them, figured out that they were gone. The parking lot patrol had seen the two of them running away from the blast, and even if no one inside the facility was left alive, there were still off-duty guards, those in charge who never even set foot inside the facility.

Alex knew he was a white-hot commodity now and needed to get out of Beijing.

Liang pulled at Alex's sleeve. "This way!"

Alex followed, forcing his tortured legs into a sprint. Then he saw what Liang was headed for, and he almost grinned. The big man had stashed his car behind a large stand of thick bushes and covered it with a pile of branches. It might have looked odd from the road, but from below it could have been a hedge.

They tore away the branches and cleared the car. Within moments they were in, and Liang fired the engine. They left in a cloud of dirt, branches and leaves, careening into the street, straightening and rocketing away from the hill and the destruction below. Liang swung them into yet another of his alleys, and turned toward the city.

The road was no less rocky and winding going down than it had been going up. The small car bobbed and shuddered as the wheels battled for traction. Liang couldn't keep the speed as high as he would have liked. It was too risky. One wrong turn and the car would tumble down the hill.

"We've got to get you to the airport and out of here. How are you doing?"

Alex looked down at his shoulder and grimaced. "I'm hanging in there. I've been worse."

"No, you haven't." Liang's face was somber, hard.

"No, I haven't," Alex agreed.

"Do you think we got them all?"

Alex looked into the mirror, watched the cloud of dust behind them for signs of life. Then his gaze swung toward the compound where smoke had all but blocked out the pile of rubble that had once been the facility. He started to say something hopeful, then bit off his words.

"We definitely did not get them all."

Behind them, the cloud parted and a long, black sedan roared after them, shooting gravel and careening wildly from side to side.

Liang looked frantically into the mirror, eyes darting between mirror and road. "Damn it!"

"Any suggestions?" Alex asked.

Liang pressed the accelerator down, taking a bit more risk for the sake of putting distance between them and their pursuers. "We'll try to lose them in the city."

"Really?"

"Sure."

"You don't sound convinced," Alex said.

Liang shot him a lopsided smile. "I'm not."

The path down the hill eventually intersected with the main road into the city. Liang barely slowed as he made that transition. One glance in the rearview mirror told Liang that the other car was still on their trail. He took the first left, then the next right, pushing the speed as hard as he could.

"Hang on," he yelled. "And maybe close your eyes."

The other car was maybe six car lengths back, and Liang took a chance. At the next intersection, he jerked the wheel to the left, at the same time yanking up on the parking brake. The small hybrid went into a skid, the rear tires sliding and at the last moment, he released the brake and gunned it. They shot down the road on the left like a rocket, scraping the curb on the right and then evening out.

Alex felt his shoulder slam against the car door and struggled to right himself as he glanced behind them. "We gained a little distance but I don't think we're gonna lose them."

"Time for reinforcements." Liang flipped open his cell phone and shouted at it. "Han Po!"

Alex watched the man's face, wondering what he had up his sleeve. Then the car skidded to the right and rounded the next corner. Their pursuers followed close behind, but Liang slowed slightly, as if leading them.

"Hey!" Liang yelled into the phone. "I need a little roadblock. You know where the Than Tan Warehouse is? Open bay three, make sure there's a truck in two, three and four. Drop the lifts."

Alex looked askance at him, eyebrows rocketed nearly to his hairline.

Liang smiled in return and made another turn.

"Keep 'em running. We've got an ETA of fifteen minutes."

With that, Liang slapped shut the cell phone and shoved it into his pocket. "I've got to get farther ahead to pull this off. Hold on tight."

With that, he raced down the straightaway, running a light and scaring a crowd of pedestrians, who had just stepped off the curb. Alex watched them scatter, half-running toward the opposite curb, half-scuttling back over the nearest curb.

The larger car followed, hampered by the thickening crowd and a badly timed car in the intersection. Liang made a hard right and gunned the engine, gaining some distance and heading back toward the more industrialized section of Beijing.

They gained a bit more distance when Liang managed to jump a curb, cut around a bus stop and force the larger car to stop and turn around before they could complete their turn. Pedestrians dived in all directions, and Alex saw the very frightened face of an old woman pass way too close to his window as they rushed past.

A large warehouse sat dead ahead. A series of recessed loading bays opened from one side, stretching from one end of the street to the other. Alex saw that there were large trucks nosing out of all but the fifth bay and Liang targeted bay number three, moving as fast as he could.

The small car was no more than ten feet from

slamming into the front bumper of the semi ahead and Alex had clutched the dashboard with both hands when the pavement dropped away and the front end of the car tilted downward. He screamed, but Liang ignored him. Then the ground dropped away suddenly, and the little car roared down at a steep angle, driving impossibly under the truck.

Liang slammed on the brakes. The car slid, shuddered and came to a halt. Liang turned to him and smiled.

"Service bay."

Alex was white and shaking as he glared at Liang. "Damn," was all he could manage.

The black sedan followed, brakes squealing, and the bay door they had come through dropped closed, sealing them in.

"Move!" Liang chuckled. "Quickly!"

Alex and Liang dived out of the car as another truck, deeper in the bay, began rolling forward. Liang dragged Alex through a door and into a passageway on the side of the service bay, just as the truck slid past and sealed the entrance. Alex heard their pursuers cursing and screaming, but there was no way they could reach the door. They were trapped like sardines in a can. The two men inside the car dived out, started yelling at the truckers. The drivers, as if confused, moved the trucks a few feet one way, then reversed, as if they didn't know what to do.

Alex followed Liang through the passageway

and under the service bays until they reached the office. A small man stood behind the desk. He looked enough like Liang to be his brother, though the glasses made his face look shorter and rounder than Liang's. He tossed a set of keys to Liang and they exchanged blessings. The next thing Alex knew, Liang was hauling him toward the door and pushing him toward a low-slung red coupe.

The pursuing car was still trapped between the trucks, its driver and passenger yelling frantically at the drivers. Liang raced the engine and tooted the horn, then piloted the red sports car onto the main avenue and sped away.

Alex didn't bother looking back, but sagged in the seat with relief. For the moment, they were safe.

24

Brin stood in the elevator, letting the recycled air and Muzak wash over her. She had been working so intently for so long that she had scarcely had time for anything else. The shift in focus had been a welcome relief, though. If she'd had to sit around and wait, worrying over Alex until he came home, it would have driven her mad. Her carefully worded request to Hershel Rand about his possible contacts in China had gone unanswered, but Brin had known it was a long shot.

In fact, her nose had been buried in research for so long that when Hershel called her, she needed a moment to even remember that she'd asked him. His voice had been full of tension and sourness when he demanded her presence in his office immediately—in regards to her request about Alex.

It wasn't like Rand to be quite so surly, and it had pissed her off, but she knew better than to ignore him and any information he might have found out about Alex was crucial. When he was in a mood like this, there was nothing to do but placate him and hope for the best.

Her heart wasn't in it—she wanted to get back to the lab. She didn't want to think about Alex until she knew what was truly going on with him and why he'd lied to her.

If she was truthful with herself, she was furious over the entire thing.

She shook her head and turned her thoughts to Rand. Was he calling her up there to reprimand her for even asking? It had to be something important for him to call her away from his own pet project, but what could it be? He'd been distracted and hard to work with ever since the package had arrived from China.

Elaine's desk was unattended again. It was starting to seem like a trend. Rand's door stood ajar. Brin marched in, her knuckles dancing briefly with the door as she passed. Rand was staring at his monitor—squinting, actually.

"Something I can help you with?" he asked distractedly, not even bothering to look up from his screen.

"I don't know," she growled as she dropped heavily into the leather chair. "You called me."

"What?" He looked up then, ripped the glasses from his nose and let them fall to the desk. His expression was pained. "Oh, Brin. It's you. Shut the door, would you?"

Brin rose, crossed the office and pushed the door shut. "No Elaine today?"

"She's taking a personal day." There was no humor in his voice. His expression was strained, almost menacing. "I received your e-mail about Alex, and as it turns out, we've been having something of a security problem ourselves as of late. I remember you once mentioning to me that he was in security consulting, so I was hoping you could help me clear it up."

Suddenly, Brin felt like the bad child, awaiting her fate in the principal's office. "I'll do what I can," she said.

"I've been in closer touch with our Chinese branch since the shipment arrived. I know we have things locked down here, but apparently they aren't having the same luck over there. Imagine my surprise when the head of security in China, a man named Dayne called to let me know a mercenary of some sort or perhaps a corporate saboteur tried to blow up our facility over there. They caught him, thankfully. He sent me this video. I'd like you to watch it and give me your opinion of things."

He pointed the remote at the large plasma screen

on the wall to his right, and pushed the play button. The video began abruptly with a scream. Brin nearly came out of her chair, barely stifling a scream of her own. The video played out, a high-definition rendering of Alex's torture at the hands of Dayne. Brin sat on her hands to stop the shaking, tried to choke back the well of tears that had nearly stopped her breath and pooled in her eyes. She didn't want to watch, but her eyes were glued to the screen. Finally, she could take no more. "Stop it! Stop it!"

Rand cut off the video, froze it in midframe for her to contemplate. "Is there anything you'd like to tell me about your husband, Brin?" His voice was softer now, barely above a growl. It was certainly menacing. "Maybe something you forgot to mention when you applied for your security clearance?"

"Is Alex dead?" she asked.

"Is he dead?" Rand laughed. "He's screaming pretty loudly on this film, so I would say not. Not yet, anyway. What happens next is up to you. If you help me with the final details of our little project, Alex may survive—though Captain Dayne is notoriously protective of our interests. If you don't help, I may have no choice but to let Captain Dayne off his leash."

"What project?" She was near hysterical now, her hands trembling and her head swimming. She had to reach Alex somehow. "The nanoagents?

I'm already helping. The research is nearly finished."

Rand typed a few keystrokes and brought an image up on the screen. "Yes, that is what they call them, isn't it? They're just prototypes, of course, but it's very close to being a fully functional delivery system. The nanoagents are just the front end of a new technology we're branching into. They represent the most efficient biological weapon in the history of science. I'm really surprised someone as brilliant as you didn't see it from the start.

"Most biologicals take time to germinate and spread. They aren't efficient because there are too many ways to combat their effects, and it's possible to get antidotes into the systems of those under attack in time to prevent complete success. The nanoagents attack a person's body on the genetic level. With the proper programming they can shut down the immune system, making the body so defenseless that even the common cold can cause death. It's based on research done right here in this lab, actually—your research."

"No." She couldn't move now. All shaking had stopped. She was frozen, unable to say anything more than that, unable to even blink.

"Ah, but it is. Your work in genetic therapy laid the groundwork for the agent. We just took the nanotechnology to the next level, allowing it to be delivered more rapidly and far more effectively. This genetic agent will attack the body within seconds of delivery. In twenty-four hours, the immune system has shut down completely. First sign of a virus or infection, the person is dead within forty-eight hours. God forbid they already have something like cancer or pneumonia. They won't last twelve hours. And by the time they determine cause of death, the agents will have spread to others, and they will die, as well—but of a variety of simple viruses and diseases."

Brin had begun to cry again. "That's my husband!" she moaned, pointing at the screen. "Why are you torturing my husband?"

"I told you what he tried to do. You and he are just lucky that he didn't succeed. So is your daughter."

Brin gasped, shaking hard and ready to faint. "Savannah?" She started to back away. She raised a hand and pointed it at Rand, then let it drop. "You bastard. You'd threaten a little girl?"

"Mind what I'm telling you. You'll bring this project to completion or you'll lose your husband. If you try to seek help from anyone they're both as good as dead. If you want to keep your family safe—do what I say."

Brin thought hard. The man was obviously insane, but that didn't mean he was stupid. She had to find a way to buy some time, and she had to get

a chance to think. She didn't know what the hell
Alex was really doing in China, or what it had to
do with her work, but she'd heard enough to know
they were all in more danger than she'd ever
imagined possible, and it was up to her to get them
out. She let her voice crack as she spoke, hoping
he'd see it as fear, and not catch the biting, bitter
taste of anger she felt in her throat.

"When I'm done, you'll let Alex go? You won't
hurt Savannah?"

"Alex will be released and your darling little
Savannah will be safe," Rand said. "What possible
use could I have for them once you've finished
your work, Brin? You are a most gifted scientist,
and I need your skills to bring the project to its
fruition. After that, Alex will be free to go. Once
the work is complete, his attempt at stopping our
project will be moot. I would, of course, like you
to consider staying on, but I understand that you
may have certain reservations after this. For the
moment, however, you will be a good little soldier,
yes?"

She knew better; no importance also meant that
there was no reason for him to keep them alive,
either. She also knew she had to buy enough time
that Alex—or someone—could fix this. She
wished she had a way to log back into Room 59,
but she remembered the threat that they'd shut
Alex out, and what if he freed himself and

managed to reach a computer? She couldn't risk putting him in further danger.

"All right. I'll do as you ask. Just don't hurt Alex anymore. And leave our daughter out of this. Please."

"They'll be safe, so long as you do what I say."

Brin turned to leave, her heart still hammering in her chest. She had never been so scared in all her life. And just the thought that someone might actually have Savannah made her heart skip beats.

"Brin?" Rand called out to her before she made it to the door.

She glanced over her shoulder guiltily, as if he were reading her thoughts. Rand was squinting at his monitor again, not watching her at all, but reviewing her husband's torture once more.

"Don't screw me. There will be no warning, no second chance. Rest assured that I do not take unnecessary risks with projects this big. You and Savannah will be watched by men who make Captain Dayne look gentle as a teddy bear. Do as I say and all will be well. Fuck with me and your life, Alex's and Savannah's will be forfeit."

She fled the office and ran down the hall to the elevator. She knew he could monitor her movements via the security cameras, but at the moment, she didn't care. She had to find out what was really going on, but more importantly, she had to know where her daughter was, that she was okay. Brin raced out of the elevator and ran almost full speed to the outdoor break area. Several startled lab technicians jumped out of her way, but she paid them little heed. Once there, she pulled out her cell phone and used the speed dial for Savannah's day care.

"Hi, Mrs. Kerr. This is Brin Tempest. I was just calling to make sure Savannah was okay."

"Of course, dear. She's just fine. Why? Is something wrong?" The woman's voice was soft, comforting.

"Nothing," Brin finally said. "Nothing at all." She paused a moment, trying to control her shaking. "You can see her right now, right?"

"She's right in front of me, having juice and cookies."

"Good. That's good. Listen, I'm going to have to work late tonight and my husband is still out of town. I'm going have my friend Karen pick Savannah up as soon as possible. You can make her show you her driver's license so you feel comfortable releasing Savannah. Her name is Karen Raisch."

"Very good, Mrs. Tempest. Savannah will be ready when she gets here."

Brin ended the call and dialed Karen's cell phone from memory. Karen was a ten-year veteran of the police department and now worked as a private detective. They'd been friends for quite a while and Karen absolutely adored Savannah.

Karen answered on the third ring, her voice reassuring in its confident strength. "Raisch here."

"Hey, Karen, it's Brin. Do you have a minute?"

"For you, Brin, I can spare at least an hour," Karen said. "What's up?"

Brin took another deep breath. "Listen, I have a favor to ask. We've got some problems at the lab and Alex is still out of the country. I know it's really short notice, but please, can you pick Savannah up at her day care and take care of her for a few days? I'll pay you whatever it costs."

Karen was silent for a long moment, then she said, "Sure, honey, I can take her—and I wouldn't accept a dime for watching her anyway. She's a doll, so that's no problem, but I sense a bit of panic in your voice. Is everything okay?"

"Not really. I can't talk now. Just please, go get Savannah as soon as possible. Keep her with you, no matter what."

"Brin, you're starting to scare me. What's going on?"

"I'll explain as soon as I can," Brin promised. "Just keep Savannah with you. And be careful. If you see anything—odd—anyone that doesn't seem right—run. Watch her like a hawk and don't let anybody else near her. I'll get to you guys as soon as I can."

There was another long pause, then Karen said,

"All right, but if Savannah needs to be protected, I should at least know what to look for."

"Just keep her safe and away from strangers," Brin said. "That's all I can say right now. *Please,* Karen. I'll owe you one. Big time."

"I'll watch after Savannah, Brin. She'll be fine. You just take care of business—whatever it is—and then give me the all clear when you can."

"Thanks, Karen," Brin said, slapping her cell phone shut before the other woman could press her for more information again. Then she slowly sank down against the wall and started to cry.

25

"I'll park in one of the maintenance spaces, inside the garage. Soo Lin has gone to visit her sister for a few days. We get up to the apartment, get you changed and bandaged up, then we're gone."

Liang drove under a hanging canopy and guided the red car into the covered spaces that were part of the maintenance department of his building.

"I've got everything I need in my bag," Alex said. "It'll just take us a few minutes to grab it."

Liang pulled the parking brake and threw open the door. He watched as Alex struggled out of the car.

Alex tried to mask his growing weakness, but he was a large man and the modified Trans Am was too low to the ground. The pain had spread from his legs and traveled all the way up to his hips. His eyes didn't want to focus, and his head pounded.

Liang stepped out of the sleek sports car and followed. He glanced around, but saw no one. They didn't know if the men in the black sedan could identify the car, but if they'd gotten any kind of look at it, they could. Didn't matter. They'd needed speed, and it was all that was available.

On the way to the elevator, they passed a man in gray overalls. He stared at them, obviously ready to say something about parking restrictions. Liang stepped forward, whispered something into his ear and pressed some money into his hand.

"Five minutes, brother, five minutes and we're gone."

The man stared at the money, tucked it into his pocket, nodded and turned away.

Once they were in the elevator, Alex relaxed a little. He leaned back against the wall and took some of the pressure off his legs. He knew that Liang was watching him, but it hardly mattered anymore. All that did matter was that Liang got him to the airport and into the air without incident.

The doors opened and Liang shot forward into the hall, Alex following slowly. He was desperate for a chance to just sit, to relieve some of the pain in his legs. They had begun to weaken considerably since he had reached China. There was no telling how far they would actually take him before they gave out altogether.

Liang raced ahead and unlocked the apartment

door. Alex stepped past him and into the back bedroom, grabbed his duffel bag and slung it over one shoulder. The added weight staggered him, made him reevaluate the strength he had left.

"Are you sure you're going to make it?" Liang looked truly concerned. "They told me to keep an eye on you—said you might not be yourself. Something I need to know?"

"I'll be fine. I have to be." Alex nodded curtly, as though that would make the statement more true. Alex stopped in the bathroom and splashed some cold water on his face, then did a quick job of bandaging up his shoulder. He changed into clean clothes, and felt almost human again. He didn't have enough time to get all the layers of blood and dirt off, but for the moment, he thought he'd pass muster.

Liang stared a moment longer, as if trying to evaluate their odds. Then he nodded.

"Off we go, then."

The two men swung into the hall, pulled the locked door shut behind them and hurried into the waiting elevator. When the doors opened, the car was in plain sight. No one was in the garage, thankfully, not even the maintenance man they'd paid off.

Liang started the engine and Alex slipped into the passenger side, arranging his bag on the floor so he'd have room to stretch his legs. A few seconds later, they were speeding down the wide avenue toward the outskirts of town. It had taken several calls, but Liang assured him that there would be a plane waiting for them, and that there would be no trouble with customs.

Alex felt the need to explain himself. More than anything, he didn't want Liang to think he was weak or inexperienced. He had put the man's life in danger by taking on this mission when he was less than one hundred percent. He owed the man something by way of explanation. And yet, there just weren't the appropriate words. Liang knew all he needed to know about Alex, the mission and his situation. Anything more would put the man in even more danger.

They reached the airport without incident, but the minute they passed through the main gate and had the terminal in sight, Liang stiffened. "We've been spotted," he groaned. "You suppose that PMC guy is hooked into the Mafia here, too?"

Alex looked behind them to where that same black car, flanked now by two SUVs, had fallen in line and were in hot pursuit. "Shit," he said. "Anything's possible. Maybe they were paying someone off. You think we can lose them? Maybe you'd better call them again and tell them to keep the engine running."

Liang flipped his phone open, clicked speed dial without looking and started jabbering into the mouthpiece. He listened for a second, and then nodded grimly. He snapped the phone shut and gunned the engine, leaving their pursuit vehicles scrambling to keep up.

"I hope those legs have a little juice left in them, brother. You may have to run for it. The plane is fueled up and ready to go, but when I told them who was on our ass, they got a little jumpy. They aren't going to be too patient."

Liang skidded in a short curve and raced for the runway.

Alex leaned out the window. He saw the plane. The engines were already revved, and Yoo Jin-Ho stood on the gangway, watching the chase. The little man waved frantically, as if he could help the car move faster. He was screaming something at them, but there was no way to make it out.

Alex dragged the duffel bag off the floor. The effort sent fire shooting through his legs. He unzipped a pocket on the side of the bag and dragged out two shoulder straps. He slung it over his back, tugged it into place and pulled the straps tight.

"Pop the latches on that T-top and blow the hatch." Liang shouted.

"You might not be able to stop and get it back." Alex grinned at him. "What do you have in mind?"

"It's not my car, and the guy who owns it," Liang shouted, "he's not here. I'll get it fixed for him. Don't worry about the car. Get that roof open, and get ready."

Alex glanced ahead. The plane was moving, and not slowly. Liang skidded in behind it on the runway. Alex stared at the plane, then back at Liang. "And you say *I'm* crazy?"

Liang just grinned. "I'm coming in straight under that plane, brother," he yelled. "You'd better be ready—you aren't getting a second chance."

Alex closed his eyes, focused and slammed his hands up, snapping the clamps on the T-top. It caught in the wind and whipped away behind them. He hoped it hit one of the pursuers in the windshield, but he didn't bother to look back. He balanced himself in the seat, hands braced on the roof, and watched as they pulled up behind the plane. It began to rise. He saw Jin's terrified face watching from the still-open hatch on the side of the plane. Liang hit the gas, and the powerful car roared forward. The plane had barely cleared them, but Liang didn't hesitate.

"I don't think they can see you from here, man. Maybe they think you missed it. Maybe they'll chase me," he shouted.

"Safe home," Alex screamed. Then he glanced up, said a silent prayer and shot his legs out like pistons. He cursed, screamed and prayed in the same breath. He reached out, caught the bottom of the door and used his momentum to carry him up and forward. He tucked his knees in close and whipped up and through the hatch. He released the rail and felt hands grabbing his waist, dragging him in. Moments later the hatch swung closed, and he felt the plane rising. He lay curled where he'd landed, his eyes closed, waiting for shots to bring them down, or the hatch to open and suck him back out.

Below on the tarmac, Liang followed the course of the plane a moment longer, then veered off. If their pursuers had seen Alex jump, they paid him no heed. All three vehicles followed Liang, the pack of cars parting to drive around the plane rather than under it.

Alex looked around and found Jin seated in a canvas cargo net, grinning at him.

"Good to see you again." Jin laughed. "That was quite an entrance."

"I'm known for my entrances." Alex chuckled. "You think we can get out of here before they get someone in the air and catch us?"

"Probably." Jin leaned into the cabin and spoke to the younger man at the controls. Jin checked his instruments, barked an order, and the pilot increased the plane's speed. They banked away from the airport and gained altitude fast.

"I called the customs officials," Jin said thoughtfully. "I am sure that I saw a black sedan and a pair of SUVs loading suspicious cargo. It was my civic duty to call in the warning."

Alex stared at the little man for a long moment, then burst into a quickly regretted fit of laughter. His sides ached, his shoulder was killing him, but, for the moment, he was alive.

Alex didn't breathe easily until the plane's wings were banking southeast toward South Korea. Jin seemed unconcerned, as if he'd done this a hundred times before. Alex sank back in his seat, shut his eyes and willed the pain in his legs away.

During the flight, Jin dragged out a first-aid kit and set to work on Alex's wounds. They needed to get him cleaned up to prevent infection from setting into his shoulder. Jin worked quickly and efficiently. He dressed the wounds, and then handed Alex a package. It was sealed in brown paper, covered in odd symbols.

"What is it?" Alex asked.

"I received a package and was told to get that to you. They said you were supposed to pick it up before you left—thought it might come in handy."

Alex opened the package. There were two small brown plastic pill bottles inside. He read the instructions on the label, and took two of one and one of the other before sticking them in his pocket. He thought about what they meant, and it all came crashing in on him. Denny Talbot knew about the MS, knew that he hadn't told them and that he'd endangered the mission by going at all. Then an image of Brin and Savannah surfaced. He shook it off.

When they touched down in Seoul, Alex waited for customs to check the plane, let the authorities check out his paperwork. There was nothing at all in his possession that could be considered illegal, so he turned his bag over to them and let them check it. Aside from a brief question on how he managed to get so injured, which Alex explained using the old serviceman's standby—a drunken bar brawl over a woman—the whole affair was done in fifteen minutes and Alex bid his farewells to Jin and made for the main terminal.

There were two hours of downtime before his flight back to the States. He knew he had to lay low, just in case. No matter how well things were going, it always paid to err on the side of caution. He slipped into the men's room, quickly washed up and changed his clothes. With his hair slicked back and wearing street clothes, he looked every bit the American tourist, if a bit under the weather. He walked into the bar then, sliding into a dark booth and ordering a whiskey. From there, he watched the door and the clock, hoping no one would notice him.

There were other Americans in the bar, all loud and full of good humor. Alex eventually fell in with them, using his businessman cover and buying them all drinks. Within a few minutes, they were chatting and laughing it up like old pals. Nobody even looked at them twice. Once they called for his flight to board, Alex was away into the night, just another anonymous American on his way home.

But he knew home wasn't exactly the same anymore. His body had gone south on him and it would have to be dealt with. He'd thought to be done with all of this once the mission was completed. But it wasn't really completed. Somehow that damnable weapon had ended up in Brin's hands. His orders had been clear. Kill everyone associated with the project. Destroy the weapon. Surely they wouldn't make him kill his own wife? Or had they already sent someone else in to do it?

All the way home, he struggled with possibilities. It was the end game, a time of diminishing options. The way Alex saw it, he had exactly two. The first was to take his family and disappear. The only other option was to go in and take out the U.S. branch of MRIS himself. If he didn't, he knew someone else would, and they wouldn't worry about whose wife was in what laboratory or about a little girl who needed her mother.

Either way, he wasn't sure he'd be able to keep them safe if the worst happened.

The flight was the longest of his life.

26

The plane touched down in the States without incident, and Alex didn't waste any time getting outside and into the first cab in line. He gave the man the address, then leaned back and tried to sort out his thoughts. It wasn't going to be easy to convince Brin to leave town on short notice. Her work was important to her and she knew nothing about Room 59. None of it would make any sense to her. She wouldn't have a choice, though, even if he had to drag her kicking and screaming himself.

There was also the separation to think of. He'd been gone too much lately, and now that he knew what he was facing, it seemed as if the minutes were more precious than ever. He was going to have to explain all of that to Brin, but not until the mission was complete. Not until he'd extracted her from the danger he knew she was in, and was certain she'd be safe.

The cab pulled up in front of his house and he tossed the driver a twenty-dollar bill and climbed out without looking back. Something was wrong. He'd known it the minute his feet hit the curb, but it wasn't until he reached the front porch that it hit him.

It was almost seven in the evening, and Brin's car wasn't in the drive. There were a couple of lights on in the house, but they always left a few on so would-be burglars might be fooled into thinking people were home. The front door was locked. Alex dug under the bushes on the left side of the porch, slid aside a flat slab of rock, poked his finger into the dirt and came up with a small key box. It required a four digit combination to open it, and he rolled the tumblers into place. It was more difficult than it should have been as his hands trembled. He was ready to curse the MS, and then he stopped, took a deep breath, and his hands stilled. It had nothing to do with the disease this time. It was all nerves.

He slipped the key into the lock and it turned easily, then he pocketed it and entered the house. He heard nothing. Closing the door quietly, he put his bag down in the hall. Then, with quick delib-eration, he made the rounds of all the rooms. He found no one, including Brin.

Alex finished his search and frowned. It wasn't

like Brin to be at work so late. Savannah had to be picked up by a certain time, and Brin hated pawning her off on a babysitter. She feared that with both parents working, Savannah wouldn't get enough personal attention. It was possible that she and Savannah had simply gone out or something, but his instincts were screaming at him that something was wrong.

He sat down in front of the computer and booted it up. As the cursor blinked and the cooling fans hummed, he wondered what he was going to face when he logged into Room 59. Denny had to know by now what had happened, and how close things had come to failing in Beijing. The mission had been sloppy, poorly executed, and he never should have accepted it. None of that was going to go over well, particularly the part where he'd kept his MS to himself until he was in too far to be recalled.

He ran through the preliminary login sequence quickly. Within moments the main Room 59 screen came to life.

"Chameleon, online and checking in," he typed. He'd used that exact same message after every mission he'd accomplished. This time it felt odd. He didn't feel like a chameleon, and he wasn't sure yet that he was even welcome in the room.

"Welcome back, Alex."

Alex took a deep breath and began to type. "Hello, Denny. I have a report."

"We know what happened already, Alex. When were you going to tell us about your condition? Didn't you think we'd understand?"

"I needed this one, Denny. You're the one who showed me Brin's company's involvement. I couldn't leave this to someone else, not knowing if they'd get the job done or if they'd come after Brin when they were done. We aren't after Brin, are we?"

"The situation is complicated. Your wife has been in here, Alex," Denny replied. "Here, in this room. She logged on to your computer, broke your security and made it into the outer room."

"And you brought her the rest of the way?" Alex shifted through emotions from surprise, to shock, to anger. "You told her what was going on without even consulting me before doing it?"

"If it had been possible, we would have aborted the mission. Under the circumstances, you were out of communication and sending Liang was the best we could manage. Brin picked up a prescription that was meant for you, and she knew something was wrong. We got our report from the medical records. None of us was happy to find out you were sick and didn't think we needed to know. We didn't tell Brin anything about what you were doing, though we did let slip that you were in the Far East. While you were keeping secrets, you failed to let us in on your cover story for this mission. Not that it matters now."

"Where are they?" Alex asked. "Brin isn't here. Savannah isn't here."

"She's probably at work," Denny typed. "Alex, we have a serious problem here. You put a lot more at risk than your life, or even your family. What the hell were you thinking? We don't operate this way. We can't afford to. Was my brief not clear, or do you think this is all just a game we're playing? If those nanoagents had been released here, or anywhere in the world, it would be too late for apologies."

"I couldn't let someone else go," Alex repeated. "I'm sorry. I don't have a better answer than that. This is my life—it's what I do. I have nothing else, and if I'm not going to be around to take care of my family in the future, I damned sure wanted to take care of them now."

"You'd better get your head straight," Denny wrote. "You are *one* man. Yours is *one* family. We aren't in this for ourselves, or have you forgotten that? This is all-or-nothing. This is us against the world. You used to be the poster child for that. I wanted you on this mission because no one could do it better, but that was you at full strength. When things changed, you should have let me know. You should have trusted me."

"I don't know what else to say," Alex typed. "I figured my career was pretty much over and had my resignation ready to turn in when you handed me this mission. I couldn't turn it down, didn't want to. I thought I could do it."

"And?"

"And I was wrong," Alex typed. "I'm just not what I used to be. I assume I'm out of a job?"

"We're still assessing all this, Alex," Denny wrote. "Your knowledge, your skills, they aren't things that can be replaced easily. That said, you have directly violated the rules of Room 59. If—and I stress the word *if*—we can find a place for you here, then there's one thing you'd better be crystal damned clear on. None of this is about you. You aren't in charge, you don't make the rules and when you are told to do something, you'll do it. There isn't any place here for rebels. We have rules and operating procedures and you know them. You willingly broke them."

"I know," Alex said. "And I appreciate that you'd still even think of supporting me after all of this, but the mission isn't over, Denny. Not by a long shot."

"What are you talking about? We have the reports on the MRIS complex. You obliterated it. Liang even managed to get a man in and verify that the lower levels were destroyed. There's nothing left of the computers or the data."

"They sent it here already," Alex typed. "They sent it to the MRIS lab right here. I found a shipping report, and I saw Brin's name on the receiving end. She's going to think she's saving the world. I have to get in there, Denny, and I have to get her out."

"Wait a minute," Denny replied. "Are you sure about this? You're telling me they've already got some kind of prototype here?"

"I still have the folder with the data on the shipment," Alex replied. "I don't know how many of their people over here are in on it, but there have to be a few. Hershel Rand, for one—he's the CEO. Apparently they are planning on bringing Brin in, though I don't know in what capacity. I know she wouldn't willingly help them release a biological weapon, but if she thought she was working on a miracle cure she'd be all over it."

"I'll send someone in," Denny replied. "You're in no condition to operate right now, even without the MS. Liang said you got pretty beat up over there. Besides that, you're too close to it emotionally—and that leads to mistakes in judgment."

"I'm going in whether you order it or not, Denny. I'm sorry to disobey orders again so soon, but this one is mine. I need to be the one to do this," Alex typed furiously.

"We *never* send in a man who is less than one hundred percent. You know that, Alex. You also know that we don't send agents on personal missions."

"This isn't a question of you sending me, Denny. I'm going. If you want to get someone ready to clean up the mess when the cripple fails, that's on you," Alex replied. "That's my wife in there, and this is my mission."

There was a long pause, and Alex thought it was over. They'd send someone in to stop him, and they'd send someone after Brin.

"Alex," Denny finally typed, "If you do this, I can't vouch for you with Kate or anyone at Room 59. You'll be on your own, and out on a very, very thin limb. Things look bad as it is."

"It's what I have to do, Denny," Alex wrote.

"I understand why you might feel that way," Denny wrote. "Don't make any mistakes. If you fail or falter, we will come in—hard, fast and final. We aren't done talking about this, and you aren't off the hook for any of this. Kate is going to blow a gasket that I didn't send a team to stop you. We're going to have to debrief Brin, too. She knows way too much, and that's on you, too. Your security passwords weren't secure enough. You also might want to check out that anonymous e-mail drop you set up—you know, the one that's absolutely a breach of security? She probably left you a thousand e-mails. If you live, you'll still have a lot to answer for, and I'm not sure you want to pay this piper. You know the penalty for disobeying orders."

Alex knew Denny was right, but he also knew the only thing he could do was to try to get in and make it right.

"I'll finish the mission," he typed quickly.
"And thanks."

Denny didn't respond, and with a weak grin,
Alex typed, "Chameleon—going offline and out."

The chat window closed, and he made his way
out through the outer room and closed that, as
well. Alex stared at the screen for a long moment,
considering whether or not to log in to the e-mail
account. He hadn't known Brin was home, wondering what he was doing and what was wrong. He
also hadn't known the doctor had called in the prescription, though thinking back he realized that he
had known, and had just forgotten. He cursed
himself for the lack of concentration. He'd always
thought that if something went seriously wrong,
his mind would get him through it—but he'd never
counted on something coming along that could
affect body and mind. He hadn't counted on
running across an enemy he couldn't defeat.

In the end, he turned off the computer without
checking the e-mail. There would be time to
straighten things out with Brin, and when that time
arrived he'd do it face-to-face. She deserved that
and he didn't think he could stand seeing her pain
or anger in the impersonal words of an e-mail.

He stood and walked quickly through the
kitchen and out into the garage. He had a small
workshop there, a place he sometimes went to be
alone. Brin had a similar retreat in a small room

off their bedroom. Hers was lined with material related to her career and a collection of books she'd been gathering her entire life and had been unable to part with. Alex seldom ventured into that room, and never when Brin was away. She'd given him the same privacy in the workshop. It was a good thing—he hadn't wanted to go off-site to stash the tools of his trade.

He stepped around to the side of the workbench and pressed hard on a small, lightly etched square on the wall panel. At the pressure from his hand it slid inward and clicked. Alex tugged gently, and a panel swung out and moved to the side, revealing a series of shelves, cubbyholes and drawers.

There was no time to infiltrate MRIS in his normal fashion. It was after-hours, and there wasn't anyone he could pretend to be to make it easier to get inside. Things could shift once he'd breached security, but for now he thought armament was more important than disguise. He strapped on a replacement for the Glock 9 mm pistol he'd lost in Beijing, and he also took some electronic devices that he could use for knocking out their security systems.

Once he had everything he needed in place, he carefully sealed the panel on the wall. His right leg ached, but his left seemed fine. His shoulder was stiff, but he thought if he didn't push it too hard ahead of time, it would work for him when he needed it.

He started to turn to his car, which hadn't been out of the garage in weeks, and then stopped. He glanced back at the house, took a deep breath and jogged back to the front hall. He grabbed his bag, took it to the kitchen and opened it, rummaging inside until he found the two brown medicine bottles. He carefully sliced one of the painkillers in half, about a quarter of the prescribed dose. Then he grabbed the bottle of Klonopin and read the instructions again to be sure he had it straight. He took two of the pills and dry swallowed them, grimacing at the taste.

He started to stash the bottles in a pocket, then caught himself and put them back on the counter. He put them in plain sight. If and when he and Brin got back home, there was no reason to continue with any secrecy. If he didn't get back, it wouldn't matter.

On his way out, he saw that the answering-machine light was blinking. He frowned. It wasn't likely that the message was for him, but he couldn't risk not checking it. If Brin was in trouble, she'd try to contact him, and the answering machine was one way to do it. He crossed the hall and hit the play button.

"Brin?"

The voice was familiar, husky and feminine. It was Karen, a friend of Brin's he'd met on several occasions. Karen was an ex-cop and a little rough around the edges, but a good friend. She'd watched Savannah for them more than once.

"Brin, if you're there, pick up. This is Karen. I've got Savannah. There was almost some trouble at the school—you didn't tell me we were playing with the big boys. I got there first, thankfully, and I had Savannah in my car when things got strange. A bunch of guys in black suits—not Feds, I'd know Feds, but not cops, either—they converged on the school. I saw them covering the exits, but we got out. I hope those other kids are okay, but I promised you I'd watch this one, and I will. When you can, let me know what the hell is going on. You know how to reach me."

The phone went dead. Alex stared at it, rewound and listened again. They'd tried to get to Savannah. That meant, at the very least, that Brin knew what they were up to. If they were trying to coerce her into working, Savannah was their best bet. If they had him, they could have used him, as well. Alex was glad Liang had ruined their chances of that.

He was also glad to know that Karen had Savannah. She truly liked their little girl, and if anyone they knew—short of Room 59 agents—could keep her safe, Karen was the one. She'd retired with honors from the force, and despite having to fight her way through a machismo-drenched hierarchy of officers, detectives and politicians, she'd made quite a reputation for herself while she was active.

The men in the suits worried him. If MRIS had

that kind of force active, then he would have to use more caution than he'd anticipated. He'd thought maybe Rand was aware, and that people from Beijing would come in and take over the operation. Now he wondered if the bastard wasn't in it a lot deeper than that.

Alex returned to the garage and slipped in behind the wheel of his Porsche. It wasn't the most inconspicuous car, but he knew it would cover the miles between home and Brin's office complex quickly. That was all that mattered. He opened the garage door, backed out and hit the road with the tires squealing. He didn't bother to close up the garage. He knew Brin would be angry when she saw it, but he thought that her being angry with him over something mundane would feel good.

He kept the sports car just barely above the speed limit, fighting the urge to hit the gas. He couldn't afford to draw too much attention to himself, and the last thing he needed was a police escort to the MRIS complex. He had to get as close with the car as he could and then go in on foot. Brin told him a lot about her work, but most of it was over his head. When she'd talked about the security systems, however, he'd perked up. He was familiar with the company that had installed them, and he knew that the lab was protected by perimeter cameras and motion detectors, as well as a state-of-the-art cipher lock system.

He was familiar with the systems because he'd been through them before. If he drove into the parking lot and walked up the front steps, they'd know he was there immediately, but he had picked Brin up several times at the loading dock, and once at a service entrance. He knew the side streets, and he had memorized the interior of the building on the two visits where he'd actually been escorted up to Brin's office and laboratories. He hadn't intended to create an internal map, but his training was too much a part of him to prevent it. He knew how to get to his wife's office, and he knew where Rand's office was located, as well. He only hoped Brin was working in her normal spaces, or if she wasn't, that he could find someone and force them to tell him where she was.

He saw the complex long before he arrived, rising several stories above the other buildings near it. There were a number of side streets, mostly fronting warehouses and industrial office spaces. Alex drove within half a mile of the complex and pulled the Porsche up in front of a small office building. There were two marked spaces with signs, and one of them read Vector Executive Parking. He took the spot marked CEO and smiled. If only Brin got out, he'd be able to tell her where to find it. If neither of them made it out, it would be found quickly and reported, and once there were reports in the system, Denny and Kate would see them and know something was wrong.

Alex left the car unlocked with the keys in the ignition and turned toward the MRIS complex. He took off at a quick trot, and was happy to find his legs cooperating and the jarring rhythm of the pace only mildly painful to his shoulder. There were a few lights on, and he knew they were on Brin's level. He sped his steps, gritting his teeth against the increased pain.

27

Brin stared at the microscope in front of her and frowned. She adjusted the lens, brushed her hair to one side and looked again. Her frown deepened, and she turned to glance down at the computer screen to her right. She'd been going over and over the research for days, and now she was so tired she had to check and double-check herself anytime something seemed to deviate. She didn't know if what she was planning to do would work, but she knew that it had never been more important that she understand a subject so thoroughly and completely.

What she had under the scope was one of the samples from China. She had begun cultures of her own, but the preserved samples that had been operating for the longest had provided the most interesting and relevant data. If she were conducting legitimate research, the long-term data would be just as important, but when the entire goal was to just see if the damned process worked, the most mature cells were the ones with the most to offer.

These weren't acting properly at all. The original culture they'd come from had consisted of cells infected with polio and then treated with the nanoagents. The healthy cells—the control group—had been used to carefully program the agents. She'd seen a dozen studies involving different diseases. Some were viral, some were blood infections, others involved cell degeneration. In every case the programmed agents had infiltrated the maligned cells and began immediate reconstructing. They were able to replicate themselves rapidly, and they locked on to the healthy patterns of whatever host or control cell they were applied to. They were miraculous, potent and the most potentially dangerous weapon she could ever imagine.

They could be programmed just as easily to mutate cells as they could to reconstruct them, and when they entered battle with healthy cells, their infiltration was even quicker and more deadly. They could defeat a human immune system in a frighteningly short period of time—or they could strengthen it against a particular disease to the point of immunity.

Now she had encountered something new. It had been nearly a week since the sample she'd created on the slide in front of her had been exposed to the nanoagents. None of the research that had accompanied the samples stretched more than a week or two in length. It generally took a matter of hours for the agents to reprogram damaged cells and reconstruct their healthy state. The Chinese researchers had chosen to run through a large range of damaged cells, record the results up until the point a healthy state was restored and then move on.

Now something new was happening. The cells on the slide had changed. They were no longer healthy cells, though they also showed no sign of the polio they'd been infected with. She put her eye to the lens again and concentrated. The cellular structure had shifted. At first glance it seemed as if there was a new infection of some sort—as if a contaminant had been introduced. Then she saw the truth. The nanoagents had not been content to reconstruct the healthy cells. When their work was done, rather than shutting down or remaining dormant, as the research seemed to indicate, they'd changed their programming.

The changes were subtle but significant. The outer cell walls had strengthened, lowering the instances of combination. Growth was steady, but the overall cohesion of the sample had suffered. Individual cells with minuscule differences in their makeup had set themselves apart, like small fortresses, and whenever two came too close, the nanoagents in each, programmed with a slightly different model of perfection, collided and began tiny wars for dominance.

Brin stared at the sample on the slide for a few moments, jotted some notes and then pulled it out. She quickly went through a number of other samples, all from the long-term cultures provided by the Chinese. It didn't happen in every case. Some of the samples were fine, despite being even slightly older than the polio slide, but others were worse. The cellular structure in a few had been demolished and an entirely new cellular life-form had begun to emerge.

Brin carefully replaced all of the samples and sat down at her computer. She entered the data for what she'd just seen. She had a cell-modeling program that had been preloaded with all the traits of healthy cells of each type involved in the research. When she entered the traits she recorded each day from her samples she got a timeline of reconstruction. The program created a model of the cell as it was at each checkpoint, mapped the changes that had already been made and mapped those that needed to be completed before the cells reached their original healthy state.

In most cases, it took less than thirty-six hours

for the cells to regenerate. Most of the case studies had been shut down at twelve days, making that the control. In biomedical research, that was an incredibly short window and wholly inadequate for results leading to the opportunity to test a new treatment on human subjects. That was why she'd begun her own research on the original samples provided. She'd foolishly believed curing disease was what it was all about. What had really mattered to Rand, and to MRIS, was cutting down the amount of time the nanoagents needed to complete their work.

What she'd just seen changed everything, or at least it should have. Though the nanoagents still appeared to be effective in most of the samples, the few that had mutated and gone on to cause irreparable damage sent huge red flags of warning shooting through her brain. She hadn't recognized the cells the mutated polio culture had created. They would probably just war with one another until they were destroyed, but if one cell proved stronger and emerged victorious, what would they have created? Would it stop there? If they set loose what they thought was a controlled biological weapon, could it mutate into something that ran out of control and destroyed life as they knew it?

In any case, she had to let Rand know. It might not matter to him, or to any of them. It had taken a big inner shift, but her view of the world had changed quite a bit over the past few days. She understood that there were men who cared very little for the lives of others, who put personal gain far ahead of human compassion and who saw her work only as a means to an end.

Once she'd finished the reports she sent the output from the cell-modeling software to the color printer in the corner. She had a few minutes to collect her thoughts, and she put them to good use.

One of the containers that had shipped out of China, the largest, was comprised of solely programmed and yet-to-be-programmed nanoagents. She opened this container and sat it on the bench. Next she pulled out a very small vial. She placed this vial into a larger tube, about the size of a lipstick container, then took the end result and filled in around it with a special gel used to insulate samples.

Brin wasn't certain when she was and was not on camera, so she worked quickly, but she tried not to make any sudden or jerky movements. She transferred a small sampling of the nanoagents to the vial, sealed it carefully, sealed the main package and placed it all back on ice. When she turned to put the case away, she slipped the metal tube into the pocket of her lab coat. She didn't know if she'd been seen, but it was a chance she was willing to take. The scientist in her wouldn't allow for the complete destruction of valuable research, and that was what was happening. She hadn't sealed the canister fully, and as she stepped away from the bench, she brushed the temperature controls on the outside of the box. It was only a fleeting touch, but she'd been planning it for hours. That glancing touch allowed her to spin the dial on the temperature control. It would take a while, maybe longer than she had, but unless something very quickly stabilized the temperature regulation system on the canister, the samples inside would be contaminated. None of the nanoagent cells were programmed to withstand extremes in heat, and she'd adjusted the thermostat to raise the temperature to over one hundred degrees. Most, if not all, of the cultures would die within an hour or two of exposure to that.

She crossed to the printer and gathered up the pile of printouts she'd created. It was time to take what she'd discovered to Rand. He wouldn't believe her, of course, not at first. He'd say she was just being difficult, and he might order something to be done to Alex. It didn't matter. In the end, Rand had a degree in biochemistry himself, though his skills had grown decidedly rusty since he planted himself in the director's seat. He would see that the research she'd brought him was accurate, and he would know the truth. It probably wouldn't stop him from going through with his plans, but that was why Brin was taking no chances. By the time he got someone in to double-check what she'd been doing, the samples would be destroyed. She just needed to find a way out before her own actions were discovered. If she didn't manage that, she knew she was living her last day on Earth, and that the same was true of Alex. She prayed that Karen would understand when neither of them showed up to claim Savannah that it was time to hit the road.

Brin nearly teared up thinking about it. She knew she might never see her family or her friends again. She wanted to scream. She wanted to slam things around and smash things until there was nothing left to smash.

She wanted Alex.

With a deep breath she turned to the door and entered the number for the cipher lock. She didn't know if the men who'd come to set up the lock somehow knew what she'd entered for her private code, but from what she'd seen and heard she thought they didn't. Even if Rand had it, without her thumbprint, he couldn't get into the lab once it was locked down, and she had no intention of keying it in for him or providing her thumb without putting up a fight. He might force it out of her over time, but she didn't need that much time. On her way out she stepped close to the wall and once again managed to brush the temperature control. There was no time to look to see precisely where she'd set it, but she knew she'd raised the temperature. It would set off alarms eventually, but no one would be able to get in to change it. They'd have to break down the door to get in, and by then it probably wouldn't matter.

The materials in the canister on her bench were delicate. One of the reasons she'd been chosen was her attention to detail, and they'd counted on her to preserve their samples and their research. They'd set up an immaculate lab with only one flaw. She didn't want to play their game anymore.

She closed the door behind herself and heard the satisfying metallic thunk of the locks sliding into place. She made a show for the security cameras, straightening out her printouts and staring at one of them for a moment as she steadied her nerves. Then she stepped into the hall and started for the elevator for what she knew would be the last time. She had one chance to convince Rand he was crazy, and just enough time, she hoped, to make sure that, crazy or not, it wouldn't matter. They'd still have the research and the data, but it would take time to rebuild their project. She only hoped they hadn't sent it to one of the other research centers MRIS had around the globe.

The building was empty and when the elevator ground to a halt on her floor, the sound echoed ominously. She knew that somewhere in the building there was a security patrol, but she was equally sure that now, at night, with only the two of them in the complex, Rand would have his handpicked men on duty. She'd seen a few of them mixed in with the regular security guards, more as the days passed. Their uniforms were more military in style than the others, and they moved a lot like Alex did, now that she thought about it. Whatever was going on, they weren't taking chances on anyone catching on. It wouldn't be long before the staff of the building had been replaced with faces Brin had never seen.

She was glad her own people were gone for the day. She'd wanted to warn them, to find a way to keep them away from the complex, but there was no way to communicate directly from the private lab, and any conversation had to be considered to have been recorded. She didn't know what or whom to trust anymore. She didn't feel safe speaking to anyone or doing anything as long as she was inside the MRIS complex.

The elevator halted on the top floor and she stepped into the empty hall. The lights were dim. The only illumination came from the open door of Rand's outer office. Brin squared her shoulders and checked her watch. She knew the climate control in the labs was set to stabilize in less than an hour, and she'd already been out for fifteen minutes. With the lid to the sample case left open, the damage had already begun.

Her footsteps echoed in the empty hall. She

knew Rand would hear her coming. He should hear her, anyway, but he'd been distracted recently, and he was used to having Elaine in the outer office to catch what he didn't have time to pay attention to.

Brin stopped in the doorway and peered around the corner. The outer office was empty. A single desk light illuminated Elaine's desktop, which was bare and clean. Too clean. Had he gotten rid of her, too? Were there too many secrets floating around the office to for an efficient secretary? Brin hoped, suddenly, that Elaine had just been let go, or that she was taking vacation time. She hoped Rand hadn't accidentally left data lying on his desk or an e-mail on screen from someone that could raise curiosity.

The hairs on the back of Brin's neck rose. Everything was moving too fast. It didn't make any sense. They had her under control, or at least they believed that they did. They had shown her Alex, so if there had been an attempt on the Chinese facility, that had failed, as well. The research they'd brought her to complete hadn't come with a short timeline, but Rand had shortened it anyway. Had something gone wrong with their plan?

Brin stepped through Elaine's office and stood in the doorway leading to Rand's inner chamber. He sat in his big leather chair, staring out the window into the darkness. It was a moonless night. All that was visible was a solid wall of darkness, and pinpoints of fuzzy light from below. She stood and watched the back of his head for a moment. She had the eerie impression that he was dead, that it had become a scene from a very bad movie and that she'd walk around in front of him to find his chin on his chest and blood leaking from the corners of his mouth. Then he spoke.

"I hope you have good news for me, Brin," he said softly. "I hope for your sake, for my sake, for everyone's sake, that you have good news."

She considered lying. None of it mattered anymore, but it might placate him for a few moments. Then she shook off the last of her fear and stepped into the room. She remembered an old quote and almost smiled. She whispered it to herself for strength. "When you're on thin ice, you might as well dance."

"I'm afraid I don't, Hershel," she said. She dropped the file folder onto his desk, not waiting for him to turn around. "Not good at all, really, though I suppose it's all relative in the world of biochemical warfare and terrorism, don't you think?"

He spun to face her and she had to fight the urge to take a quick step back. His eyes were sunken pits. His mouth was a flat, emotionless slit across a pale, too-thin face. He looked as if he hadn't eaten or slept in days. Where he clutched the arms of his chair, his knuckles were white.

He glanced down at the folder on the desktop, but he didn't move to open it or look at the contents.

"What the hell is it?" he asked.

"The results of the research you asked for," Brin answered calmly. "You wanted your nanoagents tested and I tested them. I even ran some extras, if you find the time to check the results. They don't work."

"What are you talking about?" he growled. He spun the folder to face him, but didn't open it immediately. He glared at it, then swung his gaze back to hers. "I have seen the results. I know that they work—I've seen the results. What kind of crap are you trying to pull?"

"No crap at all," she said. "They don't work like you think they do. Your boys in China aren't as thorough as we are over here—they don't have the same restrictions keeping them from juicing up human guinea pigs. Did you know that they ran their results on only twelve-day cultures? All of them! They sent us the mature samples, but they did no research beyond the moment they deemed the cells healthy. What would you do if I turned in work like that, Hershel? I don't think I'd have been working here long."

"Stop screwing around and tell me what you found," he said, his voice suddenly dull with fatigue. She was surprised to hear the spark gone from his voice so quickly, and again she wondered what it was she didn't know. She glanced quickly at his computer monitor, but the screen saver was flipping and rolling in on itself, a psychedelic pattern covering whatever he'd been reading or doing before Brin arrived.

"They don't stop when the cells are healthy," she said. "Not every time. I'd need months, maybe years to know if they ever really stop. They mutate. When the cells are all healthy, the nanoagents incorporate minute differences from their host cells. They start wars. I don't know what happens next, not all of it, but I know the cells start attacking one another, trying to become the dominant program."

Rand started laughing and Brin fell silent, watching him as if he'd lost his mind—wondering if maybe he had.

"Did you hear what I said?" she asked.

Rand tried to speak, choked on the laughter, then got himself under control. "What you're telling me the problem is, then," he managed to say at last, "is that my weapon will kill people?"

His laughter fueled her anger. "What I'm telling you, you idiot, is that if you let this crap out into the atmosphere to kill a few thousand or a few hundred thousand people, it isn't going to stop there. The people will die—the nanoagents may not. They might move on to healthier hosts. They might enter the cell walls of plants, animals, get into the water supply. The end result of it, if you just let it go, is that you, your bosses back in China, or wherever the hell this crazy mess started, are going to die. Everyone will die, and the possibility exists that the world, as we know it, will cease to exist. How am I doing? Am I talking slowly enough?"

Rand's face darkened.

"Maybe you'd like to rethink your attitude," he said. "Or did you forget where your precious husband is? You may have noticed I'm not in a great mood. My sense of humor has suffered."

"If you're still considering using the nanoagents after what I just told you, your sense of humor isn't the only thing that has suffered," she retorted. "Hershel, what happened to you? I remember when I first came here—the work you were doing was brilliant. It's part of why I wanted to work for MRIS. Why this?"

"Things change," Rand replied. "Not always, or usually, for the better. Everything I needed to know, you've just given me."

"Why?" she asked. She leaned closer, putting her hands on his desk and catching his gaze. "Why would you do this? I have a right to know what I've been part of, whose cause my work has been warped to serve."

"You don't have a right in the world," Rand snapped. "I need the samples ready to be shipped out in the morning, before sunrise. Include all your research, particularly this last part. What's in the folder?"

"Cell models," she replied. "Cell models that I thought you'd look at. They may be the model of the end of the world."

"It isn't such a great world to start with," Rand replied. "Maybe a little genetic shake-up is in order, don't you think? Maybe it's time we did a quick reshuffle of the cards. We sure managed to screw the world up the first time around, why not give some three-eyed, green-skinned lizard man a shot?"

He turned back to stare out his window. "Close the door on your way out. Get those samples ready to travel, Brin. Seal them as they were when they arrived, and back up the data on that laptop. And don't think there won't be someone watching you. There have been complications. We're going to need those cultures intact."

"And then I can go?" she asked. "I can go home?"

Rand was silent for a long moment, so long Brin almost thought she heard his heartbeat.

"Just do what you're told," he said at last. "We'll sort out the rest soon enough. If what you told me is the truth, getting out of here is only a temporary parole anyway."

Brin stared at the back of his head a moment

longer, and then turned toward the outer office. She felt calm, but she still needed a plan. She knew she couldn't return to the lab below—there was no way she was ever opening that door again. She wished she'd paid more attention to the exits and entrances to the building. There was a map on the wall behind Elaine's desk, and she hesitated, then stepped over and began scanning it quickly, hoping Rand was still staring out the window and that the lack of footsteps in the hall wouldn't catch his attention. Somehow, she didn't think he would notice.

The man acted as if he were already dead. Maybe inside his mind, he already was.

28

Alex chose the maintenance entrance. He knew he could get past the main locks on the front of the building, and the loading dock offered a tempting target, as well, but the maintenance entrance gave him the advantage of quick access to all the floors, to the electrical system and the air ducts. He was somewhat familiar with the security system from his previous visits, and he knew they'd concentrated on the main entrances and obvious weak spots, but maintenance crews would often bypass or disable security that made their job more difficult. That meant there was at least a chance the maintenance door would have fewer locks and alarms on it.

Alex was ready to do the work himself, but if he could find a way past the first line of defense without putting out any real effort, it was better. He wanted to get upstairs. His normal confidence in his own abilities was severely shaken, and he needed to see Brin and to know she was all right. He knew this was a weakness, and it grated on his nerves, but he couldn't change it. His failure in China had made clear that his ability to be a chameleon was gone, and that even defending himself might be a difficult proposition soon. His priorities had shifted, and all he wanted was for his wife and daughter to be safe.

He watched for ten minutes without moving, standing in the shadow of a locked Dumpster. He'd stashed his duffel bag behind it. No one approached the maintenance door, and he saw no sign of movement or light on the inside. Apparently, if there was a maintenance staff working after hours, it was a small and inactive one. More likely, they only came in on call after regular business hours.

When he was convinced it was clear, he slipped up to the rear door and pulled a small meter from his pocket. He flipped a switch and ran it up and down the length of the door. The light on top remained green. He smiled. There wasn't any kind of an infrared sensor on the door.

The lock was a traditional one, but the tumblers required an electronic signal to open. There was a card reader next to the door. He put the meter back in his pocket and removed his small cell phone.

It was a device carried by a number of the Room 59 agents and could do a lot more than place calls. From behind the keypad, he slid out a rectangle of plastic with a magnetic strip on it. He put it into the slot for the key cards, then pressed a combination of numbers on his phone. It would send out a series of short magnetic pulses that would override the lock.

His phone beeped quietly a few times, then he heard the satisfying clunk of tumblers, and the door began to swing open. He grabbed it, stopping it when it was open about six inches. He waited. He heard no alarms and saw no flashing lights. He slipped inside and very carefully closed the door. Then he stepped through a doorway, found a dark corner and stood still again. If anyone came to check because the door set off an alert, it would be in the next few moments. He didn't want to be caught in the open and set off an alarm before he'd even begun to infiltrate the building.

There was no sound from the interior of the building, and he saw no lights. If anyone was watching, they weren't coming forward to stop him.

Alex thought about it and shook his head. Rand wasn't stupid. By now, he'd heard what had happened to the MRIS facility in China. Even if he didn't have time to get the same kind of security forces in place, there was no way he'd leave the building manned with amateurs. His instincts tingled—whatever security was in place was most likely watching him and waiting.

He glanced into the main hall, but chose the maintenance stairs instead. He could cover the floors almost as quickly on foot, and he was less likely to be caught on a security camera or to run into a roving security patrol. He wished he'd asked more questions. Brin wouldn't have thought a thing about it—security was what he did, after all. Professional curiosity and all that.

Alex took the first two floors quickly. On the third his legs started to ache, and by the fourth he knew he'd made a mistake. The building was eight stories. He needed to find a maintenance elevator before his legs gave out on him completely. There was no point in getting to the top floors only to be in too much pain to move. Still, the elevator would be a risk. What he truly wanted to do was to start up the next flights of stairs and force his way through whoever was waiting for him, but he knew it wasn't possible. Too much was riding on the next few minutes for him to jeopardize it with his stupid pride.

He took the doorway from the maintenance stairs into the fourth-floor hall and pressed himself to the wall. A quick sweep of the walls on either side showed the cameras. Predictably, they took direct lines on the main doors and elevators. The service entrance fell in a blind spot. He saw that there was another door just to the left of his position. He had to cross the line of a camera to reach it, but only for a second, and he thought the risk was a good one. He took one quick, deep breath and he moved. He crouched low and stayed tight to the wall. Seconds later he grabbed the door and slipped inside.

The door led to a walk-through closet. It was well stocked with cleaning gear. Mops lined one wall, and gleaming buckets stood in a row beneath them. There were brooms, vacuums and a variety of antibacterial cleaners. The scent of chemicals was strong enough to make his eyes water. Alex slipped through the center of the closet and pushed through the door at the far end. It opened into a slightly larger room with deep sinks, several stainless-steel vats and the one thing he hoped he'd find. Gleaming metal doors opened on a maintenance elevator shaft.

He started forward toward the doors but stopped. Footsteps echoed in the hall beyond the cleaning locker. They approached slowly, and Alex pulled back from the elevator. He glanced around the room quickly. There were several closets, one tall locker, the deep sinks and not much else. The steps drew closer still, and he heard a deep cough. There was no time to waste.

Moments later the outer door opened. A man in gray coveralls entered the outer room with a heavy sigh. He walked straight through to the back room and pulled the door closed behind himself, glancing furtively over his shoulder as if he was afraid he'd been followed. Apparently satisfied, he walked across the room and pulled open a small vent on the wall. It appeared to be some sort of exhaust, maybe for removing unwanted airborne contaminants.

Seconds later, the man had a small object in his hand and leaned in close to the vent. There was a flash, a flicker of flame, and then the man inhaled. As he fought the rising cough, Alex nearly burst out laughing. Two hard hits later, the maintenance man tucked the small pipe back into his pocket and snapped it closed. He put away his lighter, closed the vent and walked to one of the deep sinks. After washing his hands, and his face, and then taking a long sip of the water to clear his breath, the man glanced around the room, turned and headed back to the hall.

Alex dropped. He'd been holding himself up in the overhead pipes, knees and arms jammed over pipes on either side. His muscles were screaming, and when he hit the floor his legs nearly gave out on him. He sank to the floor and sat for a moment, gathering his bearings. He felt light-headed, and the moment he took the weight off his legs they started to cramp. Rhythmic pulses of pain flared through his thighs and into his hips.

With a growl he rolled back to his feet and

lurched to the elevator. He pushed the upward-pointing arrow and listened as the machinery hummed to life. It wasn't like the dumbwaiter in Beijing. The MRIS elevators, even the service elevators, were well maintained, lubricated and tested on a regular basis by the local inspectors. Within moments the door opened, and Alex tumbled in. When the door closed behind him he leaned forward and rested his head against one wall. He stayed that way for a few minutes, and then pulled himself together.

Brin's office was on the seventh floor. She ran the entire research department, but her personal staff and offices were on the seventh. She was always joking it was high enough to have a view, and low enough to make it clear that Rand still ran the show. Alex's plan was simple: find Brin. She would know where the prototype was being kept, and if she didn't, or still didn't know what it was, Rand would know.

He was more than a little surprised at the lack of live security. In fact, it was downright suspicious. Under normal circumstances he'd have understood it, but considering what was at stake, he was surprised Rand didn't have goons goose-stepping up and down every corridor. It didn't make sense, and it made him nervous. If he'd misjudged the situation, or if he'd missed something important, not only his own fate hung in the balance, but Brin's, as well. Maybe more than that, though he believed that Denny had been dead serious about a fast strike if he failed.

The elevator rose to the seventh floor quickly, and Alex spent the few moments sorting out his memory of the building's layout. He knew Brin's office was to his right. He knew the main lab she shared with her assistants was dead ahead, and that smaller labs, incubators and computer rooms lined the halls on both sides of the main lab.

There would be more cameras, but he didn't believe he'd fall into their direct line immediately. He was in a maintenance elevator, and unless the methods employed on the lower levels were different, he'd be clear, at least until he moved away from the elevator. The car came to a stop, and he waited for the door to open. Nothing happened. Alex frowned and pressed the button to open the door. Nothing. The car sat still, not moving up or down, and he frowned.

He pulled the small meter out of his pocket and ran it up and down the wall near the doors. The first two passes brought nothing, but on the third swipe, near the panel with the numbered buttons, he got a blinking red light. When he leaned in closer, he saw that there was a small panel imbedded in the wall of the elevator. It looked new. He pulled a multitool from his pocket and flipped open a small, sharp-tipped screwdriver. Moments later the panel was open, and he faced a second panel of buttons. There were sixteen in all. A hexadecimal code. Why were the maintenance people not allowed on Brin's floor? he wondered.

He pulled out the small electronic scanner again. From another pocket he brought out a pair of tiny wire leads. He inserted them into two small slots on the meter until they were gripped by connectors inside the device. Next he placed the bare wire tips to two leads in the panel. He stood very still and waited. There was no alarm. The lights didn't change. With his thumb, he pressed a small button on the side of the device, and the digital readout on the wall panel began spinning rapidly through different combinations.

His hand trembled, and sweat beaded on his brow. He tried to steady his fingers, but the harder he worked to prevent the trembling, the more severe it became. He moved his free hand closer and rested the shaking fingers on the palm, but he felt himself cramping up. The numbers continued to spin, and he closed his eyes, concentrating.

"Damn it," he whispered. "Come on." If he shook any harder, the wires would snap free, and he'd have to start over.

Then there was an audible click, and the numbers stopped. The code that appeared was made up of the numbers zero through nine and several letters. Hexadecimal code, very difficult to break—unless you had the right key.

The door slid open, and he didn't hesitate. He stepped into the hallway before they could close behind him again. He slipped his tools back into his pockets and leaned heavily against the wall. When he glanced up again, he stopped and stood very still. There were twice as many cameras on this level. They crisscrossed the hallway and there was no chance he hadn't been spotted on at least one of them. He scanned the walls quickly and saw that there were motion detectors, as well as audio sensors.

"What the hell?" he muttered. Security on this floor hadn't been this high before. Not even close. Then it hit him. He might not have it in front of him, but he'd found the prototype. There was no other explanation for such a shift in the level of security. He wondered where the other end of all the sensors was wired, and who might be watching. He wondered if they were awake, on duty, or if maybe Rand himself had them all on a big monitor on his wall, waiting for someone to step into his parlor. He almost waved.

If the prototype was in a lab on this level, then it was in Brin's hands, one way or the other. He knew that the beefed-up security would set bells off for her, but he also knew she could be as obsessive with her work as he was with his. If she thought she was doing something beneficial, she'd kill herself trying to get it done. He had to make sure it never came to that.

The first thing was to take out the motion detectors. There was no doubt they'd already registered his initial movement, but at least he could keep them from showing the direction he traveled down the hallway. He reached into a deeper pocket on his hip and pulled out a small black box. A short metal antenna protruded from the top of it. He pressed the box to the wall and flipped a switch on the side of it. Then he stood very still. Up and down the hall the motion detector beams winked out one at a time as the device sent a coded pulse to each one, instructing the sensor chip to shut down. The power lights on the sensors didn't fade, but the beams were neutralized. So far, he'd been fortunate that the people behind the security on this level were using standard industrial-grade security and nothing too customized. The motion sensors would now show no movement on this level.

Next he examined the angles of the cameras. He needed to get close enough to Brin's office to get a good look inside, but he knew if he started taking out cameras indiscriminately it would set off alarms somewhere. He had to take out just the one he needed and remain in a very short, narrow slice of hallway, and then he needed to get the camera back online before someone was dispatched to check on it.

He worked quickly. There was a window on the outer wall of Brin's office, and only one camera watched that particular bit of hallway. He slid along the wall, found the right camera and studied it for a moment. The ceiling wasn't that high. He was able to stretch high enough to turn the connector on the back. It took a moment, and his fingers screamed with the effort, threatening to cramp up. Finally the connector separated and he pressed into the wall again. His body shook, and he gritted his teeth. He couldn't afford to slip up now.

He moved quickly back down the wall, slid to the cleared track he'd created and crossed the hallway quickly. He pressed his face to the glass window of Brin's office and glanced inside. It was dark. Her computer monitor wasn't glowing. He saw no indication that she'd been in the room recently, not even a coffee cup. He frowned.

He tried to get a look at the labs up and down the hallway, but he couldn't without disabling more cameras, and he knew he probably only had a few moments to hook the first one back up before someone noticed and came down to check on it.

Alex slipped back across the hall and moved up under the camera. He took a deep breath, then stretched up and gripped the connector again. His fingers didn't want to hold it, and sweat broke out on his brow. He stood very still, waiting for it to pass, and very slowly moving the connector up and forward. He felt it slide into place, and began turning. The camera was just high enough on the wall that he couldn't reach it without a full stretch, and his body seemed intent on folding in on itself, cramping and preventing him. He gasped and released the connector. It hung on the lip of its mated piece, but he knew it wasn't screwed in far enough. He sank down the wall. His legs trembled and his arms ached. He closed his eyes for a long moment and took several deep breaths. Then, without giving himself a chance to hesitate, he stretched up, gripped the connector and spun it. He managed to turn it three times before he had to drop back, and this time he thought it was tight enough. If not, he had no more time, or strength, to deal with it.

There had been two floors with lights visible from below. He hoped he hadn't missed Brin, or Rand for that matter, but if they were gone and the building was empty, his work would be much simpler. He had to take out the entire complex, but he'd counted on taking care of Rand while he was at it and erasing any trail to the research or the prototype. Any trail but Brin. He would get her out safe, get her home, and then they'd have to see what Denny and Kate said, and figure out what they intended to do. It was entirely possible, he knew, that he was now a target himself and their only choice would be to run.

He turned back to the maintenance elevator and punched the up button. The door opened, and he was relieved. Apparently the code was only necessary to enter the floor, not to leave it. He hoped they hadn't thought to alarm the access, letting them know whenever someone punched in the code. He pressed the top-floor button and leaned against the wall, wishing he'd taken some of the painkiller before entering the building. He also wished the elevator would move more slowly. He wasn't sure his legs were going to listen when he told them to stand.

29

In a room down the hall from Rand's office, the control panels for the security systems in the building lined one wall. A man stood, his back to the door, examining the panels. In particular, he studied the panels concerned with the new, heightened security on the ninth floor. It was a laughable system, almost childishly simple to overcome, but then, Rand hadn't really expected anyone to try when he'd had it installed. The new system had a lot of sensors, a lot of cameras and monitors to watch over things, and it made a good security blanket for Rand and his inept crew.

The man watching the monitors wasn't an amateur. He watched as a camera with the label G4 winked to black. He studied the diagrams of the seventh floor, and then returned his gaze to the dark screen. When it flickered momentarily and then came back to life, showing the empty hallway and the wall fronting Dr. Tempest's office, the man smiled.

"So," he muttered. "You're here after all. And I was almost ready to think maybe you'd do the smart thing and leave it alone."

The man turned to his left and punched a button. Another screen lit up. On the screen Alex Tempest leaned against the wall of the service elevator. His eyes were closed, and he looked anything but ready to move. The man pushed the button again, and the screen went dark. He stepped out of the security office and closed the door behind him. He was only four doors down from Rand's office, and he considered reporting in. They'd been expecting this particular visitor for almost a day, and he knew Rand would want to know the moment had arrived.

Rand thought he was in charge. But orders were orders, and his didn't involve reporting to the CEO of the U.S. office in anything but a token fashion. He had a mission to complete, and he needed to get on with it. Instead of reporting in, he turned toward the maintenance elevator and unsnapped the flap over the top of the long, thin blade dangling from his belt.

This time, Captain Dayne planned to finish off the nuisance for good.

30

Alex stood and opened his eyes. The elevator car was slowing, and he knew he was going to have to concentrate. He didn't know if Rand had beefed-up security on his floor, as well, though he doubted it. He'd know when he tried to open the elevator doors. He rotated his neck slowly, working out the kinks. At the end of this motion, just before he turned to the door and pressed the button, he stopped.

Something caught his eye that he'd missed before, something he should have noticed right off the bat. He cursed himself softly, his mind back on track and working furiously. A small glint of light reflected through a crack between metal panels in the door. A camera. Was someone watching? Was it even turned on?

Alex unsnapped the tie on his holster and freed

his 9 mm pistol, drawing the weapon. If they were watching, they'd see it and it wouldn't matter, but if they were waiting for him, it might make the difference. If no one was there, and he was just being paranoid, the gun wouldn't hurt.

It had bothered him that there were no guards. He'd been careful, but he'd been careful for a very good reason. There was a biomedical weapon in the building worse than anything the world had never seen. There was a plan for some sort of terrorist strike. There were, in theory, backers and powers above Rand's level who would be watching, and very disappointed if anything happened.

It didn't add up. The haphazard security was a sign of something, but he just couldn't figure out what it was. All of it had brought his senses back to their earlier sharpness. He crouched by the door, and then reached up to punch the button that opened it.

He didn't take time to think. He lifted the gun, held it close to his chest, then dived forward into the hall, rolling. He swept left as the blade swept down from the right, slashing the back of his biceps. He gasped, but kept rolling, preventing the blade from biting as deeply as it might have. He twisted on his shoulders and got to his feet.

Dayne lunged. He held the long, slender knife in front of him, and his eyes blazed with hatred. Alex brought the gun up, but Dayne was moving forward and lashed out, kicking the 9 mm pistol out of Alex's grip and sending it skittering down the hall. Dayne never even glanced at it. He shifted the blade to his other hand and smiled. Alex crouched low and took quick stock of his opponent's movements. Dayne was quick and agile, and the kick had been well aimed.

"You're a long way from your crater," Alex said, backing away slightly.

Dayne saw the motion and lashed out, swinging his blade in a vicious arc that Alex barely dodged.

Alex cursed and dropped back, concentrating on the one the blade that spun and was slashing back at him in a return strike. The man was as fast as a snake.

"You should have stayed disappeared," Dayne said. "A smart man would have walked away while he still could." His teeth were gritted, and the words were difficult to make out. Only his eyes were calm—every muscle in the man's body was taut like strung piano wire.

"I thought about it," Alex replied, keeping his eyes on the blade. He didn't want to make the mistake of watching Dayne's face. "But then I decided I'd rather track you down and kill you and everyone involved with this project instead."

Dayne reversed his grip on the blade, keeping it moving and twisting, a metal snake of death in his hands. It was mesmerizing, but Alex knew the trick. He shifted his gaze in quick glances at

Dayne's waist and hips. It was an old football trick, one he'd used throughout his martial-arts training. You could be fooled with a motion of the head, arms, shoulders, even the feet, but where a man's hips moved, he followed.

Dayne lunged again, and this time Alex was ready. He whipped his arm out and gripped his opponents wrist just above the blade. He yanked, pulling the man toward him, and moved a leg in a sweep at Dayne's ankle.

But his leg didn't do what he wanted. He missed slightly, and his sweeping ankle caught the other man on the calf. The blow was glancing, sending Dayne off balance, but his reaction was swift and nearly deadly. Dayne moved the blade to his free hand, and even as he tumbled and rolled past, he slashed out again. The only thing that prevented Alex from being cut was his own bum leg. He dropped as it failed to support him as expected, and the blade flashed by his face, missing by inches.

He moved back, rolling with the motion and coming back to a crouch, even as Dayne flipped back to his feet and came at him again. Fighting with this man was probably going to get him killed, Alex realized. His body had taken too much of a pounding, and his illness was making his responses slow and sluggish. He needed to look for his moment, the one opportunity he might have to end things quickly.

"Not quite feeling yourself, are you, Mr. Tempest?" Dayne gloated. "Not quite the man you were a year ago, or even a month ago. Not so sharp now that your body is failing. It's almost a shame to waste my time killing you—you're as good as dead anyway. If you'd minded your business and stayed clear, I'd have been in and out of here with no one the wiser."

"You talk a lot for an idiot," Alex said. He was trying to anger his opponent and get a break. Dayne was wound so tight he might snap, and it might be his only chance. The hell of it was that they both knew Dayne was right. Alex couldn't trust his body to respond to his commands. Any moment he might try a block or an attack, and find that he couldn't follow through. If he collapsed, he'd be dead in an instant.

"She's a pretty lady," Dayne said. "Your wife, I mean. It will be a shame, you leaving her all alone. Brilliant, too, I understand. There's always work for someone like her with the people I work for. You think she'll like me? Maybe…"

Alex shut the man's voice out. He couldn't allow himself to be baited. He needed something, anything, that could spin the odds back in his favor. As long as Dayne remained on the attack and held that damned knife, all he could do was defend and hope for a mistake. It was a bad plan, and he knew he'd need a better one.

The 9 mm pistol was fifteen feet down the slick, tiled hall. He saw no way to reach it on his damaged legs before Dayne caught him. He'd have to turn his back on the man to make the effort. Then it came to him, and he almost smiled.

Alex turned to face his opponent, crouching low. He leaned heavily to his left, favoring his right leg. He blinked his eyes, as though focusing, or blinded by sweat. He didn't look straight at Dayne. His left hand trembled.

"Leave her out of this," he said. "She isn't part of it. This is between you and me."

"Spoken like a true hero," Dayne said, circling slowly.

Alex spun, trying to keep the man in front of him, but it was difficult with only one leg supporting him. He nearly toppled, then righted himself.

"Unfortunately," Dayne continued, "I'm not made of the same stuff. I don't believe in wasting feminine beauty or perfectly viable weapons, and when I leave this complex, I intend to have both with me, one way or the other. The work isn't done, you see. What we did in Beijing has to be replicated. We have some of the files here, and we have the prototype, but if we deploy that, what will we have left? We need your wife, Mr. Tempest. I'm afraid that means our use for you— and yours for her—has come to an end."

"And yet I'm still here," Alex replied. His voice

didn't tremble as he spoke this time, but Dayne didn't notice.

Without warning, Dayne moved. He launched himself at Alex, sending a roundhouse kick at the weak knee and thrusting the blade toward Alex's eyes. The man was damned fast. He moved like a big cat, and the blade might as well have been an extension of his hand.

Alex was ready. The second Dayne moved, Alex threw himself to the side and kicked. He'd been forcing his right leg to hold his weight, pretending that there was no strength in the left, and when he launched his kick, Dayne was taken completely by surprise. He felt his foot connect and Dayne flipped over it, crashing face-first to the floor. Alex tried to spin back and take advantage of the moment, but this time the weakness in his leg was real. He staggered.

Dayne's nose dripped blood as he lifted himself from the floor and scooted forward. He still moved quickly, but he wasn't as steady on his feet, and when he turned back he didn't smile. He still held the knife tightly, and his eyes, which had been intense, had gone wild.

"You missed," Alex said softly.

That was all it took. Dayne rushed at him, slashing wildly with the blade. Alex caught his wrist again. This time, when the man tried to shift the blade toward his free hand, Alex was prepared, and snatched at it, knocking it away, and trying to ignore the bright sliver of pain in his palm as the blade sliced across his hand. It caromed off the wall and spun away.

Alex drove his wounded hand toward Dayne's damaged nose, but the man was already moving again, so he struck high on his cheekbone instead of smashing into the wounded area. Nonetheless, the force of the blow was enough to send the man staggering a step to the side, and Alex kicked out again. This time his leg obeyed and he felt the contact. Dayne's legs flipped out from under him. He dropped heavily, trying to spin and get a grip on Alex. Dayne hit hard, striking the tiled floor with his hip.

Alex backed away and crouched, ready for another attack, but instead, Dayne screamed. He'd landed badly, and Alex thought he must have snapped something, probably his hip or his tailbone. Alex stepped forward and kicked Dayne in the face so hard the man's head snapped back. The 9 mm pistol was still out of reach, but Alex lurched in the other direction and found the hilt of Dayne's knife.

When he whirled back Dayne had managed to slide to the wall and was struggling to get to his feet. Alex faced him and watched. If he'd misjudged the damage done by the fall, he might still have a fight on his hands. Dayne tried to pull himself up, screamed and started to drop.

Alex didn't hesitate. He ran forward and drove the knife blade into Dayne's throat. He felt the blade bite deeply and he twisted it, jerking up hard. The motion lifted Dayne again, and their gazes met. Alex held it for a long moment, then pulled out the blade. Dayne tumbled to the floor and tried to scream but couldn't get sound past the bubbling mass of blood and froth that had been his throat.

Alex turned away. There was a single light glowing down the hall, and he knew it had to be Rand's office. He limped toward the light, recovering his 9 mm pistol and gripping it tightly. His legs ached, and he was having trouble focusing his eyes, but his mind was clear. At least, he thought, it was clear enough.

He slipped along the wall, trying to keep quiet, but knowing that the time for such caution was probably long past. If Rand hadn't heard what was going on in the hall outside his office, then it didn't matter how much noise Alex made. If he had heard, or had been watching on one of the security monitors, then there wasn't any chance of surprise.

Alex followed the barrel of his pistol slowly around the door frame to Rand's outer office. He wasn't sure what he'd expected to find in that office, but what he expected to.

There was a woman standing at the end of the room. The lights were dim and at first, he thought it might be Rand's secretary. Then he looked closer, and his heart nearly stopped. He choked up, and he had to bite back a sudden, overpowering wave of emotion.

"Brin." The word had been barely audible, but she heard him—or sensed him.

She spun, her eyes wide and her lip trembling at the sight of him. She began to shake.

"Alex?"

She launched herself at him, crossing the room and throwing her arms around his neck.

Alex barely had time to brace himself. The force of her leap was nearly enough to topple him, but he held her tight, keeping himself upright for a few moments, one weakened leg stretched behind him to keep his balance.

Even in that moment, his arms finally sliding around her, the emotion and the pain and all the things he needed to say rushing to his lips, he kept his head. He knew she couldn't be there alone, and he knew that Dayne was not the only dangerous man in the building.

"Shh!" he whispered into her hair, clutching her to his chest and trying to spin, keeping his eye on the door to the inner office. As he spun, her hair brushed over his face, and in that moment something shifted. He brushed her hair away almost frantically.

When he cleared his vision he saw that he was too late. Hershel Rand stood in the doorway of his office. He watched the two of them coolly. His eyes were wide and his jaw was set. He raised his arm and Alex saw that he was gripping a gun so tightly his knuckles were white from the strain.

Perhaps Rand had thought he was being stealthy, waiting for the two to be distracted before making a move.

Alex saw the motion of Rand's arm, and he reacted. He still held the 9 mm pistol in his hand. Brin's body had blocked it from Rand's sight. In a single, smooth movement he spun Brin away and pressed her to the wall. He held her there with his hand on her chest and raised the 9 mm handgun. He fired without aiming, trusting his instinct to make his aim true.

The bullet found a home in Rand's chest, right below his left shoulder. The impact spun him around. There was a quick suck of air and a yelp of pain. Rand stood, leaning against the door frame, and stared down at the wound as blood soaked his shirt. He turned and looked at Brin, ignoring Alex, and it seemed as if he wanted to say something. The gun dropped from his hand and clattered to the floor, and Rand followed, sliding slowly down the wall. As he dropped, he picked up speed. He landed with a teeth-jarring thud, his eyes wide with shock and dark with fury.

Alex released Brin and kicked Rand's gun away from him. "Stay there," he said quietly, then turned to stand over the dying man.

Rand gasped, pressing his hand to the wound in his chest and fighting for air. "Wasn't destroying our lab in China enough for you? What is it with you, some sort of weird vendetta?"

"You're playing a nasty game with dirty little germs, Rand. It's the kind of thing that catches people's attention. You were ready to kill people, betray your country, hell, maybe destroy the world. Did you really think that we'd just let that go?" Alex said.

"We?" Rand asked. "Who the hell is we? Maybe if you'd made nice with the boys in Beijing, they'd have cut you in."

"The way you cut Brin in? When were you going to tell her it was a weapon? How far in did you plan on dragging her before you mentioned that you didn't have any intention of ever curing anyone with your new toy? Cut me in? It's not about money—it never was. Where will you spend it if you can't live in your own home, or if you start an epidemic? It's about all the lives you would have taken. Not just a few, but possibly millions. My problem isn't personal—it's a mission. I'm going to destroy the weapon and kill everyone associated with it."

"So it's my turn now, is it?" Rand sneered, grimacing at the pain in his chest. Blood leaked out between his fingers and most of his shirt had been stained red. "You're just going to stand there and shoot me?"

"It's what I do, you asshole," Alex said. He pulled the trigger. Rand slumped over, blood pouring from the second wound in his chest, just over his heart.

Brin stared at the man on the floor, then turned her gaze back to her husband, who she was seeing, Alex realized, in a way she'd never previously imagined. There was so much to say, but now wasn't the time. "I'm sorry Brin. This is what I do," he said. "Or at least I did."

Brin nodded, then knelt down. Rand's breath was winding down like an old clock with worn-out springs. "Rand," she whispered. "Can you hear me?"

He panted and nodded, his face filled with the desperate hope of the dying.

"Rot in hell, you son of a bitch," she said.

They stood quietly and watched as Rand took his last few breaths and died.

Alex turned to study her face, wondering what he would find there. Condemnation? Anger? Fear? He knew that any and all of those emotions would be justified and that he was to blame for that.

"I've worked on the weapon, Alex." Her eyes found his, hers glistening with tears. "Am I next? Is part of your mission to kill me?"

Alex shook his head. "Does it work?" he asked.

"It would have, yes. Not like they thought it would—the research isn't complete—it would have been much, much worse than they thought."

He reached out one trembling hand and stroked her hair. He scooped up Rand's gun and put it into his belt. He could get rid of it later, just little pieces of metal, scattered haphazardly into the ocean.

"Let's go get that thing," he said. "I need your help to destroy it without letting any of it escape. Can you do that for me?"

"Of course," she said, watching his face. "I've already started."

They returned to the elevator and rode back to the level of Brin's lab. She led the way, and when they reached the door to the lab, she tapped in her code and set her thumb on the scanner. She set the door on lockout once they were inside. She didn't want that door to reopen until she was good and ready. If anything went wrong, it would never open again. And if everything went right, she didn't want anyone disturbing them until it was complete.

It was hot in the lab, and they were both bathed in sweat within moments. Red sensors were lit on many of the panels, but no one was around to read them or heed their warning.

Alex looked at the containment unit sitting so benignly on the counter. "So, this is it, huh?"

"Was," Brin replied. "I have all the data on the laptop. I was supposed to be backing it up and sending it back to them when I was done. But I didn't do it."

"So, you knew something was wrong?" Alex asked.

"Damned straight, I knew. I mean, at first, it just looked like their data was skewed. They didn't carry the research through logically, just stopped each time it seemed to be going their way. Then, when I got a good look at this thing, saw what happened after the nanoagents did their intended job, I saw that I had a pretty unstable component. It didn't always progress as they thought it would, and they didn't care. Research like that was never meant to be presented to any medical board.

"I was going to drop the work and walk out, but they had video, Alex. They had video of you, and you were in trouble. I stuck with it when they threatened me, but only because I knew that if you didn't make it back, it was up to me."

"Can we get rid of it without putting anyone at risk?" Alex asked.

"Like I said, I've already started. It's supposed to be kept at a fairly constant temperature. I turned up the heat as far as it will go, and I left the containment unit open. It's a powerful weapon, but it isn't invincible. The extreme heat alone would kill it in due time."

"Okay, see if you can be sure it's destroyed. I'll take care of what's on that laptop. We're going to take the building out, too, but I don't want anything surviving that they might dig out of the rubble. Is there any data anywhere else?"

"Rand had me sealed off in here, no access to the company network. They didn't want anyone looking over my virtual shoulder except them. I thought they were worried about corporate spies, until I got further into it. What sucks the most is the basis for it all is *good* work. With time, with a proper study and controlled environment, amazing things could have come of this research. As it is, it's too dangerous. I don't even know if you could find a place that would be safe from someone who wanted to put it to the wrong use. It makes me sick inside."

"That's my girl!" He gave her shoulder a reassuring squeeze and was only a little surprised when she recoiled from him. "So, if I smash this thing into a thousand pieces, it'll all be gone?"

"Yeah." She thought for a moment, one fingernail tapping lightly on the temperature control of the containment unit. "Except that I can't really be sure that Hershel didn't come in here when I wasn't here. I mean, he might have made copies…."

"And he might have stored them anywhere." Alex sighed and leaned against the table. "We're going to have to be very thorough. Whatever we do has to wipe out every bit of data in this building. Take out the whole network."

"We have no idea how much data Hershel had, or where he might have hidden it. He probably didn't trust those Chinese bastards any more than I trusted him."

"Then there's really only one way to take care of this. Make sure that nothing survives, and that anyone who might remember is silenced."

"Alex," Brin said softly.

He turned to her and raised an eyebrow.

"I'm the only one who worked on it. I'm the only one, besides Rand, who knows."

Alex crossed the lab and hugged her tight. "Don't worry. We just need to get through this—it will be fine. I promise."

"And what about you?" she asked. "Will you be fine? Will we? *You* know about the weapon, too, Alex."

"One thing at a time, okay?" he said. "Let's get this handled, then we'll start figuring out the rest. It will be okay."

She studied him, as if trying to judge if he was telling the truth, then nodded and turned back to the canister on the table. There wasn't much time.

31

"You're sure that crap can't survive if we blow it to bits?" Alex asked. "I'd hate to think I just ended one threat to create another that's airborne."

"Like I said, extreme heat will kill it for sure. You're going to blow the whole building, then?" Brin asked.

Alex saw her hesitation. He knew she had years of research tied up with MRIS, stored on their computers and tucked away in their files. All the work she'd been doing, all the work her colleagues were doing, would be destroyed right along with the nanoagents. He wished there was another way. More than that, he wished she'd never been dragged into any of it.

"It's the only way," he said as gently as he could. "We have to neutralize the threat, and we can't take a chance that Rand backed up the data or kept a second sample on ice in some hidden lab you don't even know about."

He hesitated a second, and then added, "I'm sorry, Brin."

"But everyone who works here—"

"There's no one here," Alex said. "But sometimes you have to sacrifice a few people to get the job done. It's sounds cruel, but it would be worse if we didn't do what we had to do. The best thing we can manage is to get moving before people start to arrive. We need to get out."

Brin stared at him and then nodded. Alex could tell that she knew it had to be done, but she didn't have to like it. As much as she loved him, she still couldn't be sure whether his loyalties were with her or with Room 59. It hung in the air between them, in a place where nothing had ever hung before.

"Give me a second, then," she said. "I'll make sure none of it's viable before we—" She trailed off then, not wanting to put such a horrible thing into words.

Brin opened the container and withdrew a sample, got it under the microscope fast. She felt Alex's eyes on her and she wanted to spin on him, rage at him for all of this, the lies, the danger, the fear, the scent of gunpowder that still filled her nostrils. Instead, she stared into the microscope, focused and inspected the slide, checking carefully to be absolutely certain that the cultures were dead.

"We're good to go," she said at last, lifting her head. "Whatever we have to do, we can do it without releasing any of this into the air."

"Okay." Alex shoved the laptop off the table and began pounding furiously at it with the leg of the chair. He smashed at it until the case shattered, spraying little bits of motherboard about the room. When he managed to free the hard drive, he gathered it up in one hand and snagged a pair of tongs with another. Once he had the drive gripped tightly in the tongs, it was a simple matter to drop it into a large beaker.

"You have anything we can pour in here that will eat through plastic?" he asked. "The drives on the inside are layered, like thick CDs stacked one on top of another. To really get all the data out of there, we need to destroy the interior disks."

Brin glanced around the room, then said, "How about sulfuric acid?" She crossed the lab and grabbed the container and returned, twisting off the top to bypass the nozzle they normally used to apply the solution a bit at a time. She poured the contents over the drive. As the clear liquid made contact with the surface of the hard drive's case, the solution began to bubble and froth. Then she took down another bottle and said, "Stand back."

"What's in that?" Alex asked.

"Water," she said. She poured a small quantity of water over the acid and it began to spit and boil. "Sulfuric acid is exothermic," she explained. "There won't be anything but plastic soup left inside."

The beaker sizzled and bubbled, threatening to spill acid all over the tabletop. Alex watched it carefully. It wasn't that he didn't trust Brin—he wanted to see the damned thing melt. When he was sure it was done, he turned to her and tried a half grin.

"You ready?" he asked.

"Yeah." Her voice had a hollow, sad sound to it. "Where are we going?"

"Home. First we blow this place off the face of the planet, and then we go home."

"Good," she replied. "You have one hell of a lot of explaining to do, and you'd better start thinking about it now."

Alex stepped forward and pulled her to him. Despite the slight resistance she gave him, he hugged her tightly. He didn't want to let go, but he knew they weren't finished. "Get us out of here," he said softly.

Brin stepped to the cipher lock, entered the code, and the door swung wide a final time. She set it to lock behind them, and they stepped through into the hall.

Alex knew that the security cameras were still watching, but somehow he thought no one was home. If Dayne had backup, he'd have called on it when things started to go south. They must have kicked the entire security staff out for the night, or fired them outright. It was crazy, and Alex saw the desperation behind it. He wondered if maybe Dayne had come on his own, sort of a last-shot desperation tactic.

The one thing he knew he had to include in his final report was the Chinese Mafia's involvement. Some additional cleanup would have to be done to ensure that they weren't expanding their operations into completely new realms of crime like bioterrorism. It made sense, though, considering the market for weapons, that the organized-crime groups of the world would seek to profit from it all.

Alex led Brin down the maintenance elevator and out through the service doors. His duffel bag was right where he left it next to the Dumpster, and he retrieved it while she watched. He had a bad moment when he thought this left leg was going to collapse. He leaned against the trash receptacle, waiting to see if the leg would come back, or if he'd tumble to the ground.

The spasm in his leg passed and he snagged the duffel bag's handle and opened it. There were six separate charges inside. He gripped the bag tightly and turned back to the building.

"I can do this myself," he said softly. "I can tell you where the car is and you can wait for me. I have to place all six around the perimeter on the inside. I don't want the building flying all over town—I want it come down on itself, and to do that I have to get the placement just right."

She hesitated.

"But I could really use someone who knows the interior layout better than I do."

Brin nodded and they slipped back in the service doors and got to work. The building was laid out in a cross pattern, four wings shooting out from a square central lobby area. Alex chose two wings, the one directly below Brin's office and the wing opposite, to place the first two charges. He attached them carefully to the wall at the far end of each, then returned to the center. Next he did the same for the remaining two wings, leaving two charges.

"What about those?" Brin asked, perplexed. "If there are only four wings, why do we need more than four—what are they, bombs?"

"Simple," Alex explained. "We'll place these two near the center, and we'll set them off first. Then we'll trigger the outer charges a few seconds later. This will cause the center to begin crumbling, and when the force from the outer explosions pushes in, it will crumble the walls inward. If it works right, the parking lot outside might get some debris, but no one nearby will be hurt. I doubt they'll ever find Rand or Dayne, though."

"Dayne," Brin repeated. "That was his name? Alex, he was in those videos. He had a knife, and they had you—"

"Later," Alex said, giving her another short hug. "There will be time later, and I'll tell you everything. He was a bad man, though, the worst."

"What about you?" she asked softly. "Is that what you are? Are you a bad man?"

"I hope not," Alex replied, turning back to his work. "They tell me I'm the good guy."

He worked as quickly as he could. When she saw him struggle once or twice, Brin took the duffel bag without saying a word. Alex did his best to resist each time his body betrayed him because he knew that when she saw it, she was reminded of his own betrayal, or at least his failure to be honest. One lie led to the next, and it was a wonder that she still stood beside him, or waited for him at all. As close as they'd always been, he now saw what a wall of secrets he'd built between them, and despaired of ever tearing it down completely.

Finally, the charges were set. Alex checked his watch. It was nearly four-thirty in the morning.

"How soon until people start getting here?" he asked.

Brin thought for a moment.

"The main lobby opens at eight, but there are a lot of people in before that. The earliest I've been in is about five-thirty, and I only saw a couple of others at that hour. We have a little bit of time."

Alex nodded. "I want to make sure we have time to get out of here and back to the car before I set this off, and I don't want anyone wandering in in the meantime."

When the final two charges were set, he pulled a small black box from the pack. Alex attached it to the first charge, flipped up a small antenna and then pressed a button. A series of lights flashed, flickered and then burned green and steady. He crossed to the second charge and repeated the action with a second box.

"The others are set to respond to the shock of the initial blast," he explained. "It was the best I could do on short notice."

She stared at him and he flushed. Everything he said made his life of lies more clear to her. More than anything, he wanted to try to explain, but what could he possibly say that would mend the rift between them? He turned away to hide his frustration and adjusted the receiver.

"We'd better get going," he said at last.

They turned together, leaving the empty duffel bag on the floor behind them. Alex stumbled, nearly fell, and found that Brin had caught him. She slipped under his arm and supported him without comment as they hurried out the service exit, across the parking lot and down the street to where Alex had parked. Then Brin stopped.

"Alex, I have to get my car," she said quickly.

"I have mine," he said, not understanding, and she slipped out from under his arm, nearly dropping him to the pavement.

"My car is in the parking lot, Alex. Why would it be there if I'm not inside? If I'm inside, and the building blows up, they'll think I'm dead, and they'll come around with condolences. If they find me, they'll wonder why my car was in the parking lot of a building that went up in a flaming ball, but I wasn't killed." She hesitated for a moment, then turned back. "I'll be right back." She started to walk away, then called back over her shoulder, "I thought you were supposed to be good at this."

Alex watched her go in numb disbelief. She was right, of course, and it was another indication of how tired he was, and how far off his form. He'd almost made a blunder that a first-year agent would laugh at, and his wife had just saved his ass. Again.

THERE WASN'T A BONE in Alex's body that didn't hurt. The fight with Dayne had left his arms weak, his legs even more unstable than they had been in the past few days. His shoulder was so sore that his arm hung limp and nearly useless. His head burned like fire and he'd sweated through the bandages and smacked it on something during the night's adventure. It throbbed and felt as if it might burst through its bandages and explode. He couldn't tell if that was why he had trouble focusing, or if it was the MS. He had been through hell for the past few days and he had trouble sorting out what was a symptom, what was fatigue and what was a normal casualty of the job. Not knowing made him crazy and he shook it off, trying to concentrate.

He fought the urge to doze off as he waited, and he knew it was only a few moments before he heard the engine of Brin's SUV idling beside him, though it felt like hours. She parked, but left her engine running, came around and slid into the passenger side of the Porsche.

"Okay," she said.

Alex nodded. He pulled a black box out from under his seat and placed it in his lap. It was simple, three switches and a few status lights. He flipped the first button and the lights flickered. One light glowed amber, and the others flickered, then grew steady. Each was green, like the indicators on the receivers had been.

"They've found the signal," he explained. "You ready?"

"No, but do it and get it over with," Brin said. Her eyes were dark, hovering somewhere between fear over what was to come, and anticipation. Alex nodded, closed his eyes and flipped the two switches.

For the first couple of seconds, nothing seemed to happen. Brin turned to look over her shoulder toward the building, started to speak and was cut short by a flash of light. There was no sound at first, then the explosion registered and the car shook. Brin screamed and Alex put an arm around her to steady her. They turned together and watched.

What looked like a pillar of light shot up the center of the building then, seconds after the initial blast, the other four charges went off. They weren't exactly in sync, and it sounded like a string of giant, out-of-control firecrackers. There was no hint of sunrise on the horizon, so when the flash died, all that remained was a white cloud illuminated from within, and then, nothing.

"Wha—" Brin started to speak again, and it was that moment that a cloud of dust and silt began raining down on them. Another wave of energy washed over the Porsche and around it, blowing outward and shaking the windows. The small vehicle shuddered. Brin clutched at her armrest on the right and Alex's thigh on the left until the moment passed.

It was hard to see out the windows more than a foot or so.

"Wait for the dust to clear," Alex said. "It will

be hard to breathe out there for a few minutes. As soon as we can see, we'll go."

"I'll have to come back," Brin said.

He stared at her again. "There's nothing to come back to," he said softly.

She turned to him, glaring. "I know that, Alex. I'm sitting right here. I have to come back. I'm the manager of the research lab. If I just don't show up, how is that going to look? When my people show up for work, and the building is gone, they're going to be looking to me for guidance. Maybe you've seen this kind of thing too much. You sure don't seem to see the people behind your actions— not even when I'm one of them. I have to come back and help try to make sense of this."

Alex sat back as if he'd been slapped. It felt that way, actually. She was right, and not for the first time in a very short span his respect for her grew and his confidence in himself dwindled. He was starting to feel very weak and small, and he hated the sensation almost as much as he hated seeing the hurt in her eyes.

They sat in silence for a few minutes longer, then Brin opened her door and stepped out. She leaned in and caught the stricken look in his eyes, leaned over to kiss his cheek. "I'll see you at home," she called as she closed the door.

Alex sat and waited until she was back behind her own wheel and pulling away from the curb, then he started the Porsche and sat a few minutes longer. He had a lot of things to sort out.

He slapped the car into gear and pulled out onto the street, fighting the urge to gun it and race home. He wanted to, but the professional in him still held sway. If he drew attention to himself now, there might be questions. If they questioned him, they would find out who he was, and if they found out who he was, they'd find Brin, and everything she'd just reminded him of would become a serious problem.

Of all the times in his long and dangerous career, Alex thought that the next few hours, or days, were going to prove to be the trickiest and most difficult. He hoped he had the strength left to see it through.

Behind him the last of the dust settled over the rubble that had been the MRIS complex.

32

Alex pulled into the driveway and parked beside Brin's vehicle. He'd taken his time on the way, running the car through an automatic car wash while fighting fatigue and doing his best to just concentrate on getting home. He hadn't wanted to risk a ticket, and that meant driving with steady control when he felt anything but steady. Fatigue had begun to claim him. His wounds ached, and he felt his shoulder seeping blood into the bandage. His legs trembled and made working the gas, the clutch and the brake a challenge.

Brin had obviously taken less time on the trip. Her SUV was dark, and the lights in the living room were lit. He didn't know what would be waiting for him inside, but he knew he had to get in and face it. If he sat in the Porsche any longer, he thought he'd pass out, and the ache in his heart matched any that his body could serve up.

He climbed out of the Porsche without bothering to lock it. He staggered to the front door and fell against it for a moment, then gathered his strength and turned the knob. As he entered, he saw that Brin was waiting on the couch. She sat very still, and very stiff. Her back was straight, and she held a bottle of beer. There was another bottle resting on a coaster on the coffee table. Alex took the hint. He limped across the floor, trying to keep his face from registering the pain. She never looked up, never offered to help him, and didn't wince when he gasped. She sat, and she waited, and somehow he knew this was part of what was to come, and he took it in stride.

Alex tried to sit down carefully, but at last, it was too much. His legs trembled and he collapsed, crashing to the couch and nearly causing Brin to spill her drink.

Finally, she moved. She put her beer on the table and turned to him, tears in her eyes and wrapped herself around him. He started to speak, but she shook her head, and he fell silent. For a long time, she held him, and as she did, he felt some of the tension drain from his limbs, though the pain remained, a dull ache that pounded with his pulse. His eyes were heavy, but he fought for control of his thoughts.

Brin pulled back and studied him. She seemed to be searching for something, and he didn't know what she wanted to see, but he couldn't have given her anything but the honest truth of his pain and his love. He had no strength, no ability to think, so he let it all go, hoping she'd sense the truth. They'd always been able to communicate without words.

It seemed like an eternity that she watched him, then, like lightning, she hauled back and slapped him hard. Alex didn't pull back, but he was shocked. His head rang from the blow, and he felt a flush of pain on his cheek, newer and sharper than the thousand other pains. She fell on him then, pounding, one fist, then the other, beating against his chest, his arms, until one blow glanced off his shoulder and he cried out from the pain.

It brought her under control. Her eyes went wide and stricken, and she fell into his arms. She didn't speak, but he felt wet tears soak his hair and his cheek, running down his neck. When she finally pulled back slightly, he started to speak but she silenced him, this time with a hand over his mouth.

"Never again," she said softly. "I trusted you, Alex, trusted you with everything I am, everything I care about—my home, my family, our daughter. You lied to me. Not a little lie, or the kind that you can forgive, but the deep, bottomless kind of lie that will always be there, just out of sight. I won't let that happen twice."

Alex didn't answer. There was nothing to say. She wasn't asking him a question or making a suggestion. She was just laying down the rules as she saw them, and telling him how it was going to be. She had that right. He knew there was no way to argue. Everything he'd told her about his life, his work and so many other things—all of it had been a lie.

He'd told himself that it was for her own good. He knew the work he did saved lives, a lot of lives. He knew that he'd helped more than once to make the world a better place, but for the first time he wondered what that mattered if the tiny bit of the world that was his was skewed or out of balance. Was it worth it to save the world if the one person who trusted and loved you was hurt in the process, or worse than that, lost? Had his recent decisions now put Brin and Savannah at an even greater risk than they had been before?

"I love you," she said. Then she kissed him gently, and it was his turn for tears. There was so much he wanted to say, so much he needed to do, but he had no strength. He felt like a rag doll in her arms, but there was warmth there, and when she leaned in this time, much more tenderly, he felt her heart beating against his chest. He closed his eyes.

"Don't you think you'd better check in?" she whispered. "They'll be looking for you by now."

He opened his eyes and stared at her, then turned toward the computer. It sat dark and quiet, and in that moment he hated it. He hated everything it stood for, the secrecy, the lies, the pain. He hated how it had drawn Brin in, despite his years of effort keeping her apart from the darkness that made up his life. He shook his head.

"To hell with it. They will have been watching anyway," he said. "I'm too tired to report in right now. I'll do it later."

She hugged him a little tighter. "Will you ever be safe, Alex?" she asked. "Will we?"

"I don't know," he admitted. He held her, and they both drifted off, fatigue and emotional exhaustion sinking them into sleep.

When a sudden knock came on the door, Alex almost leaped out of his skin. Alex glanced at the window, but there were no flashing lights. The sun was shining. A new day had started.

"Be careful," he said. "We don't know—"

It was too late. Brin crossed the room quickly. She reached the door and flung it open, and Alex flinched. There was a curse from the door, and he saw someone step back quickly as the door flew open. Then Brin gave a soft cry, and he staggered to his feet. By the time he managed to make it halfway across the room, a small dark streak launched through the door and hit him midthigh. He shook, but stood his ground as Savannah hugged him tight.

"Daddy!" she squealed.

Karen stepped through the door, frowning, and Brin shut it behind her.

"Jesus, Brin," she said. "What the hell is going on?"

Brin laughed, but the sound had a tinge of hysteria to it, and no one joined her. Alex led Savannah back to the couch and dropped heavily onto the cushions, pulling her into his lap.

Karen stared at him, then turned to Brin and shook her head.

"When you say there's trouble, I guess it's true," she said. "What happened to him? He looks like he just came in from a war zone."

"Something like that," Brin replied, giving her friend a quick hug. "Something very much like that."

"You should see the other guy," Alex said, trying to keep his voice light. It shook slightly.

"I may ask you about that other guy one of these days," Karen said. "I came as soon as Savannah woke up. She hasn't been getting much sleep."

Alex hugged Savannah, who looked up at him as if he'd sprouted antennae. Karen had pretty much the same expression as she turned first to Brin, then to Alex, then back and shrugged.

"Everything's good now?" she asked.

Brin wiped tears from her eyes and nodded. She tried to speak, lost control again and choked on the words. Finally, she said, "As good as it's going to get, we think."

Karen shook her head and turned back toward the door.

"I'm going to go get some sleep," she said. "Your phone call kind of disrupted my beauty sleep. Give me a call next time there's a war."

Neither Brin nor Alex was able to answer, and Karen let herself out.

"Mommy," Savannah said, "What's wrong with Daddy? He's bleeding!"

Brin stared at her daughter, then turned to Alex. She smiled. "Nothing a good hug won't fix," she said. "We're just very tired, baby. I think maybe it's time we tuck you into your bed." She looked at her watch. "It's very early in the morning, so maybe just a little more sleep for you?"

Savannah looked anything but sleepy, but she nodded. She hugged Alex and rolled off of him, then turned back and stared at his shoulder. She pointed at it and frowned.

"You have a boo-boo," she said.

Alex glanced down and saw that blood had leaked through the bandages and spotted his shirt.

"So I do," he said. "I'll have to put a new bandage on it. Let's get you to bed, and I think maybe it's time for Daddy to take a shower and go to bed, too. Daddy is very tired."

"Mommy can fix it," she said solemnly. "She's very good at it. She put one on my knee, and it's all better."

Savannah leaned over and lifted the hem of her flowered skirt to show off the knee in question, and Alex reached out, tugging her hair gently.

"So she is," he said. "Very good at that, and a lot of other things. She's also right about bedtime."

He rose then, and followed as Brin led Savannah to her bedroom. They tucked her in, Alex dropping clumsily to one knee to give her another hug, and to kiss her cheek.

"Are you okay, Daddy?" she asked.

He smiled at her, but as he did, he felt a strong tug at his heart. There was so much to do—so many things that would change, maybe too fast for him to explain them.

"Yes, baby," he said. "I'm okay. It will all be okay."

He rose then, and Brin steadied him. They watched as Savannah snuggled in, grabbed her favorite stuffed tiger and wrapped herself around it. She pulled one of her pillows over her head, like Alex often did, and he had to turn away slightly. He didn't want her to see him crying and misunderstand.

"Good night," Brin said softly, turning to the door and walking very close beside her husband. He leaned on her a little bit, but tried not to put much of his weight on her. It hadn't been an easy time for either of them. They walked down the hall to the bathroom and inside. Brin pressed him to the wall and held him there. He stood still, watching, as she went to the tub and started filling it with hot water.

When she had the heat adjusted to her taste, she turned back to him and began very slowly, and very gently to strip away his soiled clothes. She unwound the bandage on his shoulder and winced when she saw the ugly, bruised wound left by the bullet. It had started to heal, but the fight with Dayne had opened it at the edges. It seeped blood.

"Does it hurt?" she asked.

"Not as much as you'd think," he replied.

She nodded and went to the medicine cabinet, returning with ointment and clean gauze.

"You'll have to try not to get this wet," she said as she applied the clean dressing. She did the same for his head. When she saw the missing patch of skin where Dayne had cut him, she looked away for a second. Then she squared her shoulders and applied antiseptic salve to the scab, covering it with another clean gauze wrap.

She led him to the tub and helped him step in, sliding into the hot water with such a sigh of pleasure that, finally, she smiled a genuinely happy smile.

"No more secrets," she said. "Promise me."

"None," he said softly. "Ever. I love you, you know."

Brin stood and unbuttoned her blouse, letting it drop away behind her. She stepped out her skirt and within moments stood naked, staring down at him. Then, delicately, she stepped into the tub and slid down between his legs, letting the steamy water wrap around them both.

When she was settled, she leaned into him, her breasts brushing his chest, and her finger stroking his cheek. She stared into his eyes again, and this time he thought she found what it was she needed.

"Prove it," she said.

Holding her tightly, and sliding her into a tight embrace, he did.

IN THE BACK OF THE FREEZER, tucked behind a bag of frozen broccoli and a steak, a thin metal tube rested. It was about the size of a lipstick container, and frosted with the cold. Brin had placed it there just before Alex arrived home. She knew she should have told him the truth, but she would allow herself this one lie. The nanoagents weren't susceptible to extreme cold, just heat. She didn't know exactly what she'd do with it—where she could go to work on it—but she knew it might be a cure. Someday.

If it was in her power, she would make her husband—and her world—right again. She had hope and that, at least, was a small start. Her memory was excellent. The loss of the data wasn't that big a deal, so long as she had the nanoagents, the possibility of reconstructing the work for good purposes was there.

If only she could win the race with the clock.

If only she could do it before they were out of time.

DENNY TALBOT NODDED to himself. He'd just received his orders from Kate Cochran. He'd know it would come down to this but he always regretted losing a good agent. The accident would be tragic and the child would be orphaned but Kate's directive had been clear.

"They know too much, she has the nanoagents, they can't be trusted," Kate had sated before issuing the order.

Denny called the agent he'd put on standby notice.

"The termination order is in effect. Do what you have to do."

JAMES AXLER
OUTLANDERS®
GHOSTWALK

Area 51 remains a mysterious enclave of eerie synergy and unleashed power—a nightmare poised to take the world to hell. A madman has marshaled an army of incorporeal, alien evil, a virus with intelligence now scything through human hosts like locusts. Cerberus warriors must stop the unstoppable, before humanity becomes discarded vessels of feeding energy for ravenous disembodied monsters.

Available May wherever you buy books.

GE08

LOOK FOR

CRITICAL EFFECT
by Don Pendleton

In St. Louis, a rogue scientist unleashes an experimental
pathogen on innocent victims. Stony Man targets the
disturbing intel and launches an offensive that stretches
from Munich to America's heartland. It's a worst-case
scenario linking a radical Middle Eastern group with
Europe's most sophisticated smugglers—along with a
killer virus manufactured for mass destruction.

STONY®
MAN

*Available June 2008
wherever you buy books.*

Or order your copy now by sending your name, address, zip or postal code, along with a check or
money order (please do not send cash) for $6.99 for each book ordered ($8.50 in Canada), plus
75¢ postage and handling ($1.00 in Canada), payable to Gold Eagle Books, to:

In the U.S.	In Canada
Gold Eagle Books	Gold Eagle Books
3010 Walden Avenue	P.O. Box 636
P.O. Box 9077	Fort Erie, Ontario
Buffalo, NY 14269-9077	L2A 5X3

Please specify book title with your order.
Canadian residents add applicable federal and provincial taxes.

**GOLD
EAGLE** ®

GSM9S

JAMES AXLER

DEATH LANDS®

Apocalypse Unborn

Reborn primeval in the fires of thermonuclear hell, America's aftermath is one of manifest evil, savage endurance and lingering hope. Traversing the lawless continent on a journey without destination, Ryan Cawdor seeks humanity in an inhuman world. In Deathlands, life is cheap, death is free and survival demands the highest price of all.

And there's no turning back. Or is there?

Available in June wherever you buy books.